THE FIRST HUSBAND

An unputdownable psychological thriller with a breathtaking twist

MCGARVEY BLACK

JOFFE BOOKS

Joffe Books, London
www.joffebooks.com

First published in Great Britain in 2023

Cover art by Nick Castle

ISBN: 978-1-80405-861-9

This is dedicated to my parents, Dorothy and Charles McGarvey, who showed their four children what a positive and loving relationship looks like. We and our spouses are eternally grateful.

CHAPTER ONE

Delhi, India — September 1988

The young American woman gripped the hand of the Indian man she loved, while the Air India ground agent printed out only a single ticket. With tears in his red eyes, the young man reluctantly picked up his fiancée's backpack and together the couple slowly walked through security towards the gates.

When the first boarding announcement for Trina Holmgard's flight home to New York was called, the couple looked at each other in a panic and Sam put his arms around her as if unwilling to let her go.

'We still have a little more time,' Trina said, trying to reassure the man she loved, her light blue eyes getting teary again. 'I'll board at the very end, right before they close the doors, that way we can stay together longer.'

'Do you have a picture of yourself that you can give to me?' said twenty-one-year-old Sam as he squeezed his soulmate's hand. Trina frantically dug through her bag and pockets. The only pictures she had of herself were on her passport and her New York State driver's license. She needed her passport to get home so she handed him her license.

'It's not the best picture of me,' she said wiping away another tear, 'but you can have it if you want.'

Sam looked at it, smiled and eagerly accepted his future wife's photo. 'You're so beautiful,' he said, admiring her picture.

'You must really love me if you think my driver's license picture is beautiful,' she said, crying and laughing at the same time. 'How will I make it through a whole year without seeing your face, hearing your voice or feeling your arms around me?' She reached up to stroke his thick dark brown hair.

A droplet of water ran down Sam's tan cheek. He brushed it away, but it was followed by another. An announcement echoed over the loudspeaker: 'Air India flight 213 for New York, stopping in Frankfurt, this is your final boarding call.'

All the other passengers had already boarded. Trina and Sam were the only people left in the waiting area. A male ground agent signaled to Trina that she needed to get on the plane immediately. She nodded to him, pointed to her wrist and raised one finger.

'I need a minute,' she shouted.

Sobbing, the couple stood up and clung to each other one last time.

'I'm so afraid of losing you,' said Sam crying.

'Why?'

'When you leave here, you'll go back to your old life and maybe you'll forget all about me.'

'Don't be crazy. I love you more than anything,' said Trina, her voice cracking. 'Sam, I'm committed to becoming your wife. Don't forget that? Please, don't cry.'

'What if you meet someone else once you're back in America? Maybe when you get home, you'll decide I'm too poor and uneducated for you.' Tears were sprinkling over his thick black eyelashes and drenching his face.

Trina tightened her arms around the man she loved to convince him that their feelings were real and unbreakable, but Sam was inconsolable. The ground agent called out to Trina one last time.

'Miss, we are closing the plane door, now,' he shouted.

'I'll be right there! Please hold it for one more minute.' She turned to face her fiancé. 'Sam, look into my eyes. I've got to go but I'm going to prove to you that I'll be back and that we will get married.'

Sam cocked his head as he looked into her big eyes. Trina reached behind her neck, and unclasped her silver necklace with an antique locket.

'Take this,' she said, holding up her most prized possession. 'You know I'd never part with my grandmother's locket. You keep it until the day we're married.' She fastened the silver chain around Sam's neck before he could protest.

He sighed and smiled. Now, he knew for sure she would return for him. 'I will never take it off. I'll wear it until our wedding day.' They kissed one last time, and she ran for the closing door.

She didn't know it then, but Trina Holmgard's reckless and ill-conceived decision to give Sam her locket would eventually trigger the death of thousands and ultimately destroy both their lives.

CHAPTER TWO

Copenhagen, 1861

Lena Jensen had agreed to marry a man she didn't love or even like — in fact, he disgusted her. The young woman's rash yet calculated decision to marry him and the deception that followed would influence the course of history and ruin the lives of all her descendants.

Earlier that day, Johan Pedersen nearly wore a hole in the old braided rug that covered the floor of Rasmussen's Silver Shop. A plain-looking young man, Johan wasn't handsome or ugly. He wasn't tall or short. His muddy-brown-colored hair barely covered his overly large head and despite the fact he was only twenty-two, it was already thinning. His pale features were unmemorable. People often forgot Johan, forcing him to constantly re-introduce himself to those he had met many times before. It was just the way it was. Johan was reliable but painfully dull — though he didn't know it.

On this day, he perspired as he paced back and forth across the tiny front room of the silversmith shop. For the tenth time, he pulled out his watch and sighed. *Why is Mr Rasmussen taking so long? I have something very important to ask Lena Jensen. I must have my silver locket today.*

For almost a year, Johan had painstakingly saved money to have a custom silver piece made especially for the woman he loved. He was convinced that presenting the necklace when he asked Lena his important question would result in a positive outcome.

The shop's front door swung open triggering the little bell attached to the top. Rasmussen heard the jingle and rushed out from the back to wait on an elderly couple who had entered the store.

Fidgeting by the front door, Johan started to pace again. *Mr Rasmussen. If you stop every five minutes to talk to customers, it will be too late for me to take my sweet Lena for a walk.*

In most people's opinion, seventeen-year-old Lena Jensen was the most beautiful girl on the south side of Copenhagen. No one was able to put their finger on what made the young woman so striking. Each of her facial features on their own was not spectacular. Her bright blue eyes curved upwards at the corners and were small and somewhat closely set. Her lips were possibly too big for her face, and her nose turned up almost a little too far. Each feature alone was ordinary, but together they created a symphony. With her magnificent head of strawberry blonde hair, Lena was envied by the girls and lusted after by the boys. For most of the young men, she was unattainable, like catching a hummingbird. Despite this, dull and boring Johan had convinced himself that he and Lena were destined to be together.

Lena and her two younger sisters worked in her family's general store after school each day. Regularly and deliberately, Johan passed the store on his way home to ensure 'chance meetings' with Lena. Whenever he *accidentally* bumped into her on the street, he was sure she was glad to see him because she always smiled and laughed at his jokes.

'What a coincidence to bump into you again,' Lena exclaimed on more than one occasion.

Johan noticed when he went into the family store, even if Lena was busy with a customer, she found a couple of minutes to offer him a free piece of candy or a cake. He was also certain she danced with him more than anyone else at the last Christmas Ball — clear signs she felt the same way he did.

The truth was, Lena Jensen barely noticed Johan and he wasn't her type at all. She had already given her heart to another — an actor from a touring theater company. Their affair had started when Lena, along with her mother and sister, had gone to see a new show. He was extraordinarily handsome and made all the girls in the audience swoon. Tall, muscular and lean with thick, wavy, dark-brown hair and a mustache to match. He moved across the stage with cocky confidence. From the second he stepped into the light, his soulful eyes instantly captured Lena's heart and she was smitten. Her skin felt hot, her heart pounded, and she could barely catch her breath as she sat in the dark auditorium. She had never felt like this before and carefully considered what these new feelings meant. Boys usually admired her, not the other way around. She realized she was in love with a total stranger — and she liked it.

Over the next few days, Lena *borrowed* a few kroner from the store's till to buy tickets to the performances. Sneaking out of the store early, she'd meet a friend on the corner, and go to the theater and sit in the front row. By the third day, the handsome thespian noticed the pretty young woman with strawberry blonde hair gazing up at him adoringly. Lena had enlisted different friends to accompany her to the first four performances, but by the fifth day, no one was available to go with her. Not wanting to miss an opportunity to see him again, she ventured to the theater alone and sat in her regular front row seat.

At intermission, she received a note from an usher inviting her to join the actor in his dressing room after the performance. Nervous but also thrilled, she interpreted this gesture as a sign that the actor felt the same way she did.

When the last curtain call was taken, Lena walked out of the theater and around the building to the stage door. Her heart pounded so intensely that she thought it might beat right out of her chest and leave a gaping hole. She approached an old man sitting on a stool outside the alley door. He was reading a newspaper and didn't hear her approach. Shaking slightly, she cleared her throat and handed him the invitation she had received.

The old man looked up at the eager young girl and shook his head with a mixture of pity and disdain. *She's much prettier than most of the other girls who have shown up with similar notes. Some of the girls were downright homely, and one had enormous feet. This one is quite attractive and smells of honey and rosewater.* He pointed to a door down a hallway.

'You sure you want to go in there, miss?' grumbled the old man while he raised one eyebrow.

'I'm sure I do,' said Lena as she lifted her chin and breezed by the man with such determination that the movement of her skirts caused his newspaper to blow onto the ground. She marched to the dressing-room door without looking back and knocked confidently, mainly for the old man's benefit. A moment later, she heard the unmistakable baritone of her actor's voice through the closed door.

'I'm getting changed. The door is open. Come in and please close it behind you.'

Lena entered the room and shut the door. The actor, seated at his dressing table, looked at her through the reflection in the mirror.

'Come in and sit down,' he said. 'I'm John. You're even prettier up close.'

Lena gave him a half-smile and felt herself flush.

'And what is your name, my beauty?'

'Lena. My name is Lena.'

In her short eighteen years, the young woman had always behaved most appropriately. On this day, however, she fully succumbed to the actor's charms right there on the worn gold brocade chaise lounge in his dressing room. When they were finished, she dressed and made sure everything was in its proper place. John walked towards her and smiled before he kissed her on the forehead and told her he hoped to see her in the audience again.

When she walked out of the theater and passed by the old stagehand she heard him mutter something that she couldn't quite make out. *I don't care what that smelly old man thinks, anyway. I'm in love, and I know John loves me.*

For the next six afternoons, Lena attended every show. Afterward, she gave a command performance on the chaise lounge in John's dressing room. On the sixth day, as Lena buttoned the cuff of her sleeve, the actor shared some news.

'I'm going to truly miss you, sweet Lena,' he said as he admired himself in the mirror and combed his thick mustache. 'Our acting company is leaving tomorrow to travel throughout Europe and then we're going back to America. We've got bookings in twenty-eight cities. I'm afraid it will be a year or two before I return to Copenhagen.'

A high-pitched ringing filled Lena's ears, and she couldn't get any air into her lungs. 'You'll be gone for a year?' she gasped. 'But I thought we were going to be together. I don't understand. I thought we would get married.'

The man shook his head wondering why all the young girls always misinterpreted his actions. He sighed as he walked over to a big black trunk in the corner and opened it. He fished out a wooden cigar box filled with several dozen beaded bracelets, each with a dangling charm in the shape of a rose. An engraving on the back of the charm read: *All my love, J.W.B.*

He extracted a single bracelet, closed the trunk and faced the visibly pale and stricken young woman.

'Put out your right arm, Lena. I've had a special gift made just for you so you will remember me.'

With great fanfare, the man placed the beaded bracelet on Lena's wrist and stood back to admire his generosity. 'I had it custom-made for you so you wouldn't forget me,' he said smiling.

Lena gently touched the charm; her fingertips ran over the roughness of the engraving on its surface. *It says:* All my love. *He does love me then.*

'My acting career requires I experience the world first-hand,' said the actor. 'I hope you didn't misconstrue the nature of our most pleasant friendship. Naturally, I have a deep affection for you.'

'But, I thought . . .' Lena said.

'Surely, you understand that I must maintain my independence for my art,' said John Wilkes Booth, as his lips grazed her forehead. A moment later, he went back to his dressing table and continued his grooming. 'It's getting late, sweet Lena. I must get changed or I'll be late for a dinner. Close the door tightly when you leave.'

She didn't remember exiting the theater, but somehow, she made it home and went straight to bed without speaking to anyone. Damning recriminations screamed from inside her head. *What have I done? He doesn't care about me. What a horribly foolish girl I've been.* That night she vowed never to see or speak of the actor again.

Lena never did speak of him — not to anyone. Less than three months later she reluctantly acknowledged to herself that she was pregnant. The changes in her body were clear, and she knew what was coming in six or seven months. The day she realized she was going to be a mother was the same day Johan Pedersen came calling with the custom-made silver locket in his pocket.

It was a windy Saturday afternoon. Lena had just finished stacking boxes of shoes in the store and was lost deep in thought over her unfortunate predicament. Johan stopped by to ask if she might be free to go for a walk. Normally, she would have doled out a piece of candy to get rid of him and tell him she was too busy, but today she was glad for an excuse to get out and get some air.

Walking along the windswept cobblestone streets of the city, Lena felt the red, yellow and brown fallen leaves brush up and swirl around her ankles. Johan chatted about the goings on around town and the local gossip, but Lena barely heard a word he said. When they rounded a corner, a gust of wind blew leaves and debris at the young couple. Johan stepped in front of Lena to protect her and seized the moment by taking her hand. Startled by his grasp, Lena was confused and wished she had never agreed to go for the walk.

'Miss Jensen, there's something vitally important I need to ask you.'

Lena looked up at his puffy, red face and into his beady eyes. *He's perspiring and breathing so hard. Why is he squeezing my fingers? I didn't give him permission to hold my hand.*

'Lena Jensen, I have loved you from the moment I saw you,' said Johan. 'I hoped that perhaps you might feel the same way about me. If you would consider becoming my wife, I can promise you a lifetime of love and security. You will never have to worry about anything, and I will always take care of you.' When he finished, he held his breath.

Lena's jaw dropped, and her eyes widened. She had not anticipated this. Before she could respond, the young man nervously pulled out a small blue box from his inside jacket pocket and lifted the lid.

'For nearly a year, I've saved up to have this made for you, dear Lena,' he proudly announced. Nestled inside the box was a shiny silver oval-shaped locket with a granulated point on each end. The locket hung from a thick silver chain and had a very fancy clasp. A picture of a heart was engraved on the front. He opened the charm and inside was engraved the words: *You Are My Heart.*

With the exception of her recent dalliance with the actor, most of the time Lena Jensen was a practical young woman. She quickly evaluated her options. *Johan did go to a lot of trouble and expense to have that locket made for me. That was sweet. But, he's still repulsive and rather irritating.*

She didn't have much time because soon the baby would start to show. After a short internal debate, with no other immediate solutions or marriage proposals on the horizon, Lena forced a smile and accepted Johan's proposition along with the silver locket. 'I will become your wife, Johan, providing you agree to marry me right away,' said Lena. 'Once I decide something, I must act on it, or I might change my mind.'

Johan clapped his hands, surprised by his good fortune and proclaimed he was the 'luckiest man in the world'. Gingerly, he placed the silver necklace around Lena's long white neck, sure that the magic of the locket had helped him get the answer that he had dreamed of.

'Promise me, you will never take this locket off,' he said. 'You'll wear it every day as a symbol of our eternal love.'

Lena agreed.

The following week, their two families met at the local chapel where Father Schmidt united Lena and Johan in the eyes of God. At the end of the ceremony, Johan kissed his new bride for the first time. He was in love. She was nauseous but relieved.

Seven months later, a daughter was born *prematurely*. Despite the baby's early arrival, she was quite large, much to everyone's surprise. No one but Lena noticed that the baby girl was the spitting image of the man she had once admired from the darkness of the audience.

True to her word, Lena wore the silver locket from their wedding day forward. It was a constant reminder of her youthful transgressions, her rejection by the actor and the loveless marriage she had entered into. She hated that piece of jewelry more than anything.

Eighteen years later, on the eve of her one and only daughter's wedding day, Lena had an idea and went to speak to her husband.

'I was thinking that we should give my beautiful necklace to our daughter as a wedding present,' said Lena. 'This locket has brought us luck and good fortune and will surely bring the same to our beautiful daughter.' It took a while to convince Johan, but he eventually agreed.

'I do hate to part with it,' Lena said. 'But it's a sacrifice I'm willing to make for our daughter.'

The next day, while Lena dressed for her daughter's wedding, she stood in front of the mirror. For the first time in almost two decades, her long neck was bare. She smiled and took a moment to congratulate herself for being so clever.

The necklace had always felt like a noose and now it was finally gone. She could breathe again.

When Lena accepted Johan's locket of love, letting him believe that the baby was his, she and all her descendants who wore the false amulet, were cursed.

Nearly six years after Lena's marriage to Johan, on April 15, 1865, in the Ford Theater in Washington D.C, John Wilkes Booth shot President Abraham Lincoln and changed the course of history.

More than a hundred years later, John Wilkes Booth and Lena's great-great-great-granddaughter would unwittingly be the catalyst that would cause a world-altering catastrophe.

CHAPTER THREE

New York City, July 1988

JFK's international terminal was packed with summer travelers, and after months of planning her trip to India, Trina was one of them. Her best friend, Jenn Fairchild, stood nearby, nose-deep in a celebrity magazine, oblivious to the airport chaos.

Inseparable since their college freshmen days at CUNY, the two young women had bonded over a mutual dream of becoming editors at national magazines like *Vogue* or *Rolling Stone*. Both were well on their way to achieving their goals. Jenn was an editorial assistant at a popular consumer psychology magazine and Trina did copy-editing for a medical trade publication. They were practically replicas of each other with one exception, Jenn's shoulder-length hair was jet black while Trina's was dirty blonde. Both were precisely five-foot-five-inches tall with blue eyes. Sharing clothes and dreams with equal passion, they were more like sisters than friends.

As they walked to their gate, Trina thought about her grandmother, Nanna Mae and the long, painful year since the old woman had died. A lump formed in her throat and she took a deep breath through her nose and blew out through her mouth.

'Put a smile on your pretty face,' Nanna Mae always said with a wink. 'It'll trick your brain into thinking you're happy, even when you're not. Trust me, Cookie, it works.'

She smiled remembering the time she and Nanna received a letter saying Trina had won a college scholarship. Her grandmother had danced around the kitchen banging two pot lids together while crowing. Later that same day, the joyous mood changed dramatically when Trina learned from a friend that the boy she secretly loved, Jake Mainelli, had asked another girl to go to the prom. Trina had been convinced that Jake had felt the same way she did and she was furious with herself for being so stupid and so wrong. Her inability to read relationships accurately was her Achilles heel and would plague her for the rest of her life. Jake was just the first of many unrequited romances that she misinterpreted. On that day, Nanna Mae had wrapped her arms around the sobbing teenager and assured her everything would be all right and Trina had almost believed her.

'There will be loads of other boys, Cookie. Way better than that stupid Jake what's-his-name,' said Nanna Mae giving her another squeeze. 'Focus on your happy news. You're going to be a college girl!'

Trina's own mother had died when Trina was two and never divulged who Trina's father was. Nanna Mae had been everything; her mother, teacher, and champion. In the winter, their small two-bedroom apartment in Astoria, Queens always had the delicious aroma of Nanna Mae's homemade soups simmering on the stove. In summer, you could smell Nanna's special coffee cake cinnamon muffins baking in the oven. Now, those comforting smells had been replaced by the faint odor of mildew mixed with stale cigar smoke that wafted up through the floorboards from the fat guy on the first floor.

Her final conversation with her grandmother played on an endless loop in Trina's head. Right before Nanna Mae died, she had given Trina her antique silver locket, the one that had been handed down for generations.

'Put the chain on,' Nanna commanded. 'It's yours now. Wear it every day, just like I always did, and one day you'll give it to your own daughter. Remember, it will protect you as it did me and all the women in our family.' Trina's eyes welled up as she put the locket on for the first time.

'Never take it off, promise me,' Nanna Mae said.

'I promise, Nanna. I'll wear it always.'

Satisfied, the old woman smiled and closed her eyes. Twenty minutes later, she was gone and Trina was truly all alone. Nanna had been Trina's chief advocate and strongest protector helping Trina to believe in herself and reminding her granddaughter that she was worthy of being loved.

Now, Jenn was the closest thing Trina had to family, and their friendship meant everything to her.

The voice on the plane's loudspeaker jolted Trina back to the mission at hand.

'Are you all right?' Jenn asked tapping her friend on the shoulder as they moved slowly down the aisle.

'Why?'

'I asked you the same question three times.'

'Sorry. Lost in thought,' said Trina shrugging her shoulders. 'I was just thinking about how much my life has changed in the last year. First losing my grandmother and using what she left me to go to graduate school and now this trip. I would never have guessed I'd be getting my master's and going to India a year ago. What did you want to ask me?'

'Now, I don't remember,' said Jenn rolling her eyes and sticking out her tongue.

Twenty hours later, after a connection in Frankfurt, the plane made a smooth landing in New Delhi, India. As the wheels hit the tarmac, Trina felt a mixture of excitement and resolve. Years earlier, when Trina's grandfather had a fatal heart attack on the Long Island Railroad, her grandmother had focused everything on her granddaughter, giving up her own dreams. Trina was taking this trip in her grandmother's honor. She was going to see all the places Nanna Mae had dreamed of going but never had the opportunity. The Taj Mahal was on the top of the list.

Though exhausted after checking into their small, marginally clean hotel, the two American women ventured out into the decaying quagmire of Delhi. Buildings appeared to crumble before their eyes while deteriorating sidewalks and roads were overrun by too many people. Bodies, both human and animal, moved in every direction yet went nowhere. Indian women in colorful saris, arms stacked with shiny yellow-gold bangles, colored dots on their foreheads and tiny jeweled studs in their noses created a spectacular rainbow.

Roaming livestock darted in and out of alleyways looking for scraps of food or water. Gas exhaust puffed in clouds of thick black smoke out of tailpipes as sirens blared. Car horns honked incessantly for what appeared to be no reason at all. The air was filled with a mixture of odors, some good, most bad; a combination of gasoline, cigarettes, cooking meat, curry and the stench of rotting, putrid garbage. Worst were the flies. Massive numbers of big, fat, black flies landed on food and faces, flying into eyes and ears.

'Cover up and maintain a low profile when you're walking around India, ladies,' their New York travel agent had warned. 'Delhi is not New York, respect the local customs. Young, single Indian women do not walk alone without a chaperone, so don't draw attention to yourselves.'

The two friends tried their best to blend in with the locals donning headscarves, long skirts, long-sleeved shirts, and sunglasses to hide their light eyes. They were significantly taller with much lighter complexions than the locals, and their camouflage did not work well.

No matter how the women tried to cover up, scores of young Indian men catcalled to them and made lewd comments in Hindi and English. The women were poked, squeezed, pushed and groped. Warm, rough hands grabbed at their thighs and thrust between their legs. Fingers brazenly grabbed at their breasts or cupped their buttocks. Hands jutted out from the crowds and reached under their skirts and up the front of their shirts for a quick squeeze.

'Here's how it's going to go. If one more guy puts his hands anywhere near my upper thighs,' said Jenn defiantly raising her knee in the air, 'he's going to feel this right where it hurts. Remember, I've been taking kickboxing for the past three years. Might as well put it to use.'

In addition to the young men, the two Americans were constantly pursued by beggars — some missing a hand or a foot, hobbling around on makeshift crutches often constructed of misshapen pieces of wood or tree branches. Bands of emaciated children in tatters, followed and encircled the women pleading for money or food while reaching for the women's skirts and pointing towards their own open, hungry mouths.

'*Baksheesh. Baksheesh*,' the children cried shouting the Hindi word for 'donation'. Heartbroken, that day Trina and Jenn gave away everything they had in their pockets.

The next morning the two women went to Agra, to see the Taj Mahal. The enormous white structure constructed almost entirely of marble was one of the things Nanna Mae had read extensively about and obsessed over.

'Depending on the time of day when the light changes, the Taj Mahal is supposed to look completely different, Cookie,' Nanna had said. 'Promise me you'll go at different times.'

As evening approached, Trina and Jenn walked through the chaotic streets towards one of the 'man-made wonders of the world'. They passed under an oversized, ornately carved stone archway and there it was, the majestic Taj Mahal.

'Wow,' said Trina as she placed her hand on her throat and touched her locket.

'Incredible,' said Jenn, eyes wide. 'I've never seen anything like it.'

The evening light hit the building in such a way that it glowed. At some angles, it appeared two-dimensional, as if it was painted onto the horizon. The warm colors of the sunset cast a bright orange melon-colored hue over the entire building. Long reflecting pools leading up to the structure mirrored the building's colorful reflection in the water below.

'It's so beautiful,' said Jenn. 'I'll admit it, I'm impressed.'

The next morning, they went back for the sunrise show. This time the Taj went from orange to pale yellow and finally to a bright iridescent white. From there, they grabbed a cab to the central bus depot to take a twelve-hour bus ride north to Kashmir.

'And don't forget, when you go to India, Trina, make sure you stay on a houseboat in Kashmir. I've read all about them in that *Travel and Leisure* magazine,' Nanna Mae had said, showing Trina the article. 'It's in the north of India near Pakistan, but tourists can't always get there because of politics and warring tribes, it says — so only go if it's safe.'

'You've got to be kidding me,' said Jenn when she saw the condition of the bus they would take to Kashmir. 'It's a freaking school bus and there's no air conditioning. It looks like it was built with spare parts.'

The driver put three people in seats meant for two. Jenn was crammed against the window, Trina next to her and a fat middle-aged Indian woman wearing a royal blue sari was on the aisle. When all the seats on the bus were filled, the driver lined people down the center aisle.

'Oh my God,' said Trina, 'those poor people have to stand in the aisle the entire trip.'

'They don't even mind. Look at their faces,' whispered Jenn. 'Like it's normal. Buckle your seatbelts. Next stop, hell,' shouted Jenn to Trina over the noise. 'Oh, what a surprise, there *are* no seatbelts. We're going to die on this thing!'

The rickety school bus wound its way along the steep, treacherous, rocky mountain roads. Misty air made the visibility difficult. Driving at dangerously high speeds, the driver did not slow down on the jackknife turns. Trina and Jenn clung to each other while they both gripped the metal rail on the seat in front of them.

'The lunatic driving this heap of junk is going to send us right off the side of this mountain,' yelled Jenn over the noise of the engine's grinding gears. 'I've read about buses going off mountains in India. It's a regular thing. They lose like one a week!'

CHAPTER FOUR

Kashmir

In the morning, the bus passed a sign that said *Srinagar*, the city they were going to in Kashmir. The vehicle made a left turn into a large bus depot and came to an abrupt stop. Yanking open the door, the bus driver released the exhausted passengers from their twelve-hour misery. Trina looked out through the filthy window and bit her lower lip.

The chaotic depot was a combination of junkyard and dusty outdoor market. People milled about buying and selling food, water, jewelry, scarves, dresses, frogs, pottery, dogs — even medicine. In stark contrast, the scene around the depot was a lush, verdant green, bordered by majestic snow-capped mountains in the far distance.

Over to the left, a group of men lined up holding signs saying *Houseboat* in different languages and waving pictures of boats and rooms for rent. 'Speak English?' they yelled at Trina and Jenn. '*Deutsche*? *Habla español*? *Parle français*? Aussie? Kiwi?'

'We're Americans,' shouted Trina smiling. The men grinned and gave her a thumb's up. 'Welcome, pretty American lady,' they shouted back. 'You want houseboat? You need room? I got nice boat.'

While the women sifted through the houseboat look books, the Indian salesmen got more aggressive and thrust additional pictures and testimonial letters in different languages into the women's hands. The sales pitches grew more animated and the volume, frenzy and shoving escalated.

From behind, over all the noise, a calm, cool male voice called out, speaking perfect English. The tone was steady and reassuring, mixed with a tinge of amusement. 'Good morning, ladies. You look a bit confused. Perhaps I could be of assistance to you.'

The women spun around. A smiling twenty-something Indian man, holding a brown clipboard, clicked his ballpoint pen. He wore khaki shorts and a green Izod Lacoste golf shirt with its collar turned up ever so slightly. His curly dark-brown hair was neatly combed and his thick black eyelashes made him look like he was wearing eyeliner.

'He looks like that actor from the class we took on silent movies,' whispered Jenn. 'What was that guy's name?'

'Rudolph Valentino,' Trina replied without missing a beat.

'How did you remember that? You're a freak, you know that?'

The man with the calming voice had a welcoming smile and two rows of straight sparkling white teeth. Holding his clipboard and pen, he looked very official, like a cruise director.

'Welcome to Kashmir. My name is Samir but everyone calls me Sam,' he said with confidence and a sly grin. 'Do you need some help in choosing a place to stay? Our convoluted process here makes perfect sense to us but can be very confusing to foreigners.'

As he spoke, Trina felt her anxiety level diminish. In five seconds, the young man had made all the crazy disappear. The crowd of barkers began shouting things to Sam in Kashmiri.

'Yes,' she said over the noise of the crowd. 'We have no idea what we're doing.'

Sam smiled and gestured for the ladies to follow him away from the other men.

As the three walked away, the barkers raised their fists and yelled at Sam. The young Indian stopped, walked over and faced the barkers and shouted back at them using big hand gestures. One of the men stepped closer to Sam and pushed him. Sam stumbled and fell. It looked like a fight was developing until two older men intervened and stopped it. They helped Sam up and spoke to him sternly for a minute. Brushing himself off, Sam walked back to the Americans.

'Are you okay?' said Trina. 'What just happened?'

'Nothing,' said Sam, flushed and clearly distracted. 'Just a misunderstanding. Some of my *neighbors* need to learn better manners. Most of them are illiterate jerks. Don't give them another thought.'

When they were out of earshot from the others, Sam turned and faced the two women. Trina stared at his face. There was something unusual about him. He wasn't traditionally handsome, but something drew her to him — his voice. The timbre and pitch were soothing, sounding as if he had been born and raised in a fancy neighborhood in London.

'I'll bet you're both from America,' said Sam looking Trina over from top to bottom. She felt herself blush. Their little exchange did not go unnoticed by Jenn.

'How did you know?' said Trina trying to compose herself.

'It's the backpacks and the shoes,' he whispered. 'Everything else looks the same but those are the tell.'

'And maybe,' said Jenn with a sly smile, 'you heard us shout to those guys back there that we were American?'

Sam laughed again. 'That was another helpful clue,' he said with a twinkle in his eye. 'It can be very confusing to choose a place with all those guys screaming at you,' said Sam. 'Do you want to be right on Dal Lake?'

'I promised my grandmother I'd stay on a houseboat,' said Trina.

Sam nodded and told the two women about the different neighborhoods and the vastly different price levels of accommodation.

'We can do about thirty-five US per night for the two of us,' said Jenn. 'Will that get us a nice boat?'

Sam clapped his hands and smiled. 'Yes,' he said, 'thirty-five dollars is a perfect amount. I know of a very special houseboat right in the center of everything. It is quite beautiful, nicely maintained and costs exactly thirty-five US per night and it has the best cook in all of Kashmir.'

The two women looked at each other and smiled.

'It sounds perfect,' said Jenn.

'It turns out,' Sam said, 'the cook on this particular houseboat happens to be my mother, and this boat belongs to my family. Of course, you may want to look at some other options.' He gestured to the mob of barkers still waiting to pounce. The women stepped away to talk privately.

'What do you think?' whispered Trina.

'I think he played us,' said Jenn.

'You don't want to deal with those shouting guys again, do you?' said Trina. 'I say we go for it.'

Jenn nodded and the two women walked over to Sam.

'We look forward to meeting the best cook in Kashmir,' said Trina to the Indian with a smile.

He loaded their backpacks into an old green and white Volkswagen van and they were off.

While he drove, Sam described the nuances of the landscape while pointing out local flowers. He explained the history and development of over one thousand private houseboats that dotted and lined the lake. 'Dal Lake runs on a waterway economy,' he said. 'People live their lives on the lake and get around by small boats. Houseboats sell everything from bread to leather goods to plumbing supplies. Restaurants, gas stations and hair salons all have storefronts on the lake.'

Sam stopped the van in front of a simple tan and white rectangular houseboat. Streaming banners of blue, yellow and green flapped in the wind from the flat roof. A big white sign with red lettering hung across the top that said *Zahra's Palace*.

'Wait here,' he said as he got out of the car, 'I'll let my family know we are here.'

'He's one smooth operator,' Jenn whispered to Trina after Sam left. 'While those other guys at the depot were fighting with each other, he marches up with his clipboard and snags us away in under ten seconds.'

'We needed to find a houseboat anyway, and he seems perfectly nice,' said Trina. 'I think he's kind of cute.'

'I knew it! You *like* him?'

'Don't be ridiculous. Shhh, here he comes.'

Sam opened the car door. 'Good news. Everything is ready. My parents are waiting inside.' He carried their backpacks onto the boat, and the two women followed him up the gangplank. Once inside, they were greeted by Sam's father, a small, wiry man with black hair flecked with gray, wearing a traditional white skullcap and long white gown. Sam's diminutive mother stood behind her husband in a long brown dress fitted over loose pants. Her dark hair was mostly covered by a yellow, orange and green print scarf. Sam's parents waved and bowed their heads as they welcomed the women to their houseboat.

'Neither of my parents speak much English but I'll be around to translate,' said Sam. 'There are four bedrooms on our houseboat. Each room could sleep four, but at the moment, you are our only guests. For now, you'll have the place to yourselves. My family and I live on another small boat down the road. While you stay with us, I'm at your disposal for your entire visit, day or night.'

'That's wonderful,' said Trina looking in his eyes and blushing again.

'Come,' said his father as he beckoned the women to enter the sitting room of the houseboat.

The front room was round, and while it looked old and dated, it contained three plush velvet maroon chairs and an ornate wooden coffee table in the center. Woven murals depicting life in Kashmir hung on the walls. Thick, colorful, reddish and gold handmade Indian rugs with black accents covered the wooden floors. An old crystal chandelier was suspended from the ceiling.

The dining room was equally opulent, but visibly worn. The oval dark wood table, surrounded by four upholstered chairs had such a high gloss finish the women could see their reflections. Thick drapes were secured by cords with dangling tassels. An exquisitely carved china cupboard was against one wall and showcased colorful hand-painted dishes. Jenn noticed many were cracked.

Sam's father led them to their bedroom. It was small with two twin beds, each with a hand-carved wooden headboard. Bright white, green and yellow floral cotton bedspreads covered each bed. A fan turned briskly over their heads, creating a cool breeze in the room. On the ceiling, around the fan, was a mural of hand-painted vines, leaves, and birds. Down the hall, there was a tiny, immaculate bathroom with the smallest white pedestal sink the women had ever seen.

'Who knew they made sinks that small,' whispered Jenn. 'It looks like a birdbath for a sparrow.'

They took another lap around the boat that was to be their home for the next few weeks and noticed every wall was lined with books, hundreds, maybe thousands of books from floor to ceiling.

'Sam, please tell your parents we think Zahra's Palace is beautiful,' said Trina.

'And, that we will be very comfortable here,' added Jenn.

Sam translated the compliments to his parents who both smiled.

For the first time since her grandmother had died, Trina felt like she was exactly where she was supposed to be — in Kashmir.

CHAPTER FIVE

In the morning, when the women walked outside onto the deck, Sam was leaning against a tree, sketching a building design in the notebook he always carried.

'Good morning,' he called out as he put his book into the waist of the back of his pants, 'I've been waiting for you to wake. We'll bring your breakfast now.'

'Sam, what's the deal with all the roosters crowing in the morning?' asked Jenn.

Sam laughed. 'In Kashmir, the birds are considered nature's alarm clock,' he said chuckling. 'Prepare yourselves for their sweet song every morning. You'll get used to it.'

'Not a chance,' said Jenn making a sour face and crossing her eyes.

'After you eat, we'll start our tour.' Sam ran off down the road and five minutes later, he, along with his mother and father, appeared in the road carrying trays of food towards Zahra's Palace. Sam had an ornate black lacquer tray that held a sizable ceramic teapot, cups, spoons, a small pitcher and a bowl filled with sugar. His mother brought a metal platter with bread and jam. His father carried a large ceramic dish containing sliced pears, and bunches of large purple grapes. Jenn's eyes lit up when she spotted a small bowl nestled on the fruit tray.

'Look,' whispered Jenn, 'they brought us candy. Yay.'

'You're a sugar addict, you know that?' said Trina.

'There are worse things.'

'Sit. Eat. Relax,' said Sam as he opened the door to leave. 'I will be back in forty minutes to collect you for our water tour today where you will learn all about the history, customs and architectural wonders of the region.'

Alone in their private houseboat palace, the two friends ate far more than they should have.

'Did you eat all that candy?' asked Trina noticing the small bowl was empty.

'They were delicious,' said Jenn laughing and licking her lips. 'They eat sweets for breakfast here. It's so civilized. I think I love Kashmir.'

Forty minutes later, Sam poked his head into the dining room, saw the empty plates and smiled.

'I told you my mother was the best cook in all of India. Now you know I was telling the truth,' he said as he led them outside. 'Are you ready for the best tour of your life? Today you will see Dal Lake from the water. We'll take that small boat,' he said, pointing to a long narrow red vessel with three large gold throne-like seats in a row positioned down the center of the boat. A decorative tarp was slung overhead to protect passengers from the sun.

The women climbed onto the waiting boat and took their places in the elegant center seats.

'I feel like Cleopatra sailing down the Nile,' said Trina as Sam took his seat in the back by the motor.

'Kashmir,' Sam explained shouting over the engine, 'is often called the Venice of India.'

Boats sailed past them going in every direction. Families taking children to school, men commuting to work, women shopping. Sam steered their boat down canals where they spotted old men playing cards outside a waterside barber shop. Further along, a group of teenaged boys bought cigarettes at a waterside convenience store. On another boat they saw a woman purchase loaves of bread from a floating bakery. Sam waved to almost everyone and shared stories of some of the houseboats they passed and the personal lives of their inhabitants.

Throughout the day, Sam proved to be a thoughtful and attentive guide, describing every aspect of Kashmiri life, pointing out the tiniest details on wildlife, vegetation, religion and architecture. The young Indian man seemed to be well versed on almost every subject from world events, politics, music and history. On top of his command of almost any subject, the women also learned he spoke five languages fluently.

On the houseboat that night, Trina and Jenn were treated to an extravagant meal of lamb kebabs and grilled vegetables. Moments after they were finished eating, Sam magically appeared to collect the dirty plates and review the itinerary for the following day.

'Tomorrow, I'll take you to see the sites of Kashmir on land. Did you know Srinagar is a city of over one million people?' he said.

'Can I ask a personal question?' said Trina.

'Of course, anything. I have no secrets. Well, maybe a few,' Sam said smiling.

'You speak five languages, you know about astronomy, architecture, world history, literature, science, even philosophy. But, you told us you stopped going to school when you were twelve. How did you learn all this stuff?'

'I was kind of wondering that, too,' Jenn chimed in, suddenly interested in his answer.

Sam stood up straighter, puffed his chest out a little and smiled broadly. 'I have a secret weapon, a photographic memory,' he said pointing to his head. 'I can remember anything I read, forever.' He pointed to the walls of books. 'Thousands of tourists have stayed on our houseboat over the years. From the time I could walk, I interacted with foreigners and learned their language. Pretty soon, I did all the communication with our guests and helped build my family's business. I read in other languages, too. My older sister also speaks English and German, but she's married now and lives across the lake.'

'You learned to speak all those languages by yourself?' asked Jenn.

'Every year, new tourists would come from different parts of the world, and they always left their books behind,' said Sam. 'I read everything, novels, history, biographies, language books, textbooks, even instructional manuals. I can take a vacuum cleaner apart and put it back together.'

The two women laughed and Sam chuckled at his own joke.

'There were also many travel books to read as well.'

'I'm impressed,' said Jenn, 'and that almost never happens.'

'Me too,' said Trina. 'I can't even remember the Spanish I took in high school.'

Sam grinned proudly clearly enjoying their admiration.

Later, when Jenn and Trina were alone on the houseboat getting ready for bed they discussed their host.

'He's pretty amazing,' said Trina while brushing her hair. 'You'd never expect to find someone like him here in India, in the middle of nowhere.'

'You like him,' said Jenn narrowing her eyes. 'You always fall for them too fast.'

'That's not true. He's intelligent and extremely nice. Don't you think so?'

'He seems a little too proud of himself.'

'He taught himself five languages, Jenn. Five.'

Jenn rolled her eyes as the two climbed into their beds and turned out the lights. When she closed her eyes, Trina pictured Sam's face and wondered what it would be like to kiss him.

CHAPTER SIX

In the morning, Jenn, Trina and Sam went on a land tour through the crowded, chaotic city streets. After a while, Sam pulled over and drove up a long rocky road leading to an ancient temple. He stopped the car in front of a large stone archway fitted with a thick black iron gate. 'Now, ladies, we must climb.'

Out of breath when they got to the top, Jenn pulled out her camera and asked another tourist to take a picture of the three of them. Linking arms, Trina, Jenn and Sam smiled for the photo as if the three had been lifelong friends. At one point, Trina walked off by herself to drink in the quiet majestic mountains in the distance. A wave of sadness overcame her. *Everyone said it will get easier, but it still hurts every day.*

Sam's voice broke her spell. 'It's time for the next stop on our tour.'

Sam pointed out landmarks and local highlights, farms, trees, plants, architecture, and the history of everything. He discussed the complexities of the government in India both nationally and locally and gave them a tutorial on how the Indian legal system was set up after the British left.

Lastly, he shared his definite opinions on global politics including his feelings about their American president,

Ronald Reagan. 'He's very old,' said Sam. 'America is such a young country. Why do you have such an old president?'

The two Americans didn't have an answer. Trina wondered what Sam might have become had he gotten a good education and grown up in the United States or Europe.

That night, two Italian women in their fifties arrived and occupied one of the other bedrooms in Zahra's Palace. In the morning, Sam took his new larger group to see 'incredible sights' in the western part of the city. The Italians were both retired high school English teachers from Napoli.

'You have boyfriends?' asked one of the Italian ladies making a clucking sound.

'Most of the men in New York,' said Jenn, 'are so filled with self-importance that there's only room for one in the relationship.'

'That about sums up my love life, too,' said Trina grinning. 'Finding a good man isn't easy.'

The Italian teachers talked about their high school students, and Jenn and Trina laughed over how similar it sounded to high school in America.

'It's universal. Teenagers are rotten,' said Jenn.

'How about you, Sam?' asked Trina. 'What were you like as a teenager?'

'I did a lot of reading. I was always thinking about my future,' said Sam. 'The other kids accepted that they would do what their fathers did and what their grandfathers did before them. I wanted something more. I'm going to move to London or Germany or maybe even America and open a rug store or become an architect.'

'Of course, you will,' said one of the Italians. 'You can do anything you want. What about you, Trina? Tell me about your wonderful life in New York.'

Not a naturally funny person, Trina had to work hard to make people laugh and often failed. Jenn effortlessly managed to elicit a chuckle from everyone without breaking a sweat. Trina desperately wanted to make Sam laugh. She thought hard and remembered an incident that even Jenn didn't know about.

'There was a guy who lived in my building in Astoria,' she said as she got up in front of the group. 'He used to travel for work for months at a time and apparently wasn't very good about paying his bills. One Friday afternoon, in the middle of August, he came home after a long trip to Asia. New York City was in the middle of a wicked heatwave.'

'And, New York during a heatwave is like being on the face of the sun,' Jenn interjected making the others laugh.

'Anyway,' said Trina, taking back centerstage, 'this guy hadn't paid his electric bill in eight months, so the power company had turned off his electricity. He had no lights but more importantly, no air conditioning. He called the power company at four forty-five p.m. that Friday and demanded they turn on his electricity.'

'Good luck with that,' said Jenn laughing. 'Nobody does nothing at five o'clock on a Friday in New York.'

Trina kept going with her story, becoming more animated as she progressed. 'Con Ed said the earliest they could turn his power on would be in five days. My neighbor started screaming into the phone and threatened to blow up the power plant if they didn't turn on his electricity immediately. Fifteen minutes later, thirty cops, a SWAT team, and the FBI banged down his front door.'

'Oh my God, that's what happens in America when you don't pay your electric bill?' gasped one of the Italian ladies.

'It's a felony to threaten a public utility. They led him out of his apartment in handcuffs,' said Trina with a smile. 'We never saw him again.'

Everyone laughed, but Sam laughed the hardest and that made Trina feel good.

CHAPTER SEVEN

The days passed quickly and soon it was the day before Jenn had to leave for her trip home. Trina hadn't yet decided if she would travel around India by herself or stay and explore more of Kashmir. Sam hoped she would stay in Kashmir.

Jenn wanted to go shopping before she left, and the three of them walked through the downtown market stalls on the hunt for the perfect souvenir. Jenn decided to buy a couple of saris to take back to New York so Sam offered to take them to another area where he knew of several good dress shops. Trina begged off to run a few errands on her own and they made plans to meet up later at a nearby market.

'Let me do all the negotiating for you,' Sam said to Jenn before they went into the first store. 'If you do it, they'll rob you, but if I do it, I'll get you the best price.'

The two developed a system. Whenever Jenn found something she wanted to buy, she would touch it and wink at Sam. That wink was his cue to begin the negotiation. At the second shop, Boutique Jawad, Sam got into a long and spirited conversation in Kashmiri with the owner as he was negotiating.

After a while, Jawad's voice grew louder as did Sam's. Jawad threw up his hands and got red in the face, so did Sam. Finally, Sam handed the angry shopkeeper the money, and he and Jenn walked towards the exit. As they stepped out onto the street, the owner shouted something at them. Sam looked over his shoulder at Jawad and glared as he took Jenn by the elbow and guided her away from the boutique.

'What was that all about?' asked Jenn who had remained quiet during the whole altercation.

'That guy is a jerk,' said Sam. 'He said I had no business being here and that I should let tourists pay what they are willing to pay. That's the way Jawad makes his money, dumb tourists paying too much. He also said some bad things about my father. He'll be sorry he said that.'

Jenn grimaced.

'Don't worry,' said Sam putting a smile back on his face. 'There's nothing to worry about. Let's find Trina.'

Carrying overflowing bags of colorful dresses and shawls, Sam and Jenn arrived at the market and spotted Trina across the plaza, seated on the ground in a circle, playing with a dozen local children. A little boy galloped around tapping the other children on their heads, saying something as he passed each one.

'Look at your friend over there,' said Sam smiling. 'She's having such a good time with the children.'

'That's Trina,' said Jenn, 'she's really just a big kid.'

'She's as beautiful on the inside as she is on the outside,' said Sam, causing one of Jenn's eyebrows to go up.

Later, when they got back to the houseboat, Sam excused himself to help his parents prepare their evening meal. Jenn asked Trina to take one last walk with her before it got dark. The sun was low on the horizon as the day traded places with the night. When the women walked down an alley, an odd-shaped figure lumbered towards them. The shadows along the path and the advancing sunset made it difficult to see clearly who or what was coming. The strange figure was only a few feet in front of them when they saw exactly what it was.

An old man was walking a brown chicken wearing a blue collar tethered by a bright blue leash. The old man smiled proudly, nodded at the women as he and the chicken walked by. Once the odd couple was out of earshot, the two friends burst out laughing.

'India is freakin' crazy,' said Jenn trying to catch her breath. 'You'd never see that in New York.'

'Don't leave tomorrow?' said Trina. 'Send a telegram to your office saying your flight got canceled. Make something up.'

'They'll fire me if I don't show up,' said Jenn as they turned to walk back to the houseboat.

'I'm going to be all by myself.'

'You'll have plenty of company,' said Jenn smiling knowingly.

'What are you talking about?'

'Sam,' Jenn said. 'I see the way he looks at you. When he tells stories, he tells them for you. He gets so happy when he makes you laugh. He told me he thought you were beautiful on the inside and the outside. Clearly, he doesn't know you like I do.'

'He said that?'

'And, my gut tells me, you like him, too. When you told your little tale about your neighbor and the electric company, it was like you were doing a private audition for him.'

'I was not,' said Trina looking away.

'Whatever you say.'

Trina felt herself redden, that full body flush she used to get in high school whenever she'd see Jake Mainelli in the halls.

'He *is* kind of cute,' said Trina, 'but it's not going anywhere. We come from different worlds, and soon I'm going back to mine. I'm certainly not going to stay here in Kashmir.'

'You still have another month here,' said Jenn laughing as the two friends climbed onto the deck of their houseboat. 'A lot can happen in a month.'

After dinner that night, Trina learned Sam was a diehard Bruce Springsteen fan just like she was and when he sang part of a Springsteen song with an Indian twang, it made the women laugh so hard they gasped for air.

'I know everything about American music,' said Sam boasting. 'I love rock and roll. A lot of our guests give me their old music cassette tapes. Tapes are my second favorite treasures after books.'

In the morning, before he drove Jenn to the bus depot, his father spoke to him. 'We've not had a lot of business lately, Samir,' said his father. 'See if you can pick up a few people today.'

'I will, Papa. I'll get ten people, I promise.'

'That would be nice,' said his father. 'By the way, when your mother went to the market this morning, she heard from Mrs Padar that someone threw a big rock through Jawad Boutique's front window. Smashed the whole thing. What's happening in the world? He had to board up his shop and close it.'

'Serves him right,' said Sam as he walked out the door. 'All he does is cheat people anyway.'

Later at the depot, before she got on the bus, Jenn handed Sam a bag filled with her cassette tapes to add to his collection.

'I can't take these from you,' said Sam.

'Who are you kidding?' said Jenn with a smirk. 'I'm done with them anyway. There's a Springsteen in there, too. You can return them to me when I come back.'

As the words left Jenn's mouth, she knew she'd never see Sam again. He knew it, too, but they pretended anyway.

'Be careful,' shouted Trina as Jenn's bus pulled away. Still waving to her friend, Trina told Sam about all the groping they had experienced when they had walked around Delhi.

Sam shook his head and apologized for the behavior of the men in his country. 'I would have killed those guys. Every single one of them.' Sam spoke with fire in his eyes. Trina smiled. He wanted to protect her. That's when she decided to spend the next four weeks in Kashmir — with him.

CHAPTER EIGHT

As Jenn's bus disappeared in the distance, Trina and Sam walked back to the car without speaking. Jenn had been gone for only a few minutes, and already Trina could feel the dynamic between them had changed.

'You're lucky to have a good friend like Jenn,' said Sam. Trina nodded. They sat in the car in silence for a minute.

'I'm going to take you somewhere special today,' Sam said. 'That way, we won't miss Jenn so much.'

'You're the boss,' said Trina.

'Leave everything to me,' said Sam with a grin. 'I'll take you somewhere on the lake.'

They stopped at Sam's family's houseboat to pick up the keys for the small boat.

'Wait in the car, I'll be right back,' said Sam.

'Can I see where you live?' asked Trina. 'I'd love to see how a typical Kashmiri family lives.'

'It's nothing to see.'

'Please, I'd like to.'

Sam shrugged his shoulders and they stepped onto his family's small empty boat. Trina noticed the boat was old and the wood appeared to be rotting in parts. Sam opened the door to the main living space. It smelled of mildew. On the left side of the small room was a wooden table with four chairs. Two worn upholstered easy chairs flanked the far wall. Yellowed sliding glass doors led out to a deck on the water. The kitchen was outside with only a tarp overhead. His parents' bedroom was big enough for a full-sized bed, a single standing lamp and nothing more. Sam's room, entered from the outside at the other end of the boat, contained a bunk bed that he used to share with his sister until she got married. A single light bulb hung by a wire from the middle of the ceiling.

Sadness washed over Trina when she saw that Sam and his family had next to nothing. Compared to the way Sam and his family lived, her apartment with Nanna Mae was a palace.

An hour later, Sam's red shikara glided towards several tiny verdant islands in the middle of the lake.

'I'm taking you to my most favorite place today,' said Sam with a wink.

He ran the shikara up on the shore, and pulled the boat up onto the muddy bank. Then he turned and reached out his hand to her. When she took it, an electric current went through her body and it startled her. That was the first time she had ever physically touched him and she didn't know what to make of it.

Sam led her to a secluded spot surrounded by red flowering bushes. He opened his backpack, spread a blanket on the ground, and unpacked their lunch. When he finished setting the meal out, he looked at her, raised his arms in the air and shouted, 'Ta-da!'

'A feast,' said Trina smiling.

'For a queen,' Sam replied as he bowed and gestured for her to be seated.

'Tell me more about your big plans for your life,' said Trina.

'I've started saving up a little money. I don't have much yet, but I think eventually I'll go live in Paris or Frankfurt,' he said. 'Nothing will happen for me if I stay here.'

'But what about your family?'

'I'll be rich and successful and I'll come back to visit them,' he said. 'I won't spend my whole life on the houseboat. By six, I could speak English fluently and did most of the communication with our guests. At seven, I mastered conversational German, and by the time I was fourteen, I could converse in French, Italian, and Spanish and did all the talking for my parents. I even know a few words in Japanese. *Konnichiwa.*'

Trina laughed. 'You're amazing.'

'I was incorrigible,' said Sam laughing, 'but I loved the attention.'

'I think you still do,' Trina said teasing him.

'Guests gave me their old books, hats, toys, or money as parting gifts. When I got older, I got clothing, shoes and cassette tapes. I've acquired an impressive Western wardrobe. I have six pairs of Italian sunglasses and golf shirts with little crocodile emblems in every color. I even got a pair of Birkenstocks from a Swiss guy.'

'What does your family think about all the tourists?' Trina asked.

'My father just wants their money,' Sam said laughing and then imitated his father. '"I don't care which country has the most beautiful women, Samir, or what country makes the best sunglasses," my father would say. "All I care about is that they pay their bill — in cash"'

Trina laughed at Sam's almost perfect impersonation of his father.

'But here's the thing, everything I know I learned from other people,' said Sam. 'I've never experienced anything for myself. That's why I must move away. Over the years, I have collected hundreds of names and addresses from many of our guests. I know they will help me make some connections.'

'I'm sure they will.'

'I'll probably get a job in Europe or Australia or maybe even America. Then I can visit you and Jenn,' he continued. 'I'll open my rug store and maybe go to a university and study architecture or hospitality.'

'It sounds like a great plan,' said Trina.

'Everybody will know me. I'm going to be famous.'

Trina smiled as Sam laid out his detailed yet scattered and unrealistic dream. His enthusiasm and attention to detail made her believe that somehow, he would make things happen. When he finished sharing his life plan, Sam looked at the Swiss watch on his wrist. 'It's so nice to have someone to tell these things to. My parents don't understand,' he said.

'I loved hearing about all of it,' said Trina smiling. 'You're inspiring, and I know you'll do something extraordinary one day. I bet you will be famous and everyone will know who you are.'

Sam smiled, a woman who appreciated his talents. 'Now, you must tell me about your plan,' said Sam.

Trina thought for a moment and then looked away. 'I don't have one,' she said quietly and her eyes filled with tears. 'You've heard me talk about my grandmother. She was my whole family. This necklace is all I have left of her.' Trina lifted up the silver locket that hung around her neck.

She told him about her life growing up in Astoria, Queens, just across the river from Manhattan but so very different. Sam listened to Trina's story without interrupting.

'I was shy in school but always got good grades, especially in English, because I loved to read, just like you,' she said. 'Reading was my escape, and it's what led me to become a writer. Through books, I could live in other people's lives, people who had families.'

'Family is important,' said Sam. 'One day you'll have your own family and then you can do all the things you missed out on.'

'I don't even know my father's name. Holmgard was my mother's name. Other than Jenn, you're the only other person I've ever told about that,' said Trina. Sam reached over and took her hand and held it firmly.

In one fluid move, he leaned over and kissed her — a long, gentle kiss. A wave of warmth overtook her body as she leaned in and kissed him in the same way.

'You know something,' said Sam sitting back and looking at her. 'You might be the most beautiful girl I have ever known.'

Trina blushed as he leaned in and kissed her again. 'I don't even know how old you are. Maybe I'm too old for you,' she said coyly.

'You're not too old for me, I will turn twenty-one on September first,' said Sam.

'I can't believe it. That was Nanna Mae's birthday, too,' said Trina.

'See, it's in the stars. The moment I saw you, I felt something powerful. It was like, whoosh,' said Sam. 'You're smart, beautiful, and kind. I'm already sad thinking about you leaving in a few weeks.'

He kissed her again but this time a long and passionate kiss that she responded to in kind. Feeling his body next to hers, skin touching skin and being in his arms felt oddly right.

Later, when the shikara sidled up next to Zahra's Palace, Sam jumped out and reached back for Trina's hand to help her off. Sam's mother was walking towards the houseboat at that moment and saw her son with the American woman. She noticed he held the American's hand a second too long.

'Samir!' yelled his mother in Kashmiri. 'Get to the bus depot. No more idle time with the guests. We have empty rooms to fill. This one American isn't going to cover our bills. You need to find more people. Do you hear me?'

'I know, Mama,' he said. 'I'm going soon. I promise to bring back enough people to fill all the empty rooms.'

'Would you like to accompany me to the bus depot?' Sam asked Trina. 'We'll have to keep it a secret though. My father said I have been spending too much time with "one of our guests" and not enough time bringing in new customers.'

CHAPTER NINE

Sam wore a yellow golf shirt, khakis, boat shoes and his favorite pair of Ray-Ban aviator sunglasses.

'What do you think?' said Sam to Trina. 'Do I look like Tom Cruise in *Top Gun* in these glasses?'

Trina giggled as he led her to a particular spot to wait. Soon, a dirty yellow coach pulled into the courtyard and was immediately surrounded. The symphony of shouting went into full throttle. As the tourists descended from the bus, Sam waited until they appeared sufficiently agitated and he moved in for the kill. Within minutes he had secured a group of Brits for his family's boat. The scene looked familiar to Trina and she realized it was exactly the same as on the day she and Jenn arrived.

That night, after Sam and his parents served dinner to their guests, Sam stayed on for several hours chatting about sightseeing plans for the week. Trina watched him, in awe of how easily he was able to charm the entire group.

By ten, the Brits, exhausted from their long trip said goodnight and went to their rooms leaving Trina and Sam alone in the lounge.

'Now I know how I ended up on your houseboat,' she said. 'You're very clever, aren't you?'

'Many people think I'm also charming and handsome, too,' he said playfully as he moved closer to her.

'Oh, you're charming,' Trina teased, 'but handsome might be a bit of a stretch.'

He hung his head. Trina moved towards him and lifted his chin and kissed him. Sam wrapped his arms around her and pulled her in close, and they kissed again, deeper and more passionately. Trina's body felt like it was on fire. Without speaking, she took his hand and led him back to her room and quietly closed the door.

In the morning she was awakened by the familiar crowing of roosters, and she smiled. Lying in bed alone, she thought about their first night together. She had only known Sam for three weeks, but she felt more connected to him than any man she'd ever met. With every conversation, she felt more grounded, and her heart opened further. The final test had been last night, and he more than passed.

Everything had been perfect with one exception. He had to leave her in the middle of the night to return to his family's boat before anyone noticed he was missing. 'My parents wouldn't understand,' he whispered. 'I don't want to leave you, but I must. It's better this way.' He kissed her one last time and then he was gone.

Trina stared at the spinning ceiling fan over her head. *I'm falling in love with a guy who only finished the fifth grade. Is this really happening?*

For the next week Sam took Trina and the other houseboat guests on tours around the region. In the evening, he would say a formal goodnight and leave. Later, after everyone had gone to bed, he'd quietly sneak into Trina's unlocked room. They'd whisper, kiss, laugh and make love as quietly as possible, holding each other tightly until it was time for him to leave.

CHAPTER TEN

Because of his family's business and the proximity of his mother and father, finding time and places for Sam to be alone with Trina was difficult. There would be terrible gossip if anyone saw him spending too much private time with the American blonde, so he came up with a plan and went to speak to his father.

'I've been doing some research, Papa, on how we can grow our business,' said Sam. 'You know Dharamshala, where the Dalai Lama and Tibetan refugees live?'

His father nodded.

'Thousands of travelers go there every year,' said Sam. 'We should develop reciprocal hotel partnerships. We push people to them, and they send people to us.'

Sam's father listened to his son's idea and gave his blessing for Sam to make the trip the next day.

'One day, Samir, you'll do something of great importance in the world,' his father said.

'Also, Papa, the American woman, she's going home tomorrow. I'll drop her off at the bus on my way out.' Sam's father was not sorry to see the young woman go after his wife told him what she had seen.

Sam had chosen Dharamshala because he had heard no one there cared if you were white, black, Asian, Muslim, Jewish or Christian. Creating hotel partnerships would bring in business for his family — and the trip would also give him time alone with Trina.

'We'll have a romantic road trip,' he said as he outlined their itinerary that night while they lay in bed. 'It will be like a honeymoon. We can be totally out in the open there,' he said. 'We wouldn't have to hide from anyone.'

Trina's heart was full. *Sam is what I was supposed to find here. He's the reason I came to India.*

The next morning, they drove for hours, laughing, talking, and singing old Beatles songs as loud as they could. When he pronounced a lyric with an Indian twang, she found it endearing, and it made her laugh.

'Did I tell you that my father was originally from Egypt?' Sam said. 'He came to Kashmir many years ago to work, met my mother, and they fell in love. I was actually born in Egypt while they were visiting my father's brother. If I wanted, I could get a dual citizenship from both Egypt and India.'

'You're so international, like James Bond,' she said laughing and giving him a kiss.

They held hands the entire ride, sharing their most intimate secrets and dreams, opening themselves to each other like they had never done before.

'It was the universe that brought us together,' said Sam.

'I think you're right,' said Trina smiling at him.

When they arrived in Dharamshala, the air smelled clean, and the views of the snow-capped lower Himalayan mountains in the distance created a magical backdrop.

McLeod Ganj, the section of Dharamshala they were going to, looked nothing like the rest of India. The main cobblestone and dirt road that rambled through the center of the town was filled with small dilapidated cafés, shops, and bars, many flying flags with peace signs. 1960s rock and roll music blared from almost every establishment giving the compact ramshackle city the appearance of being locked in a mid-twentieth-century time warp.

The Tibetan people were warm and welcoming and young children danced around the couple as they walked. The street was dotted with groups of young Tibetan men with shaved heads wearing long robes in various shades of red.

The young lovers walked through the courtyard of the Dalai Lama's residence passing statues and giant prayer beads the size of small suitcases.

It was in this courtyard that Sam took Trina's hand for the first time in public.

'We need to find a place to stay,' said Trina. 'I'll pay for it.'

'I can pay,' said Sam, the smile disappearing from his face.

'If I had stayed on your houseboat I would have been paying thirty-five dollars a night,' said Trina. 'Here we can get a room for only fourteen dollars. I'm actually saving money.'

He looked into her blue eyes and nodded. 'When I'm a big success, I'll take you to the penthouse at the biggest hotel in London.'

The next few days passed quickly, and soon, to the young couple's surprise, it was time to leave. On their last night, after they finished making love, Sam was uncharacteristically quiet.

'What's wrong?' Trina asked reaching over, putting her arms around him.

'I keep thinking about you leaving for America,' he said, as a tear trickled down his cheek. 'The days with you have been the happiest of my life. When you leave, my life will be nothing. Trina, I'm so in love with you.'

'I love you, too,' she whispered back. 'Let's not talk about me leaving now,' she said as she kissed him. 'We have tonight, and we still have our drive back to Kashmir.'

'You are so beautiful. I want to spend my life with you. I want to marry you, Trina,' said Sam as he pulled her closer.

'We're soulmates. The odds were against us ever finding each other, but we did,' said Trina, kissing him again. 'Something stronger than the two of us made it all happen.'

'I found you, remember?' Sam said proudly. 'When you got off that bus my heart nearly beat out of my chest. It wasn't an accident when I approached you and Jenn. I never leave anything to chance.'

The two lay in bed devising a plan on how they might build their lives together under what seemed like impossible circumstances.

'How would we ever make this work?' said Trina. 'We're from two completely different worlds. New York City and Kashmir couldn't be more opposite.'

'I'm Muslim, and you're Catholic,' said Sam. 'My family would never accept you.'

'Maybe they'd get used to it,' said Trina. 'Especially after we had kids.' Sam grinned and she blushed.

'Religion always gets in the way. Sometimes, I wonder if there even is a God,' said Sam.

'Me too,' said Trina nodding.

'That's another way we think alike,' said Sam. 'We can make this work if we love each other enough. You trust me, don't you? I can do anything, once I put my mind to it.'

CHAPTER ELEVEN

Back in Kashmir, Trina rented a room on the other side of the city where no one knew them and they could stay together on her last night. Sam dropped her at the hotel and went to see his parents. When he walked through the door, his mother and father sat motionless in separate armchairs.

'Mama? Papa?' asked Sam. 'What's wrong?'

'Sit,' his father said giving his mother a stern glance. 'Your mother and I have not been happy with your behavior and attitude lately. You've been acting like you're some important big man and spending too much time with certain guests, especially the women. Neighbors are talking. Your mother is embarrassed.'

'I don't care what the neighbors say,' Sam said. 'Tell me who is gossiping. I'll shut them up.'

'I will not have it,' his father continued, his voice rising, 'and it stops now.'

'I bring in new customers every day,' said Sam getting angry. 'I run tours that keep them happy. I just secured deals with six different hotels in Dharamshala. I make all the money for this family.'

'I appreciate all those things, Samir,' said his father, 'but I cannot tolerate the other behavior. You will not spend time alone with the women. Is that clear?'

His mother remained silent while the father and son's debate escalated into a shouting match.

'You are an arrogant and ungrateful son,' his father bellowed.

'I hate it here,' Sam snarled. 'You're uneducated and poor. There's no opportunity for me. I hate this miserable houseboat. I deserve more, and I'm going to have it.'

Sam walked out slamming the door and left the boat. He wanted to get back to Trina. The full moon was bright and he could easily see his way. He walked quickly to work off his anger and to get to her as soon as possible. He stepped over the garbage that littered the streets on the way to his van. Since he had met her, everything had changed. Before he had ignored the poverty around him but now it was all he could see.

It was late when his car pulled up near Trina's small hotel. Still shaken from the unexpected fight with his father, Sam asked Trina to go for a walk with him. He guided her along a deserted dirt road to an empty dock on the lake. He pulled out a thin blanket and a couple of beers from his backpack. The two lovers laid down and gazed up at the giant yellow orb in the sky.

'Stay with me for a few more weeks,' Sam begged. 'When I think of you leaving. I feel pain in my chest.'

'My love, you've asked me a hundred times. I can't. I have a job, and I'm supposed to start grad school next week,' she said. 'I used up all the money Nanna left me to pay for school. If I don't leave tomorrow, I'll lose my job and my deposit.'

'I can't breathe without you. Don't leave me.'

'I love you so much,' she whispered.

'I need to ask you something,' Sam said summoning up all his courage. He took a deep breath, sat up on his knees and pulled her to a sitting position.

'Will you marry me and become my wife? You won't ever be alone. We'll start our own family, the one you always dreamed of. I'll always be with you, forever.'

Trina thought her heart might burst. She knew she belonged with him but was at a loss as to how it could work. She touched the surface of her locket with her fingers. Sam's proposal had to be a sign from her grandmother, and she told herself to open her heart and listen.

'But, where would we live?' said Trina. 'I can't live here.'

'I would come to New York with you and open a rug store like I had planned,' he said. 'You know I'll be a huge success and make lots of money for us and always take care of you.'

Trina looked deeply into his dark eyes. 'I will.'

'You'll marry me?'

'Yes. Oh my God, this is so crazy,' said Trina laughing and crying at the same time.

'I am the luckiest man in the world,' Sam cried out as he leaned over and kissed her.

For the rest of the night they planned their lives. The possibilities were endless even though the obstacles were enormous.

'There's going to be a lot of paperwork to fill out, and I have to find out about the rules for visas and marrying someone from another country,' Trina said making a list in her head. 'It will take me about a year to finish school, make all the arrangements and get the money, documentation, and approvals set up.'

'A year is so long,' Sam said.

'We both need to be patient. Right now, I don't have enough money to buy you a plane ticket. If we're going to do this, we need to do it right.'

They walked back on the deserted streets to Trina's hotel room for one last night in each other's arms. Now that they had pledged to marry, the night felt different.

In the morning, when she opened her eyes, she found Sam staring at her. 'Good morning, my wife.'

'What are you looking at?' she said blushing.

'You're so beautiful when you're sleeping,' he said as he climbed on top of her and they made love one last time.

Knowing his parents would be out, Sam stopped at his house and left a note for them saying he had gone to take care of some business in Delhi.

Fourteen hours later Sam and Trina were at the Delhi airport. Holding each other by the gate, Trina wept, while Sam clenched his jaw fearful that once she left she would forget him. Tears sprang from his eyes and rolled down his face. His voice caught in his throat as he tried to speak. Seeing him in such distress, Trina desperately wanted to make his pain go away. That's when she got the idea. She put her hands up behind her neck and unclasped her silver locket.

'Wear it until our wedding day,' she said as she put the chain around his neck. He closed his eyes and nodded — that gift changed everything. Now he knew she *would* come back for him. Moments later she ran for her plane and was gone.

Standing by the gigantic picture window overlooking the runway, Sam watched his future wife's plane taxi down the airstrip and take off. He played with the charm hanging around his neck thinking that soon he'd be going to America.

After boarding the bus to Kashmir, he took a seat in the back near a bunch of boisterous Australian girls. He looked out the window and smiled, dreaming about his new life in New York.

He considered the brightness of his future for a few more minutes and then started a conversation with the Australians. They were funny and loud, and Sam spent most of the long, tedious bus ride making them laugh. By the time they arrived in Kashmir, he had four new paying guests for his houseboat.

One of the Australian girls was particularly pretty and Sam gave her a wink, flashed her a smile and wondered for a moment what it might be like to live in Australia. *I could open a rug shop in Sydney. I've always wanted to see a kangaroo.*

CHAPTER TWELVE

'Miss? Miss, are you all right? Can I bring you anything?' The Air India flight attendants had taken note of the distraught blonde woman who had been last to board in Delhi and were doing their best to comfort her each time they passed.

Trina shook her head and waved the kindly flight attendant away. She blew her red nose and wiped away the tears. *No one can help me. The man I love is on the other side of the world and I'm alone.*

Three days later, still jetlagged, she was back to work at the small medical publishing company on Madison Avenue and 38th Street. Piles of manuscripts and yet-to-be-published articles were waiting for her on her desk. Urgent projects had been handled by co-workers but the rest, six weeks of day-to-day stuff, lay in one massive disorganized heap.

'I'm going to be working until ten o'clock every night,' said Trina to a co-worker when she saw the backlog of paperwork. All day, people stopped by her desk to ask about her trip but she only had one thing on her mind — Sam. She ached for him, and her stomach was churning. She couldn't focus on anything, especially not the files on her desk.

At lunchtime, Trina went to the post office to get some pre-paid international stationery so she could write to Sam several times a week. She passed a newsstand and scanned the headlines. The Olympics were about to start in Seoul. Vice President George H.W. Bush was the favorite to beat Michael Dukakis in the 1988 presidential election in November. At the post office she purchased twenty pale-blue onion skin paper envelopes each with a red-and-blue chevron-patterned border on the outside. On her way back to her office, she stopped at a little coffee shop for lunch and began her first letter.

September 15, 1988
My Love,

I can't believe it's been almost four days since I've touched you. I think about you from the minute I wake up until I fall asleep at night. I got nothing done at work this morning because my brain was completely focused on you. People stopped by my desk and talked to me, but I didn't hear what they were saying because my mind is always focused on you. Does that happen to you, too? I go over every minute that we spent together in my mind so I can re-live it. Everything reminds me of you. Sounds and smells, colors and even the moon.

I'll tell you my little secret — I miss smelling you. Does that sound crazy or weird? You smell delicious, by the way.

I miss the breakfasts on the houseboat and even those annoying roosters in the mornings. In New York, we use an electric alarm clock to wake up and not poultry. Ha! Maybe I should get a rooster. My New York neighbors would chase me out of my building if I did that.

I miss you and love you so much. I'm getting all my pictures developed this week. I'm going over to Jenn's tomorrow night. She's already developed hers and I'll get to see her pictures of your handsome face.

I start school tomorrow night. Working full time and going to school is going to be tough. I love you, my darling and future husband. I guess that means you are my fiancé. I have a fiancé. How cool!

Love always and forever,
Trina

She was about to lick the envelope but stopped and dug into her bag and pulled out a bright red lipstick. Carefully coating her lips with extra gloss, she placed a big red kiss on the blue paper next to her signature. Satisfied, she smiled, sealed the envelope and put it into her satchel to be mailed on her way to the office.

* * *

The next night after work, Trina stopped at Jenn's apartment on East 35th Street on her way home. Jenn lived in an old walk-up building and had a bottle of white wine, two glasses and a plate with cheese and crackers sitting on the coffee table when Trina arrived. Jenn poured two generous glasses of wine and plopped cross-legged on the couch next to Trina.

'Okay, let's have all of it. I want to know everything that happened after I left Kashmir,' Jenn demanded. 'Every bit of juice, leave nothing out. I will decide what's important. I've got lots of time and plenty of wine. OK — go,' she said with a hearty laugh.

Trina got comfortable on the sofa, leaned back, picked up her glass and took a ceremonial sip, milking the moment in the spotlight for all it was worth. She told Jenn the story about her month with Sam in Kashmir; the secret island where they kissed the first time, the night on the docks, their romantic trip to Dharamshala and sneaking around the houseboat at night so Sam's parents wouldn't find out.

'You really think his parents didn't know what was going on?' asked Jenn.

'We were very careful,' said Trina. She told Jenn about her last few days and their awful teary goodbye at the Delhi airport. 'It felt like my heart was being cut out of my chest. He was so upset that I gave him my locket.'

'Wait. What?' shouted Jenn doing a spit take with her wine. 'You gave him your silver locket!'

'And my driver's license.'

'But you never take that thing off. You love it more than anything,' said Jenn as she paused to consider what she had just been told. 'Why did you give him your license?'

'He wanted a picture of me. It was all I had.'

'You're holding something back,' said Jenn suspiciously.

Trina took a deep breath and let it out slowly. 'He asked me to marry him, and I said . . . yes. We're engaged,' said Trina with a big smile.

Jenn's eyes rounded and her mouth opened wide but no sound came out. 'Oh my God,' she finally shrieked.

Trina told her about their plan for Sam to move to New York the following year. Jenn remained unusually quiet and listened without interrupting, remembering the time she saw Sam have that bitter fight with the sari shop owner.

'I want you to be my maid of honor,' continued Trina.

'Of course, I will, you know that,' Jenn replied brightening. 'That was truly big news.'

Jenn leaned over and gave Trina a hug. 'You want to see my pictures now?'

Jenn took out a yellow and red Photo Hut envelope that contained her newly developed pictures from India. As the two friends looked through the images, they reminisced about their great Asian adventure and talked more about the wedding plans.

'You took me totally by surprise,' said Jenn later that evening. 'You know I love you and I'm a little protective of you. I can't believe it. Trina, oh my God! You're going to be a bride.'

Jenn hugged her friend and regained her usual good humor because she knew in the end, the wedding would never happen. There were too many obstacles. When Trina came back down to earth, she'd realize Sam was just an exotic vacation fling. Jenn had one of those when she had gone to Peru the previous year. Pedro had been an attentive and skilled holiday lover during her visit to Machu Picchu. Eventually, Sam would just be a pleasant memory for her best friend and things would go back to normal.

CHAPTER THIRTEEN

New York, 1988

Tired and famished when she arrived home in Astoria after her night class at NYU, Trina opened a can of lentil soup and heated it up in an old dented pot on the stove.

Sitting at the kitchen table, she pulled out a blue envelope with red and blue chevron trim and began to write. Over the next few weeks, she would write a letter to Sam almost every day. A few times, she sent two letters on one day. With each passing week, her feelings intensified making it difficult to focus on anything besides the man she loved who was thousands of miles away. Staying on task at work and in her new writing classes was proving to be a challenge.

Each night she raced home from work or school hoping a letter from Sam had arrived, but there were none. Trina wrote to Sam religiously for the next four weeks, yet still, after a month, she had not received a single letter from her paramour. *What if he doesn't love me anymore? I should have received at least one letter by now. What if he met someone else?*

That night, when she got home from school, Trina pulled out a fresh blue envelope.

October 10, 1988
Dear Sam,

It's been nearly five weeks and I've not heard anything from you. It can't take that long for a letter to go from India to New York. Why don't I hear from you? We pledged our lives to each other that last day in Delhi. Do you not have enough money for the postage? If that's a problem you must get word to me so I can help you with expenses. Your silence is scaring me. I love you so much but when I don't hear from you it makes me crazy. If you love me then why don't you write? I need to hear from you, now.

Jenn says I'm being silly and that I need to be patient, that sometimes, international letters take a long time. It's possible but it's been so long. I NEED TO HEAR FROM YOU. NOW. I mean it. Please write soon. I miss you so much. My heart is breaking.

Love you always and forever,
Trina

She included her customary lipstick kiss at the bottom but she could feel anger coursing through her body.

On her way home the following night, Trina's pace quickened and her heart beat faster as she got closer to her apartment building. Entering the vestibule, she thrust her key into the mailbox lock. When the little bronze metal door creaked open, it revealed several blue *par avion* envelopes nestled within a bunch of junk mail.

'Yes!' she screamed grabbing the mail from the box. *One, two — oh my God, there are five. He loves me!*

With the letters clenched in her fist, she raced up the stairs two at a time to her apartment. Five minutes earlier she had been sad and angry, and felt gullible and used. When she opened her mailbox, her world was suddenly brighter. She was loved.

She sat on the couch and organized the envelopes by date so she could read them in the order they were written.

Picking up the first one, she waited a moment to savor the feeling and then carefully tore open the delicate blue paper.

September 12, 1988
Dearest Trina,

I stopped at the post office in Delhi to pick up some envelopes so I could write to you on this bumpy ride back to Kashmir.

Leaving you today at the airport was difficult. When your plane left the ground, I thought my heart would break in two pieces. Then I touched the locket around my neck and it was like you were there, telling me everything would be all right and that you would come back for me.

One day, we will have a family just the way we said and we will have a perfect life. Forgive my bad handwriting. This bus is bouncing around and I'm writing while leaning on a book. The bus is very crowded but at least it's given me a chance to find some new customers for the houseboat. I met some backpackers from Australia. I'm happy to report they will all be staying on my houseboat for a week, maybe more. My father will be happy.

See, Trina, I'm already starting to make money for our future. I will make as much as possible and save it for our new life in New York. I have a goal now. You are my goal. I might even make some extra money finding customers for other houseboats and make commissions.

That's about all I have to say since I just left you at the airport and nothing much has happened. I will write to you tomorrow.

You are my heart,
Sam

All is forgiven. He totally loves me. He said I was 'his heart'. Aww. Why did I doubt him? The heavy physical weight that had been on her for the past few weeks slowly lifted. She felt light, happy, giddy, almost drunk. A dark fog had lifted and the world was beautiful again — rainbows and butterflies.

Wanting to pace herself and savor each letter, she poured herself a glass of white wine and inhaled a deep breath. Grabbing the multi-colored afghan blanket that Nanna had lovingly knitted years before, she wrapped it around her shoulders and curled up on the couch to begin the next letter.

September 15, 1988
Dearest Trina,

Three long days since you left me in Delhi. As much as a person can miss someone, is how much I miss you.

While you were here, Kashmir was filled with colors. Everything smelled better, tasted good. The sky was bluer, the grass greener, even the grumpy old man who runs the bakery seemed nicer. While you were here, it was like being in heaven. And now, Kashmir is only a place. But I will make the best of it because I know we have a plan to build our lives together. A year seems like a long time but when you think about it, it's only a small part of a lifetime.

I have made a deal with three other houseboats and I will be looking for customers for them and make commissions. I'm thinking of taking a free class in bookkeeping, too. There is a school here in Srinagar that teaches all sorts of accounting classes. If I'm going to run a rug shop or a café in New York, that might help. I need to prepare for my life in America.

Think of me as often as I do you — which is every minute.

You are my heart,
Sam

Trina took a big gulp of her wine. *Everything is fine. He loves me.* She had worried that he might meet another woman, another tourist. Now, after reading his letters, she knew he was devoted to her and all would be good. She opened the third letter. This one was a little different. It started out about her, but then his writing turned to his family's boat business and how he was trying to make more money from the tourists. The majority of the letter was about what he was going to do once he got to New York — how he might open a rug shop or take classes in accounting or architecture. He hardly mentioned their mutual dreams of a life together and focused mainly on his fantasies of his life in America.

She leaned back on the couch. She loved that he worked so hard and was always trying something new, but she liked it better when the letters were more about her. She felt her insecurities creep up the back of her skull. *He is everything I want, and I mustn't sabotage this relationship with my usual doubts and crazy thoughts.*

Pouring herself another glass of wine, she opened the fourth letter. She let out a sigh when she realized that this one was filled with more pledges of his love for her. *How could I have doubted him? He does love me.*

The final letter lay unopened on the coffee table. She picked it up slowly and held it in her hand for a moment. She wanted to make this one last. Who knew how long it would be before new letters arrived? She pictured Sam's face, took a deep breath and slit open the envelope looking forward to the magic carpet love ride she was about to take. But it wasn't a love ride. It was a documentary on fixing up a houseboat, giving tours and serving meals to visiting tourists in Kashmir. There was no mention of their great love, only paragraphs about taking an inventory management class, working so hard on the houseboat and finding people at the bus depot to make more money.

Why is he telling me about all the guests? I don't care that there's a couple from Switzerland or three sisters from Rome staying on Zahra's Palace. Does he like one of the sisters? Is he trying to tell me something?

Stop it, Trina. You always do this.

She put the letter down and tears welled up in her eyes as she talked herself off the ledge. She picked up the blue paper and re-read the last few lines.

> *I'm always thinking of how I can build my business while I make a good life for us.*
> *You are my heart,*
> *Sam*

Trina stared at the blue paper and tried to focus on the last line: 'while I make a good life for us. You are my heart.' *He did say 'us' and he said I was his 'heart'.*

She felt a little let down and was sorry she had saved this letter for last. His first letter had been romantic and with each one, they had gotten progressively less romantic. The last one talked mainly about the houseboat and hardly mentioned her at all.

Insecurity had always been her undoing. Fears of inadequacy routinely lurked in the back of her mind and undermined her success, especially with men.

Nanna used to warn her about that. 'Why do you always doubt yourself, Cookie?' her grandmother would say. 'You're a beautiful smart girl. As far as I'm concerned, you're practically perfect. Relax. Have a little fun. You're your own worst enemy.'

Nanna was right. Don't let your stupid baby fears ruin this relationship like all the others. He wrote about the houseboat and his classes because that's what he's doing. Some letters are going to be romantic and some will just be news. Get over yourself, his next letter will be amazing and romantic.

Then she remembered that one angry letter she had written to him when she hadn't received anything and instantly regretted it. She pushed all the crazy thoughts out of her head and focused again on the mound of open blue letters in front of her. She pulled out a blank sheet of blue *par avion* stationery and began to write.

> *October 21, 1988*
> *Dear Soulmate,*
>
> *When I opened my mailbox today I found not one but five letters from you. Until today, I had not received anything. I was going insane. When I didn't hear from you, I thought maybe you didn't love me anymore. That's why I wrote that last cranky crazy letter to you. I was upset and scared because I hadn't heard anything.*
>
> *Forgive me for doubting you, just rip that letter up, don't even read it. I'll have to get used to the slow Indian*

mail service. I guess it could take a couple of months for a letter to get through. Being apart from you is torture and I think about you all day long. I love you with all my heart.

All my love (and kisses),

Trina xoxoxox

She loaded up her lips with red lipstick and placed a big red kiss on the inside of the letter next to her name. She had to keep him wanting her.

CHAPTER FOURTEEN

It had been nearly six months since Trina and Sam had parted at the Delhi airport. Despite the distance between them, her love for him had only grown stronger. She missed looking into his eyes and ached for the feeling of his arms around her. She loved him even more after six months of being apart than the day she had left him in India.

Grad school was going well and Trina liked her teachers and classes. Soon she would finish her coursework and apply for a bigger and better journalism job where she would make more money and bring her true love to New York. Working all day and going to school at night with studying and papers on the weekends had at times been overwhelming. But, she kept her eye on the prize — Sam. All the hard work would be worth it when she landed that dream job at one of the top magazine companies in New York — Hearst or Condé Nast. Without a degree from the right school, those two organizations wouldn't consider hiring someone for an editorial job. Trina's undergraduate degree from city college was not considered the 'right school', but a master's from NYU could be the golden entry ticket. A better job meant more money and she could bring Sam over much sooner.

She still regularly wrote to her future husband several times a week but lately had noticed his letters came less frequently. She needed to hear from him and be reassured. When she didn't get a letter her mind would wander into dark places creating all sorts of scenarios of Sam romancing other women. When she opened her mailbox and saw blue envelopes, her doubts faded away. One thing she was desperate for was to talk to her soulmate, to hear his voice, to melt from his laugh. It had been more than six months since they had actually spoken to each other and in her next letter, she suggested that Sam pick a time to do their first phone call . . . *I need to hear your voice, my love. International calls are so expensive. It will cost ten dollars for the first three minutes and then five dollars for each additional minute, but it will be worth it. I've saved up. We'll just have to keep the conversation short, OK . . .?*

Sam's family's houseboat had no phone. He would have to take the call at the Western Union office. Trina would call the following Sunday, when phone rates were cheapest.

Kashmir was ten and a half hours ahead of New York. On that particular Sunday morning at eight a.m. New York time, Trina carefully dialed the international number of the Western Union office near Sam's home. After eight double rings, a man's voice answered and said something in Kashmiri followed by 'Western Union'.

'I'm calling from America,' Trina shouted into the phone.

'America? One minute,' said the man. She heard a lot of garbled noise and then after ten seconds . . .

'Trina? Is it you?'

Her heart pounded as his voice electrified her entire body. A wave of relief and gratitude washed over her and made her limbs tingle.

'Yes, Sam, it's me. Oh my God, I've missed you so much. It's so good to hear your voice. Every night I dream about all the time we spent together in Kashmir, just the two of us. It was so incredible. I love you so much,' she said rapidly, tears filling her eyes.

'I play the films of you in my head every day and think about the time when we will be together again,' said Sam. 'I can't wait until we're married and living together in New York.'

'Me too. I love you.'

'Trina, I've got so much to tell you. I've been doing research on importing rugs and how to set up a rug business in New York,' he said, his words tripping over themselves. 'I've even lined up different local Kashmiri vendors to work with me. They're all ready to send products to the United States and be my suppliers. I'm hoping I can get some merchandise from Delhi, too. I've got everything figured out. It will take some time but I was talking to my cousin and he told me that . . .'

Trina listened to Sam while she kept her eyes on her watch. The time had passed so quickly and their call had already gone for fifteen minutes. So far, it had cost her about seventy dollars. She needed to wrap the call up or she would be eating nothing but peanut butter and jelly sandwiches for the next few weeks.

'I've made lots of contacts for my import business,' he continued. 'I talked to all of our foreign guests about my plans and got their opinions. They all think my idea is very sound and clever.'

'Sam, I haven't gotten many letters from you lately.'

'I've been so busy, with all the guests, my love. You know how crazy it gets here.'

'I know but . . .'

'One of our guests told me that diners in New York refill your coffee for free. For free! I want to go there and sit all day and drink my free coffee. Then, I'll take the ferry to Staten Island. I heard that's free, too. Maybe I'll get my free coffee and take it with me on the free boat and—'

'I'm sorry to interrupt, Sam, but we've got to finish. The call is five dollars a minute and I think it's already cost about seventy-five or eighty dollars,' she said.

'I'm such an idiot. I was so excited to hear your voice and it looks like I did all the talking and all I wanted to tell you is a little about—'

'Sam, seriously, I have to go.'

'Oh, sure, sure,' said Sam. 'OK, then, Trina. It was so good to hear your voice. Write soon.'

'I love you,' said Trina a second later into a dead phone.

She leaned back on her bed. At first, hearing his voice was like slipping on a pair of cozy worn-in slippers. He sounded so happy to hear from her but he talked only about his rug business and living in New York. *Did he say he loved me or that he missed me?* Most of the call was about how much profit he would make on his rugs. He never asked how she was.

That familiar little worm of doubt crawled around Trina's brain as she did a mental inventory of their relationship. For the last six months, she calculated she wrote four or five letters for every one she received from him. The tone of his writing had changed over time. They used to be about their relationship but more recently they focused exclusively on him and his future life in America. *Is he in love with me or is he in love with New York? Am I his soulmate or am I only the way for him to get out of India?* She wondered if he went to the bus depot every day looking for a new woman to romance, that maybe he was having an affair with another girl. Trina's imagination ramped up into overdrive. *That would explain why he didn't write. Maybe he writes to ten different women around the world. He might be in bed with someone else right this second. He probably has women all over the world and he's just waiting for the one who moves first? STOP IT, TRINA. You're going down that rabbit hole again. You always do this. Always. Nana warned you.*

About to go over an emotional cliff, Trina inhaled and then exhaled the way her grandmother had taught her. When she finally calmed herself down, she reached for Sam's most recent letter dated March 22, 1989 and re-read it. It was like so many of the others, all about the houseboat guests and the tours he was taking them on. How he was working so hard and even started cooking some of the meals for the guests. Then, his conversation turned to his future in New York. How he had been reading everything he could get his hands on about New York City and how he tried extra hard to pick up American tourists at the bus depot so he could learn more about the United States.

He said he wanted to go to the Empire State Building, Lincoln Center, and Yankee Stadium to see an American baseball game. He wanted to eat a hot dog from a real New York City hot dog cart and go to Little Italy, the Statue of Liberty, Chinatown and Grand Central Station. He planned to spend hours walking around Central Park and take a carriage ride. He told her that the week before he had guests staying on the houseboat from New York who had given Sam their address and told him to get in touch once he got to New York. Apparently, they promised to buy some rugs from him. As always, he signed his letter with his customary: 'You are my heart'.

Trina put the letter down and her eyes started to burn.

He had the chance to send something to me through those New Yorkers who stayed on his boat and he didn't even think of it. Everything is always about him — his new life, what he's going to do, the friends he's going to make. It isn't about 'me' or 'us', only him.

Trina felt nauseous as she wondered if everything he told her was a lie and if it was all a set up for him to get to America. *I've been so stupid and gullible. Those walks through the gardens, the passionate nights, the boat rides, the tenderness, the laughter. Is he my soulmate or is he using me to get to a better life? He always said he never does anything by chance.*

Teetering on the verge of a full meltdown, Trina called Jenn for a reality check.

'I think Sam's using me,' shouted Trina into the phone as she sobbed. Without stopping for a breath, she told her friend about the phone call and the change in tone of Sam's letters. She read several of them to Jenn and they spent the next three hours dissecting them line by line.

'First of all, I think you are overreacting,' said Jenn. 'You haven't been face-to-face with him in a long time. It's possible he's using you, but that's a pretty devious long-term game he'd be playing. I don't think Sam is that diabolical. He was a nice, sweet, smart guy who was totally infatuated with you.'

'You really think so?'

'Look, there's nothing wrong with your American citizenship being an appealing factor for him,' said Jenn. 'Plenty of men go out with women because they're beautiful or have a good body or big boobs. And, loads of women marry men who have a lot of money and are successful.'

'I guess,' said Trina sniffling, beginning to calm down.

'Wanting to come to America doesn't mean he doesn't love you,' Jenn continued. 'The American citizen part is just an extra cherry on top.'

'You really think so?'

'My mother always said, you can love a rich man as well as a poor one,' said Jenn. 'So what, if a new life in New York is part of the attraction? You're blowing this out of proportion.'

When their call ended many hours later, Trina was calm until she re-read Sam's last letter and got angry and paranoid all over again.

He's using me. I know it. He played me.

She thought about all the moments they had shared. The trip to Dharamshala, their nights under the moon, his kisses. For months, she had been reliving and clinging to all those romantic scenes and building them up in her mind. Now, she saw everything through an entirely different lens — one of deception.

I'm just the vehicle for him to get to the United States and get his American citizenship. That's all he wants.

With tears running down her cheeks, Trina snatched up his letters in her hand. She was about to throw them all into the trash when she remembered Nanna's locket. She had given it to Sam in that reckless moment of passion at the Delhi airport. Not a hundred percent sure about Sam's true motives, she knew one thing — she had to get her locket back, no matter what.

I told him he could keep it until the day we got married.

Shit.

* * *

April 5, 1989

Dear Sam,

Hello my darling. I just re-read one of your letters today and it made me miss you more than ever. I'm looking forward to seeing you soon and hoping I can book my trip to India sometime in July. Only four more months until we're together again. Still saving up for it, my love. I can't wait to see your handsome face and feel your arms around me.

Soon, we'll begin our lives together. I can't wait for you to hold me again. In the meantime, I have a favor to ask of you. I know I gave you my locket to keep until I came back but it reminds me of my grandmother and I've been missing her so much lately. Would you mind terribly sending it back to me, now. We'll be together soon, anyway. Thank you for understanding, my love. You know how much I loved Nanna Mae.

Kisses.

Love always,

Trina

She coated her lips with red lipstick and planted a big red kiss next to her name like she always did.

Three weeks later, in early May, she got his response. He wrote about the usual stuff, houseboat guests, his future life in New York . . .

I've been reading all I can about America and watching movies, too. I saw a movie called Wall Street *and read a book called* Bonfire of the Vanities. *There sure are a lot of crazy people in New York with a lot of money. Money makes people do terrible things.*

About the locket, you promised I could keep it until we got married. It gets me through the days and nights without you. I never take it off because it's like having a piece of you with me. You told me I could keep it until our wedding day. I promise I'll put it on your neck right after we say our vows.

You are my heart,

Sam

When she read his response, she made her decision. She would have to go back to India to get the locket herself. Only then, when she looked into his eyes, would she know what was in his heart. He was either her soulmate — or a world-class liar.

The next day she booked a July flight to Delhi and wrote to him about her arrival.

Sam was surprised and delighted Trina was returning to him. Everything was finally coming together. In no time, he'd be living in New York.

CHAPTER FIFTEEN

India, July 1989

Two and a half months later, an old yellow bus lumbered towards the depot in Srinagar, Kashmir. Trina wiped her clammy hands on her shirt and wondered if they were wet because she was excited to see Sam, or scared to learn the truth. Regardless, she told herself, the main objective for this trip was to retrieve the locket.

As the bus stopped with a screech, Trina peeked her head out the window. She scanned the crowd and caught a glimpse of Sam, standing in his favorite spot, apart from all the others. He was smiling with anticipation and holding an enormous bouquet of yellow and white flowers. His creamy tan complexion was offset by a crisp white linen shirt. She noticed his thick wavy brown hair was longer and thought it looked sexy. He was taller and looked more mature than she remembered. He looked good.

When he spotted her through an open window, he smiled from ear to ear and waved. Their eyes locked and Trina felt her breath involuntarily quicken.

I had forgotten how nice his smile was. And his eyes. He looks genuinely happy to see me. He brought me flowers. Aww. Was I completely wrong about him?

Despite all the crazy negative thoughts she had been having over the past weeks and months, at that moment she was very glad she was there and smiled and waved at him with genuine enthusiasm.

He ran over to her window and reached his hand out. She extended hers and when they touched, electricity shot up her arm. The sensation confused her even more. She waited for all the other people on the bus to disembark using the time to take several deep breaths.

When she climbed down the steps into the bright sun, a grinning Sam bowed and presented his flowers.

'I can't believe you're really here,' he said as he stepped back to get a better look at her. 'You know I'd pick you up and kiss you if I could, but there are too many people around. You've grown more beautiful in the months we've been apart.'

Trina blushed. 'Your hair is longer, it looks good,' she said, vaguely aware that her doubts about him were fading.

'I've missed you so much,' said Sam. 'I couldn't sleep this whole week thinking about your arrival. My beautiful Trina is finally here.'

She looked up into his dark, gentle eyes rimmed with those thick black lashes and smiled. 'Come on,' she said with a grin, 'let's get out of here. I'm starving and desperately need a bathroom.'

Sam grabbed her backpack and bags and carried them to the van. They had to be careful. They couldn't kiss or hold hands or anything like that or news would go directly back to his father. They casually walked towards the van like two friends. He started the engine and drove out of the depot. Five minutes later he pulled over to the side of the road, switched the engine off and turned to face her.

He leaned over and gave her the most loving kiss she had ever received in her entire life and she kissed him back in the exact same way. With his arms around her, and his lips on hers, all her concerns dissolved.

He told her everything was arranged for Trina to stay on Zahra's Palace. She would have the same room that she had the last time. As they drove, Sam chattered on about all the upgrades and improvements he had made to the boat and was eager for her to see his handiwork. When they stopped at a little café for some lunch, Sam talked nonstop, filling her in on a year's worth of information in less than an hour. Trina smiled as each detail was shared: his classes; boat renovations; new business ideas and all the guests he had procured.

When they got to the lake everything was just as Trina remembered. She looked out on the beautiful water with its rows and rows of houseboats. Chickens, roosters and an assortment of other animals roamed about without a care in the world. Sam honked the horn three times when they pulled up to Zahra's Palace and Sam's mother and father came out and waved.

'Welcome,' said Sam's father looking at her skeptically as she climbed out of the car. 'Not many people come back here.'

'Tell your parents that this time I'm only here for a week because of my job,' said Trina. 'It takes a full day to get to India from New York and then another day to get from Delhi to Kashmir. I only get two weeks off from work and I spend four of the days traveling. This will be a quick trip, but I'm glad to be here.'

Sam translated all of what she said to his parents and thought he detected a look exchange between them.

'Tonight,' said Sam's father, 'my wife will make something special for you to eat, in honor of your second visit.'

'I can't wait,' said Trina smiling. 'But now, I need to lie down for a few minutes.' Sam's mother and father nodded and gestured for Trina to board the houseboat.

His father turned to his son and spoke to him in Kashmiri. 'Come home with us and let the American rest.'

'I'm just going to help her get settled and show her all the improvements, Papa. I'll only be a few minutes.'

'I don't want any funny business, Samir.'

'Ten minutes, Papa.'

With that, his parents turned and walked down the road towards their own houseboat. Sam proudly showed Trina around the boat and pointed out the gleaming new wooden rails he had refinished.

'I did all the work myself,' he said. 'Don't they look elegant?' He pointed out each spot on the boat where he had made an improvement. The floating hotel gleamed. Outside, the boat was freshly painted and Sam had made a new sign with lights that said: *Zahra's Palace*. Underneath it said: *The Best Cook in Kashmir*. Trina was truly awed by the breadth of his skills and made appropriate sounds of admiration. Sam was visibly pleased. *For someone so young he's really quite remarkable.* He showed her to her room, placed her backpack on the chair and leaned over and kissed her.

'I can't believe you're really here,' he said, as he wove his fingers between hers. He leaned in and pressed his body against hers and that's when Trina's body made the decision before her mind had rendered its verdict.

'I've missed you,' she said as she kissed his neck again and again, his powerful arms embracing her.

* * *

That evening, Trina was in the dining room with some other guests from Sweden, a married couple in their late twenties with their four-year-old daughter. The adorable little blonde girl entertained the group throughout the meal and Trina spent most of the night playing with the child. Sam lovingly watched his fiancée interact with the little girl out of the corner of his eye and wondered who was having more fun. *One day, she'll be a great mother for our children.*

When the dishes were cleared, Sam and his parents said goodnight and left. The Swedish family retired to their room and Trina went to hers. She washed her face, changed into her nightgown and laid down on the bed to wait for him. They hadn't discussed it, but she knew he would come to her.

Twenty minutes later she heard a faint creak and then a soft shuffle on the floor outside her door. The knob turned slowly and Sam stepped into the dark room. 'I told my parents I was going out with some friends,' he whispered and took off his shirt and pants in two quick moves. He stretched out on the bed next to her. With his body pressed into hers, the same old intoxicated emotion overcame her, so thick you could cut it with a knife. Everything felt familiar. It felt right. She remembered now what had drawn her to him.

'It's like a dream that you're here,' said Sam. When Trina kissed his neck, she felt the chain of her grandmother's locket against her lips. With all the emotions of the day, she had completely forgotten all about it.

'You're still wearing it,' she said casually as she touched it with her fingers. 'I wondered if you wore it all the time, like you said in your letters.'

'I've never taken it off. Not once since you left,' he said. 'It makes me feel close to you when I feel it against my skin. It's like you're with me even when you are not. This was the greatest gift you could have ever given me. It's made being apart bearable.'

A little voice echoed inside her head. *Get the locket.*

'That's why I gave it to you. Now that I'm here, can I have it back?' asked Trina.

Sam sat up in bed, his hand on the locket. 'You promised I could keep it until we said our wedding vows. I've dreamed of putting this around your neck on our wedding day, just like your great-great-grandparents did.'

Trina rolled over and turned her back to him. 'But I gave you the locket to prove that I would come back and here I am. Isn't that enough?'

'Let's not talk about that now,' he said as he flipped her over and kissed her. For the next few hours, he tenderly made love to her and all of Trina's insecurities and misgivings slowly faded.

In the morning, Trina woke up alone, and replayed their conversation from the night before. The lovemaking had been incredible, even better than she remembered. Sam had been adoring and gentle and she found herself more confused than ever. He acted like he really loved her, not just her American citizenship. Still, several times she tried to get him to give the locket back to her and each time he dodged the question.

'I have an idea,' he had said as he pulled her closer. 'Why don't we get married now while you are here?'

'What?'

'We could get married in Dharamshala the day after tomorrow,' said Sam. 'Then we could be together always and I'll give you the necklace.'

'You want to get married? Now?'

'It would be easier for me to come to America if we were already married,' said Sam. 'We could elope. Wouldn't that be romantic?'

'And then you'd give me the necklace?'

'Of course, my love, that was our agreement. If we elope, I won't have to argue with my parents about you not being a Muslim,' said Sam. 'By the time they find out, we will already be married and it will be too late for them to do anything.'

'Where would we do it?' she had asked wondering just how far he'd go and calling his bluff.

'I'll make all the arrangements,' Sam had said. 'Don't worry about anything. We can leave tomorrow and soon we will be husband and wife.' As he slipped his arm around her waist and drew her into him and kissed her, his thoughts were on his future. *I'm going to America and my life will be incredible.*

CHAPTER SIXTEEN

Kashmir, July 1989

The next morning, sitting alone at the breakfast table on the houseboat unable to get food down, Trina tried to take her mind off what she was about to do. This wasn't an ordinary day at all. Today, was her wedding day. She looked at her reflection in the mirror hanging on the wall.

I'm getting MARRIED today. I only came here to get my locket. What am I doing?

They had agreed to keep their marriage a secret until they both agreed the time was right to share the news. She looked into her own eyes in the mirror. *This is either the smartest thing you've ever done or the stupidest. He's either your knight in shining armor or a duplicitous con artist. But which one? Which is he?*

To throw off his parent's suspicion, Sam told them Trina had received an urgent telegram from America: her cousin was extremely sick and she had to return to New York immediately. The last bus of the day had already left. The American offered to pay Sam to drive her to Delhi so she could catch her plane to New York.

'You are going to take her all the way to Delhi?' said his father. 'That's a twelve-hour trip. That's crazy. Why would you do that?'

'Papa, it's an emergency,' said Sam. 'She's my friend, and besides, she offered to pay me a lot of money to take her there. And, she'll pay for all the gas, too. While I'm there, I can visit my friend, Ariff, for a few days. You remember Ariff, don't you, Papa?'

Sam's father grumbled, and he shook his head. The American woman was trouble. He wanted to forbid his son from going but he could see the look of determination on Sam's face. At least the American would finally be gone from his houseboat, and he hoped this time it was for good.

Trina tried to wrap her head around what was happening. Only a few days earlier, she had been at her desk in New York editing a men's fitness and grooming book. Now, she was about to travel into the mountains and marry her Indian lover. *This is crazy.* With her head spinning, she recognized the ridiculousness of the situation and started to laugh out loud picturing Jenn's incredulous face. *Wait until Jenn hears about this. She'll lose her freaking mind.*

With the van packed, Sam drove away from Zahra's Palace for what he thought was his last time as a single man. When he saw his parents again, he would be Trina's husband and on his way to becoming an American.

'What are you smiling about?' asked Trina touching his arm as the van sped down the road.

'It's my wedding day, and I'm about to marry the most beautiful girl in the world,' he said. He held the steering wheel with his right hand and reached out to hold her hand with his left. She pushed her fingers through his and squeezed.

In the early afternoon, they arrived in Dharamshala. Sam had it all set up through some of the contacts he had made on their trip the previous year. They were to get married at four p.m. Before the ceremony, they checked into the same small hotel they had stayed in the year before. Trina went to their room alone to clean up after the long car ride and change into her wedding outfit. Earlier, they had stopped at a dress shop, and she bought an embroidered white sari with pink and gold accents. She put it on for the first time, and slipped on a pair of matching flat white beaded shoes. She ran a comb through her hair, pinned it up, and covered her head with a white and gold shawl. She put on some lip gloss and took one last look in the mirror. *Am I really doing this?*

Sam stood nervously in the hotel lobby wearing a pheran, a long loose traditional Kashmiri white linen gown. On his head, he wore a bright green turban. When Trina laid eyes on him, she thought he looked like an Indian prince and her heart fluttered.

Sam's eyes opened wide when he saw his beautiful bride for the first time. Always mindful of the details, he smiled and pulled a small bouquet of wildflowers from behind his back and handed them to his bride with a sweeping bow.

'Flowers for the beautiful bride,' he said. 'You are the most perfect woman that ever walked on this earth.'

Trina blushed. *He does love me. This is a good thing we're doing. We're going to be so happy.*

It was time to go. They left the hotel and walked through town to a tiny one-room government registry office.

'We will be married in a religious ceremony later, but we must first register here,' said Sam to his bride. 'I will receive the official documents of our marriage from this office in thirty to ninety days or more, you never know. This is India.'

Trina nodded while opposing inner voices battled inside her head. *Run away! But he loves me, doesn't he?*

In the registrar's office, the two young people signed some papers and then headed over to a small Buddhist temple where a monk with a shaved head and a red-orange robe waited to marry them. Two other monks came into the room to be witnesses.

Sam took Trina's hands as the first monk took his place in front of them. The priest held a small book and read passages in a language Trina didn't understand. The monk said something to her and waited for a response.

'You have to say "yes" now,' whispered a smiling Sam to his bride.

'Yes,' said Trina, as she nodded her head thinking it all a bit ridiculous. Then the monk said something to Sam and waited. Sam looked at Trina.

'Yes,' he said as he looked into her eyes. The monk smiled, mumbled a few more phrases, bowed to each of them and shook both their hands. Then he leaned over and whispered something to the groom. Sam nodded and pulled out two very thin silver wedding bands from his pocket and smiled at Trina.

'I never forget anything,' said Sam. 'One is for you and one is for me. I guessed at the size.'

The monk conducting the ceremony said a few more unintelligible words and waved his arms in the air. Sam lovingly put a silver ring on her finger, and she did the same with his. It was all over so fast and the monks left the room.

'Are we married?' Trina whispered to Sam as they stood alone in the room.

Sam leaned over and kissed his bride on the forehead. 'We are,' he said smiling. 'You are now my wife, and I am your husband. Soon, we'll begin our new life together in America.'

'I can't believe we just did this,' said Trina smiling nervously, trying to calm her conflicting emotions.

'Are you sorry you married me?'

'It all happened so fast; that's all.'

'Soon, we'll be together all the time. Once we're in America together everything will be great. You'll see.'

Later that night after they enjoyed a wedding supper together and received congratulations from everyone at the hotel, the newlyweds sat in bed talking.

'Remember, I can't do anything to bring you to America until I receive the marriage documents from you. I did some research on this, US Immigration can be difficult, especially when it comes to foreign marriages.'

That night as they undressed, Sam unhooked the locket and placed it around his wife's neck as he had promised. Trina sighed with relief; the locket was back where it was supposed to be, and she vowed never to take it off again. That evening in bed, all of her concerns about Sam disappeared as their bodies became one again. *I was crazy to think he didn't love me. He does. He totally loves me.*

The following morning, the newlyweds drove south towards Delhi. They had a final few days together as husband and wife before Trina flew home to arrange for her new husband's passage to America.

'Just think,' said Sam, smiling at his new wife while squeezing her hand, 'a year from now, we'll be together in New York City.'

CHAPTER SEVENTEEN

Delhi, July 1989

The newlyweds arrived in the sprawling city early the following evening and planned to spend two days and nights there for a short honeymoon before Trina took her flight home to New York. They stopped at the airline office in downtown Delhi to pick up Trina's tickets. A mob of angry travelers stood inside, outside and all around the Air India storefront. The crowds prevented Trina and Sam from getting anywhere near the entrance.

'What's going on?' Trina asked a woman standing nearby.

'It's a bloody nightmare, is what it is,' said a woman with a posh British accent. 'The airlines have screwed everything up. They overbooked all the flights to Europe and America by the thousands. Everyone's stranded.'

'They can't do that,' said Trina. 'I have to get back to New York. I have to be at work on Monday.'

'The airlines in India do this all the time,' said a second British woman joining the conversation. 'Usually they only bump a few people, but this summer, it's thousands. There was a riot out here yesterday. People were fighting and throwing rocks and bottles, and then the police were called.'

'What am I going to do?' said Trina to no one in particular.

'We heard people are organizing chartered buses to Germany,' said the first British woman. 'We might do that. Come with us, and you can pick up a flight to the States from there. All the airlines are overbooked; there's not a seat to be had for another two weeks.'

'Then, we'll have more time for our honeymoon,' said Sam leaning over and kissing the top of Trina's head. Surprised, the two British women looked at Trina and then at Sam.

'You two are newlyweds?' blurted out one of the women. 'Congratulations! I'm Emily, and this is my sister, Olivia. When did you two get married?'

With much fanfare, Sam told the women about their elopement and how he and Trina had met for the first time a year before, and had fallen madly in love and continued their relationship through letters. He told them about the locket and how it was the one thing that got him through the long months of missing her.

'That's so romantic,' said Emily nodding to her sister.

'When Trina came back to visit, we decided we couldn't wait any longer, and we got married,' said Sam. 'I'm moving to New York, and I'm going to import Indian rugs and open a rug store.' He told them about the plans he had for the expansion of his single store into a rug empire. 'I might even have cafés in my stores so people could have something to eat while they shopped for new carpets.'

The two British ladies got a kick out of Sam's enthusiastic storytelling, and the four decided they would all hang out together while they waited to get out of Delhi.

For the next five days, each morning the four new friends trudged across Delhi through the hot sticky summer heat to the Air India office only to be told to come back the next day and try again. Sam sent a telegram to his parents telling them that the van had broken down in Delhi and it would take a few days until he could get it repaired. Trina sent a telegram to her office in New York explaining the delay and praying her company would accept her explanation.

The next morning, when she and Sam went to the airline office, she received good news. They had a seat for her on the eleven p.m. flight that night with a stopover in Frankfurt. She was told to return at four p.m. to pick up her tickets. Trina was elated while Sam was suddenly and unusually quiet.

'What's wrong, love?' asked Trina.

'I know you have to leave, but I'm going to miss you terribly,' said Sam taking her hand.

They went back to their cheap Delhi hotel to meet up with Olivia and Emily who were waiting for them at the hotel café.

'Guess who got a seat on the eleven p.m. flight to Frankfurt tonight?' said a smiling Trina.

The British ladies hugged and congratulated her, and told Trina that they too were leaving on a bus that night through Iran and bound for Europe. The four sat down at the café to have a beer and celebrate their last few hours in India together.

'It's quite amazing really,' said Emily. 'I've known you two for only a few days, but it feels like a lifetime, doesn't it?'

'Soon, we will all be going in different directions,' said Olivia. 'We'll be riding in a bus across the Middle East to England. Trina will be flying to New York, and Sam, you'll be heading up to Kashmir. Right now, here we are, sitting together at this tiny café in Delhi drinking a beer. In just a few short hours, we'll be in disparate corners of the globe.'

'Sam, tell us more about your family's houseboat,' said Emily. 'It sounds beautiful.'

Sam obligingly described the boat in detail with Trina occasionally chiming in. Soon he segued into his plans for his life in America. While she listened, Trina noticed Sam never mentioned her in any of the future scenarios. Not once, it was only about him and the things he was going to do, the places he was going to see. Sam went on and on and on.

'I always knew I'd end up in America or Europe,' Sam said. 'It was my destiny. I almost married a French girl a year and a half ago and moved to Provence. I would have opened a rug store there, of course, but . . .'

A bolt of clarity hit Trina between the eyes as she grappled with the piece of information she had just learned. *A French girl? He never mentioned a French girl or that he almost married her.* Trina grew quiet while she tried to make sense out of what Sam had just said. The British women didn't notice his comment and they and Sam continued their convivial conversation. At three o'clock, as planned, Sam excused himself to go across the city to pick up his wife's plane tickets. Before he left, he leaned over and kissed her on the top of her head.

'Take care of my little wife while I'm gone,' he said to the British ladies as he ran off. 'I don't want to lose her.'

'He's scrumptious,' said Emily leaning over the table towards Trina as they watched Sam disappear down the road. 'He's so bright and he obviously adores you. You're a lucky girl.'

'He's lovely, Trina,' said Olivia. 'Every guy I meet is either unemployed, lives with his mother or worse. Your darling husband is so ambitious with all those ideas about importing rugs and opening restaurants. He's quite the entrepreneur. It must be difficult for you to leave him now, right after your wedding.'

Trina pressed her lips together.

'Don't worry, hon,' said Emily, 'he'll be with you soon enough.'

Trina looked at the two women for a moment before she spoke. Different realities were competing for space in her brain. 'Let me tell you something. Tonight, I'm leaving on the eleven o'clock flight to New York and that will be the last time he ever sees me. After today, he will never hear from me again,' said Trina with no emotion in her voice.

The British women gasped in unison. 'What do you mean?' asked Emily.

'You don't know him the way I do. He's an excellent liar, and puts on a good show,' Trina said icily. 'You don't know it, but everything he says is a lie. It took me a while to figure it out because he's so manipulative, and I was naive and stupid. What you don't understand is, he never loved *me*. He only wants to get to America and get out of India. It could have been me. It could have been anyone. And apparently, it could have been a *French girl.* I'm nothing more than his ticket out of this dump of a country.'

Noting the British women's shocked expressions, Trina explained further. She told them the story of her first trip to Kashmir and how Sam had romanced her and showered her with compliments.

'He said all the right words to make me believe he loved me and I fell for it,' said Trina. 'Over time, his love letters went from prose about adoring me to long narratives on the great new life he was going to have in New York; how successful he was going to be; and all the friends he was going to make. After a while, his letters were only about him.'

'But how can you be so sure?' said Olivia. 'He seemed genuine to me.'

'Why did you come back to India if you had so many doubts?' asked Emily. 'Why did you marry him?'

'I had to get my grandmother's locket back. I thought when he saw me in person, he would give it to me, but he was playing the long game, and I underestimated him. Now that I know the truth, he'll never see or hear from me again, ever.'

'You married him just to get your locket?' said Emily in disbelief.

'It was my grandmother's and it means more to me than anything or anyone,' said Trina. 'He'll get over it. He'll find a new woman within a week. I'll bet he's got a back-up bride already lined up.'

The British women exchanged skeptical looks. They couldn't believe the charming guy they had just spent the last few days with was as duplicitous as Trina had made him out to be.

'Tonight, I'm going back to New York to resume my life. If he writes, I will never answer. One day, he'll stop writing, and that will be the end of it.'

'What if he goes to New York to find you?' asked Emily, who like her sister was shocked by Trina's story. 'What if one day you want to marry someone else, then what?'

Trina let out a mocking laugh before she responded. 'He'll never be able to scrape together enough money to get out of India. No one in America will ever know about my marriage. One day, if I meet someone else that I want to marry, then I'll marry him. No one will ever know about Sam.'

Emily and Olivia stared at their American friend.

'He brought this all on himself. I'm not the bad guy,' Trina said, wanting them to take her side. 'When I say goodbye to him at the airport tonight, that will be it. He'll be erased from my mind permanently.'

As Trina uttered those last chilling words, a smiling Sam walked up to the group waving an Air India ticket folder.

'Got your tickets, my love,' he said leaning down and kissing the top of her head. 'You are officially confirmed on the flight to New York tonight. One day soon, I'll be able to say the same thing.'

'Thank you, sweetheart,' cooed Trina shooting a warning look at the other two women.

The British ladies stared at the smiling man sitting across the table, who was completely unaware of what was about to happen. Whether Trina was right about Sam or not, the women knew Sam was in for a whole lot of pain, and they felt genuinely sorry for him.

* * *

The four travelers said their goodbyes and wished each other safe journeys. Trina and Sam began the last leg of their trip together to the airport. They held hands as they walked into the terminal and checked Trina's luggage. Sam walked with his wife to the gate and sat close to her while she waited for her flight to board.

'Tell me again how you are going to grow your rug business in New York and how you'll become the best skater in Central Park,' said Trina, driving the invisible knife only she knew about, deeper. Sam chattered on, happy to take her for another ride on his American fantasy train. There was nothing he liked more than talking about his future life in America. With each sentence he uttered, he further cemented her suspicions and her final decision. *You played me — now I'm playing you.*

Overhead the loudspeaker blared, 'Air India flight 670 to Frankfurt is now boarding at gate twelve.'

'I should get going,' said Trina without emotion.

Sam looked ill. 'I didn't think it was going to be so hard this time. Now that we are married, I thought it would be easier, but my heart is still breaking thinking about being separated from you,' he said with tears in his eyes. He reached over and gently pulled her into him to give her one final kiss.

Automatically, she started to kiss him back but stopped herself and pulled away saying she needed to board. 'Goodbye, Sam.'

'How long do you think it will be before we see each other again?' he asked, reaching for her hand.

'I don't know. As long as it takes, I guess,' she said pulling her hand away. 'I've got to go, they're boarding, and I can't miss this flight.'

Trina turned and walked to the entrance. As she walked past the ground attendant her right hand reached up and touched the locket hanging around her neck.

She never looked back.

CHAPTER EIGHTEEN

Trina had hours to process her decision during her long flight home. She had been so sure he would return her locket once she arrived in Kashmir. When he wouldn't, it had taken her by surprise. But soon he charmed her. Once again, she believed that he truly loved her, until earlier that day in Delhi when he divulged that he had almost married a French girl. That's when she knew the real truth and finally saw him for who he was — a con man.

I had every right to get back what belonged to me. He manipulated me, not the other way around. I was his free pass out of India. Anyone with a beating heart and American citizenship would do. I finally see him for who he is. I'm so stupid.

She thought back to the beginning of her relationship with Sam when she believed she was so in love with him and she thought he was with her. *I was PATHETIC. He must have laughed when he received my syrupy love letters.* Faint nausea started in her stomach as her mind replayed different memories. *It was all so obvious. Why didn't I see any of it?* She was almost as angry at herself for being such a sucker, as she was with him. Almost.

Sam had expertly orchestrated everything. All those hours he spent waxing poetic on life or nature or telling me about the history of India.

What had initially seemed like his simple pride in the many languages he spoke, she now saw it as him boasting. Now, she thought his strong opinions on world politics, from a kid who had never left his tiny village on the lake, was laughable. The nausea enveloped her as she thought of all the times she let him touch her body, the nights they lay together, the times she held him, and he held her. *He was faking the entire time. He used me.*

She thought about the dozens of stupid simpering love letters she had written to him and all the phony lies she had received back. '*I love you, Trina. You are my heart,*' he had signed off on each letter. *It was all a big, fat lie. He carefully fabricated a story meant to convince me that he loved me so I'd bring him to America. I hate him. Would he have pretended to love me after he got to New York? Now, he won't have the chance to screw me over. I'll have the last laugh, not him.*

Trina turned and stared out of the window of the plane at the clouds, big balls of cotton hanging in the sky. She wanted to stop thinking about him and tried to clear her mind by focusing on the peaceful wispy clouds. It worked for only a minute and her anger reared up again.

She got up out of her seat, walked down the aisle to the lavatory, went in and locked the door behind her. She stared at her face in the mirror. Her eyes were red and the skin on her face dry and blotchy. *You look like shit. Do what you came in here to do.*

She looked down at her left hand and saw the glint of her shiny silver wedding ring. She tugged it off, dropped it into the plane's toilet, leaned over and pushed the flush button. With a grumble and swoosh, her silver ring vanished, and the last remnants of Sam were gone. She rubbed her naked ring finger glad to have it gone and looked in the mirror at her reflection again.

He'll wait for eternity for the letter from me that will never come. Every day he'll go to the post office looking for a blue envelope from me, but it will never be there. Each day forever, there will be nothing.

Furious thoughts of retaliation ricocheted around the confines of her skull. *I'll be home soon and will put India and Sam out of my life forever. Once I land in New York, I will never think about him again.*

The plane ride was her time to try, convict and hang him. After that, Sam would cease to exist.

* * *

Many hours later, a physically and emotionally exhausted Trina arrived at her apartment in Queens. She dropped her bag in the hall, walked directly to her bedroom and opened her top dresser drawer. Dozens of light blue *par avion* envelopes with the chevron trim filled half of the drawer. Next to them were photos of Sam and Trina, taken the year before in Kashmir. She picked up the letters, walked to the kitchen and put them in her empty sink. From the cabinet overhead, she pulled out an oversized box of kitchen matches.

She struck a match and lit the corner of one blue envelope and watched as it hungrily spread across the paper in colors of white, gold and green. Holding the corner of the burning paper up to another envelope she saw the flames leap from one to the other. She threw them both into the dry sink and opened a nearby window so the fire alarm would not be set off from all the smoke. One by one she added another envelope to the pyre until there was a small blaze in her sink. She could feel the heat.

As she watched them burn, a calmness enveloped her. She had destroyed the last remnants of Sam, and she felt nothing. When the letters were mostly ash, she turned on the faucet allowing the streaming water to put out the remaining embers.

She looked at the photos one last time. *We looked so happy then. The two of us laughing in a garden or smiling at a café. Sam posing — always posing. He was a world-class poser.*

She took a pair of scissors from the kitchen drawer and cut the pictures into little strips and threw them into the garbage bin. Then she scooped up the burned wet paper in the sink and put the debris in a plastic bag along with the shredded photos. She took the trash to the chute in the hall and dropped it in. It banged and tumbled down the metal shaft into a dumpster somewhere far below.

It was done. Sam and every trace of him were gone, permanently and forever.

CHAPTER NINETEEN

New York, August 1989

Trina's first Wednesday back at work was a blur. The jet lag was worse than she remembered and it was days before she felt normal again. Getting back into her regular routine after the tumult of the trip felt good. True to her commitment, she didn't think about Sam after she burned his letters. Her ability to 'compartmentalize' as Jenn would call it, was unwavering.

Jenn was tied up with a work conference that week, so they had planned to meet for drinks on Friday night.

Trina would speak of Sam only one more time, the night when she got together with Jenn. Her best friend was the only person who knew about him, and Trina knew she would demand all the details of her trip to India. It would be the one and only time she uttered his name or let any thought of him into her head. After that, she would never speak of him again.

On Friday night Jenn and Trina walked into Charley O's off Madison Avenue. The pub was jammed with young people eating free bar food for dinner so they could spend what little money they had on alcohol. Jenn spotted a group of people who were about to leave and flew across the room to hover nearby. Within a minute, the group got up, and Jenn secured the table.

Jenn always makes things happen, thought Trina. It was one of the qualities she liked the most about her friend. *No one ever takes advantage of Jenn.*

They each ordered a glass of Chardonnay and a couple of appetizers while Jenn chatted about work for a few minutes. When the wine arrived, Jenn got serious.

'OK, let's cut to the chase. I can see you're wearing your locket. Did he give you a hard time about it? Tell me everything, leave nothing out,' she demanded. 'Go.'

'There's not much to tell,' said Trina looking around at the crowd in the restaurant.

'Are you kidding me? Why do you think I'm here right now? It's not for the little hot dogs and the crappy wine. We're not leaving until I hear everything.'

'Why do you care so much?'

'Excuse me? You've talked of nothing else for over a year, and you flew halfway around the world to see this guy. I want to know what happened,' Jenn said as she popped a meatball into her mouth.

Trina filled her lungs with air and looked into her friend's eyes. Jenn knew the whole backstory and she knew Trina's early concerns. The two friends had discussed Sam a million times. Trina had read all of Sam's letters to Jenn over the phone and they had spent hours dissecting the meaning of each sentence.

'You know I thought if I went to India in person, he would give me my locket back. I thought it would be easy,' Trina said. 'But, when I asked for it, he refused and said he would only give it to me after we got married. So, I called his bluff. I wanted to see how far he would go.'

'Wait, what?' said Jenn, eyes round.

'So . . . we drove to this remote village and . . .

'And?'

'I married him and got my locket,' said Trina with no expression.

Jenn's mouth gaped open, a horrified look on her face but she said nothing. Jenn's loss for words slightly amused Trina. Jenn rarely had nothing to say.

'Close your mouth. It was the only way I could get it back,' said Trina.

'You married him,' said Jenn. 'Holy shit. Now, what are you going to do?'

'Nothing,' Trina said. 'There's absolutely nothing to do.'

'But . . . but, you're married to him,' cried Jenn, 'are you going to get divorced?'

'No.'

'What if he shows up on your front doorstep in five years looking for his wife?'

'That's never going to happen,' said Trina with a resigned look. 'He'll never get out of India. He doesn't have a pot to piss in. Besides, when I signed that marriage registry, I used a fake signature. You could barely make it out. It's a non-issue. For me, the marriage never happened. No one else knows besides you and me.'

'And him,' said Jenn.

* * *

Within a month, Trina's trip to India was only a vague unpleasant memory. She threw herself into her job and focused on her graduate classes and final thesis for her degree. When she got her diploma, she would apply for a bigger, better job. She was determined to be an editor at a top publishing company.

One evening, bone tired after a long day at work, Trina walked up the front steps of her apartment building and put her key in the front door. She went into the vestibule to get her mail and there it was. Stuffed between a few bills, some junk mail and a menu from a Chinese takeout place was a light blue envelope with red and blue chevron trim. She had so well compartmentalized her association with Sam and put him out of her mind that she was genuinely surprised to see the letter in her mailbox. She grabbed all the mail and walked up the stairs to her apartment.

Dropping the mail on the kitchen table, she changed out of her work clothes. Sweatpants and T-shirt on, she looked through the pile and opened the bills first, tossing the junk into the garbage and glancing over the new Chinese menu.

The blue envelope was still on the table. She picked it up and for the first time noticed Sam's handwriting looked like a childish scrawl. At one time, receiving a blue envelope had made her heart race and filled her with joy. Now, she felt nothing. She didn't even want to read it. It meant as much to her as the junk mail she had just thrown away. Less. *I'm more interested in the new menu from Hunan Wok than I am in his letter. Ha!* She was about to toss it into the bin when she changed her mind. She went to her closet, pulled out an empty red shoebox and put the unopened letter inside. Closing the lid, she put the box on a high shelf in the hall closet.

One day, Jenn and I will open that letter together over a bottle of wine and have a good laugh. He thought he was so clever; smarter than everyone. He must have thought I was a fool. It turns out, I'm the one who has the last laugh — a long silent laugh that he'll hear forever.

CHAPTER TWENTY

Kashmir, August 1989

Back on his houseboat, Sam missed his wife. He liked thinking of the blonde American as his wife. It made him feel grown up and important. No one knew about their marriage. They had agreed to keep it a secret until everything was in place for his move to America. He was dying to tell his parents, but he didn't tell a soul — fewer complications and recriminations from family and friends.

It had been more than a month since his wife had left India. He had written to her twice but had not yet received anything from her. *The damn mail system in India is so inconsistent. Sometimes letters take a week, sometimes, a month. Soon, I won't have to put up with the backward way of life here in Kashmir. I'm going to live in the most exciting city in the world.*

While he waited for the day he would join his wife, Sam stayed busy with his family's business and filled rooms with new guests each week.

'I re-grouted all the tiles in the bathrooms, Papa,' Sam said. 'Tomorrow I'll install new lighting in the hallways, and next week I'll start refinishing the wood floor in the sitting room.' Keeping busy helped him pass the time. He didn't mind doing all the hard work because soon he'd be gone and his parents would have to pay someone to have things done to the houseboat.

Sam's parents noticed their once irritable and sometimes self-absorbed son now appeared content, even happy. They hadn't seen him this cheerful in a long time. Until recently, Sam had been so restless and dissatisfied with his life in Kashmir — he always wanted more.

'It is because he's so smart,' said his mother to his father one night. 'His mind makes him impatient. But lately, he has been very calm.'

'Maybe he's finally growing up,' said his father. 'It's time for us to find him a wife.'

'Several local families have already enquired about our son as a potential husband for their daughters. And, why not? He's nice looking, intelligent and his family owns a houseboat. Any girl would be lucky to marry our Samir.'

'Yes, but he's also hot-tempered,' said her husband. Then he shrugged. 'Maybe a wife will calm him down.'

They agreed to begin a serious search for a bride the next day.

As another month passed, Sam was so busy with work on the new boat, entertaining tourists and fantasizing about his future American life that he almost didn't notice there had been no letters from Trina, until the day he did. It had been eight weeks since his wife left him and he hadn't received anything from her.

Later that night, Sam got out a blue envelope and wrote a long letter to his beloved Trina.

October 14, 1989
Dear Little Wife,

It feels like a lifetime since we were together although it's been barely eight weeks.

I was thinking — I might go to the university in New York. I could study architecture or medicine or maybe become a pilot for some big American airline. Your husband the architect or the pilot, how does that sound?

Kashmir is the same, nothing changes. I've been working night and day with my father fixing up the boat. I won't be here much longer so I'm doing as much as I can to help my family before I go to America.

The big problem we have now is the tourist business has slowed. Remember we talked about the political issues here? It has gotten worse and there are more problems on the border with Pakistan. People have been killed and tourists don't want to come to Kashmir anymore. They're afraid. Last week a bus filled with Indians and tourists was pulled over by some crazy group and a few tourists died. That's not good for business. Why can't everyone live together peacefully, like you and me? We come from entirely different cultures, you're a Catholic and I'm a Muslim and look at us — we're married! Everyone should be like us.

My beautiful wife, I know you are busy getting things organized for me to come to America but please write. I haven't received any letters and I miss you. This time, I don't have the locket to keep me company. It's probably the terrible Indian mail system that's slowing things down but please write soon.

Maybe I will be in America for Christmas and we can go to Times Square on New Year's Eve. 1990 is going to be the best year of our lives, you'll see.

You are my heart,

Sam

He carefully wrote her name and address on the outside of the envelope and sealed it. He smiled and looked up at the sky. His future was so bright it almost burned his eyes.

CHAPTER TWENTY-ONE

Kashmir, November 1989

Three months had passed since his wife had left for New York and Sam had still not heard from her. He became increasingly anxious. Letters between them had never taken this long before. His mind tried to make sense out of her silence and came up with the worst possible scenarios, all ultimately pointing to his wife being dead. Frantic, he imagined all sorts of awful possibilities.

What if she's sick or injured? What if she was hit by a car or one of those yellow New York City taxis? She could be in a hospital unconscious. No one knows I'm her husband — they wouldn't know to contact me. She could be dead. There are so many guns in America. What if someone shot her? Surely, she would have written to me by now if everything was OK.

STOP IT, SAMIR.

She's just busy with school and work and planning my arrival.

He calmed himself down and started a brand-new letter to his wife.

November 5, 1989
Dear Little Wife,

I'm very worried about you. I've not heard from you in three months. I know you would have written to me if you could so I must conclude it's because you are sick or possibly worse.

You need to write to me and tell me that you are all right. I've imagined all kinds of terrible things. You wouldn't believe the crazy ideas I've had. I remind myself that we're married and soon everything will be fine when we're together again in New York. Please, write to me immediately. I'm going crazy.

You are my heart,
Sam

* * *

On a cold and dark evening a few weeks later, Trina walked along the streets of Astoria to her apartment. Thanksgiving was coming up, and she had met friends earlier that night for drinks to kick off the holiday season. After a couple of glasses of wine and some laughs with her co-workers, she was feeling rather merry. She entered her apartment building, stopped in the vestibule and opened her mailbox and saw another light blue envelope waiting inside. Its presence irritated her. She grabbed all the mail and went up the stairs.

Once inside her apartment, she opened the hall closet, pulled out the red shoebox on the upper shelf and put the unopened envelope inside with the other unopened blue letters and replaced the lid.

* * *

December 16, 1989
Dear Wife,

Why is there this deafening silence? Four months ago, we said our marriage vows and pledged our lives together and in four months I have not heard from you. I get nothing. My worst fear was that you were hurt or dead— a horrible thought. I wondered if you were in a hospital and couldn't write.

I asked myself if I did something wrong to offend you? Are you angry with me? Trina, I'm your husband and you have to know that I love you. I continue to hope that there will be a letter waiting for me at the post office tomorrow.

You are my heart,
Sam

* * *

February 8, 1990
Wife,

I have sent you twenty-two letters in the past six months with no response from you. When we got married, you committed yourself to me and became my wife. I continue to be a devoted, loving and loyal husband to you, yet I hear nothing. What am I to think? None of my letters have been returned, so I don't think you are dead.

Did you find another man? I demand to know. Have you found an American man and now love someone else? Was our marriage a joke?

Please, Trina, write to me. Remember all of our plans and all the loving nights we spent together. I won't divorce you. You are already my wife and you can't change that. Maybe this is all a misunderstanding on my part. Please write to me and tell me everything is fine.

You are my heart,
Sam

* * *

April 26, 1990
Wife,

After nine months without a word from you, what am I to think? Maybe you have died or have amnesia and don't remember me.

This letter is to remind you of who I am and who you are. I am your legal husband and you are my wife. We were married in Dharamshala in July 1989. You went back to New York to arrange for my official documents so we could live together as husband and wife in New York. We fell in love on our first trip to Dharamshala, although I think I fell in love with you the first day I saw you at the bus depot. We spent so many nights in each other's arms. I hope this letter will remind you of the love and passion we shared. I can't take this any longer.

Trina. Please, you need to contact me.

You are my heart,

Sam (your legal husband)

* * *

July 18, 1990

Trina,

I now know you have turned your back on our love and betrayed me. I've been waiting for a year. It has been like torture each day waiting and hoping a letter from you will come, but it never does. After a year, it's obvious that your silence is not an accident. It's intentional and cruel.

Let me be clear. You are married to me, and I am your husband. Nothing can change that. As your husband, I have rights. In front of God, you promised to love and honor me for the rest of your life. I have our marriage documents that prove we are married. I will not be ignored, and I will not be tossed away like a piece of garbage. DO YOU HEAR ME? *You have no right to do this. I have done nothing but love you with all my heart and soul. We signed a marriage certificate and you committed yourself to me. I expect to hear from you immediately.*

You are my heart,

Sam

* * *

October 26, 1990
Wife,

Funny, I still cling to the idea that you are my wife. After more than a year with only silence, I know I won't hear from you. I have given up all hope.

I have been through so many lonely days and nights wondering and waiting. I've sent you over thirty letters and nothing. What changed you from the loving, sweet and beautiful wife I married to the cold-hearted bitch you have become? You can't just walk away from me like that. I am legally your husband whether you like it or not.

What kind of woman marries someone and then disappears? You are without a soul, without a conscience.

Know this — one day, I will find you. I will track you down and take my wife back. You made a promise to me when I put the wedding ring on your finger. If you know anything about me, you know I never forget anything. One day soon, when you least expect it, I will get your complete undivided attention, of that, you can be sure.

Your husband,
Sam

CHAPTER TWENTY-TWO

Kashmir, 1992

Bloody political fights on the India–Pakistan border had gotten worse. Bus travel into Kashmir had become too dangerous for most tourists. Only the real adventurers braved the hostile route to get there and made it all the way into Srinagar. Bombs or guns were often found hidden in the undercarriage of buses, and bandits held up, robbed and sometimes killed the people inside — not a great incentive for pleasure travelers.

Day after day, Sam went to the depot looking for a stray guest to bring back to his houseboat. More often than not, he came back alone. These days, only locals and their relatives got off the buses. The few visitors that his family depended on to survive were a rarity. Things were getting dire; everyone in the region was hurting.

Sam's father worried how they would survive and hoped the fighting would stop and things would go back to the way they were with everyone getting along. He was equally concerned about his son. During the past few years, Sam had become despondent, withdrawn and angry. When he wasn't keeping to himself, he was surly and even nasty. He refused to consider getting married and forbade his parents from bringing up the subject.

'He's always sad and angry,' said Sam's mother to his father. 'He takes no pleasure in anything anymore. Even when I make his favorite foods, it doesn't change his mood. I'm worried.'

What his parents didn't know was that in the two years that had passed since Trina had disappeared, Sam was fueled only by his anger and his desire for revenge. He wanted to know what had happened to her, but more importantly, he wanted her to feel the same pain he felt. The last moments with his wife had been beautiful, so he determined that she must have been lying to him all along. Each passing month of silence only furthered his hostility and bolstered his desire for retribution.

His worried parents, unaware of their son's marriage, watched him slowly deteriorate, with no idea of why. Life used to excite their son, but now, he had no joy. He was often rude and even impolite to the rare houseguests they were lucky enough to get. Sam had become a bitter, angry young man and it was all a mystery to his family.

'What's wrong with you, Samir?' his mother pleaded. 'You're not acting like yourself. You're never happy anymore.'

'This is who I am now, Mama,' he replied. 'If you don't like it, then don't talk to me.'

'We found many local girls who were interested in a marriage with you, but you refused to consider any of them. I don't understand you at all.'

Knowing they had to do something soon or they would lose him, his father wrote to his older brother in Cairo and asked for help. His brother, a successful mechanic with a small Egyptian air cargo company, had pulled a few strings to get his own son, Sam's cousin, into an air mechanic training program. Sam's father hoped that his brother might be able to do the same for Sam. He needed to find something that would give his son purpose and a goal. He thought that going to school in Cairo would give his son the new adventure he longed for.

'I don't want you to send my son away,' complained Sam's mother after the letter was sent.

'Samir's sharp mind needs more than an empty houseboat in Kashmir,' said his father. 'If he stays here with us, he'll wither on the vine.'

A month later, a letter came from Cairo.

Dear Brother,

Greetings. With regards to Samir, there are not many opportunities for training programs. I don't know if I will be able to get him into one.

Still, I know he speaks many languages, and that might work in his favor. They look for people who have language skills because mechanics and pilots need to communicate with people from so many countries. I can't promise you anything, but let's get Samir to Cairo for a while and see what happens. I will help him find a job and make some inquiries with my contacts. I will arrange for a free seat on one of our cargo planes for him, so you don't have to pay for his transport.

Your devoted Brother,
Ali

That day, when Sam returned to the houseboat after doing some errands, his father told him they needed to have a serious talk.

Does my father know something about Trina? Is she dead? Sam braced himself. As angry as he felt towards her, he hoped that she was alive. If she were dead, he wouldn't be able to show her how he felt, and he wanted the opportunity to do that.

His father told him about the letters he exchanged with Sam's uncle in Cairo. 'Your cousin is doing very well in an aviation program, and your uncle thought in time, there might be a chance for you, too,' said his father. 'No guarantees, Samir. I have saved up a little money. We will use that to get you started in Cairo.'

'Papa,' said Sam, 'I can't take your money.'

'It's my decision. I'm sure you will be accepted into a school once they meet you. When you are a big success, you can pay me back,' said his father. 'Then, you might get a job with one of the airlines. Maybe you'll fix engines or even fly jets for Air India,' he said laughing. 'Or maybe you'll fly private planes for rich millionaires from Saudi Arabia or Greece. Wouldn't that be something, Samir?'

Whatever it was, his father knew it would be better than his son wasting his time on a houseboat with no guests. Despite his all-consuming anger, Sam was moved by his father's gesture. For the first time in a long while, he started dreaming again. Besides, a move to Cairo was one step closer to her.

I would be a great mechanic or maybe even a pilot. I'll be the best student that school ever had and fly rich people in private jets to parties all over the world. I'll wear a uniform with gold buttons, and a captain's cap. People will respect me and look up to me.

* * *

Two months later, on the day he was to leave, he got up early and said goodbye to some of his neighbors. His sister and her husband came across the lake to wish him safe travels. Sam hugged his parents and got on the bus to Delhi to begin his new life. The last time he had taken this long bus trip, he had been with his new wife. It reminded him of how she had deceived him and ruined his life.

He was almost as excited about going on a plane as he was about going to another country, neither of which he had ever done. When he boarded the cargo plane, the captain greeted him. Sam noticed the pilot's tailored uniform and how the other crew members treated the pilot with deference and respect.

In the jump seat, Sam buckled his seatbelt. Minutes later, he would be up in the clouds for the first time. He braced himself as the plane taxied down the runway and felt it miraculously lift ever so gently off the ground. Soon, they were in the sky surrounded by white vapors. Out of a window, looking down on the ground, he could see dots and lines that were the houses, buildings, and roads far below. *I'm in the sky. Things are going to change for me. I can feel it. I will get into a program in Cairo. I'm going to be someone important, wealthy and maybe even famous.*

Then, I'm going to find my wife.

CHAPTER TWENTY-THREE

Cairo, 1992

'What do you think, Samir?' said his uncle as they gazed up at the pyramids of Giza. 'Have you ever seen anything like them? They are thousands of years old.'

'Truly magnificent, Uncle,' said Sam looking up at the humongous tombs. 'Imagine how difficult these were to erect without modern equipment.'

'I never get tired of looking at them,' said his uncle. 'How they were able to move those giant stones, I'll never know.'

Many of Sam's houseboat guests had described the pyramids to him. Now, he was finally the tourist and would have his own stories to tell. He stared up at the amazing structures and realized that, until this moment, his entire worldview had been secondhand. Everything he knew came from other people's stories, whether spoken or written in books.

From now on, he promised himself, he wouldn't hear about the world from others. He would see everything for himself. He would be the adventurer and storyteller and write his own chapters. 'One day, Uncle, I'm going to walk on the Great Wall of China, London Bridge, the Vatican, and the Empire State Building.'

Sam had been in Egypt for a week and was still acclimating to the frenetic pace of Cairo. He had been to Delhi many times, but Cairo was a different beast altogether. More modern than Delhi, it attracted a broader cross-section of travelers from all over the world.

Sam's uncle soon arranged a job for him at a small restaurant in a busy tourist area in downtown Cairo. His uncle knew the owner and convinced the man to give his nephew a chance because of Sam's language skills and his experience working with tourists.

'He barely speaks Arabic,' complained the owner.

'Who cares about Arabic?' said Sam's uncle. 'You want Western tourists to come into your café. They don't speak Arabic. Sam speaks at least five Western languages. He can get people inside your restaurant to spend their money. In the end, isn't that what you want?'

Along the main street, each restaurant had a front man, sometimes two. Like the barkers in the bus depot in Kashmir, their job was to procure customers. Standing in front of the restaurant, Sam's job was to entice tourists to come in to have lunch or dinner. Sam had two weeks to prove his value.

Women were easy marks. Sam flashed a smile at them and spoke in their language. That put them at ease and many of them chose his café over the others for their meal. Even the male tourists relaxed when Sam chatted with them in German, English or French.

The restaurant owner observed an uptick in traffic at his restaurant and more money in the register at the end of the week. Unlike the other guys who worked out on the street for him, Sam developed a rapport with the tourists, and he noticed they came back to the restaurant a second and third time.

One night, Sam had a conversation with a couple of teachers from New York and convinced them to eat at his café. After their meal, the teachers who had expressed interest in Kashmir, stopped on their way out and invited Sam to join them later for a beer. He caught up with them after he finished work and spent the evening drinking and swapping stories. Before they left, Sam asked them for a small favor.

'I have an old friend who lives in New York, a woman named Trina Holmgard,' Sam said. 'For many years, we wrote to each other quite often, and then one day her letters stopped coming. I'm worried that something has happened to her.'

'Maybe she moved,' said one of the teachers.

'It's possible but that doesn't explain why I stopped hearing from her. My address remained the same. I worry that something bad might have happened. Since you live in New York, I wonder if it would be possible for you to go to her house and see if she is all right?' asked Sam. Charmed by the young man, the American teachers accepted their investigative assignment and promised to go to the address in Astoria, Queens when they got home.

As the months went by, Sam's restaurant sales pitch made a considerable impact on the profit of the café. He had nearly doubled the amount of business coming into the restaurant and asked the owner for more money. At first, the café owner balked, but then he realized that all the restaurants on his street served the exact same food for the same price. Sam could easily get a job with one of his competitors and bring in extra business for them. Ever since Sam started working for him, his restaurant had turned a nice profit. He even had the extra cash to buy his demanding and sometimes sour-faced wife the gold bracelet that she had wanted. After he gave his wife the bangle, she had been much more pleasant, and his life was much improved. He carefully evaluated the pros and cons and decided to give Sam the raise he asked for.

With more money in his pocket, Sam saved and sent money to his parents. Meanwhile, his uncle and cousin continued to work various angles with the hope of getting Sam into one of the travel industry training programs. His uncle, who was a well-respected employee at his air cargo company, pulled in some favors, paid cash under the table to some administrators and got his nephew an interview.

On the morning of his meeting, Sam put on his best and most Western-looking outfit. He shaved with a new razor, combed his hair and said a little prayer even though he didn't believe — just in case.

He arrived on time at the four-story brick building, took the elevator to the third floor and walked down the hall to the administrator's office and knocked on the door. The fifty-something, thin, dark-skinned interviewer behind the desk was a man of few words.

Sam tried to charm him. It didn't work. He tried to impress him with his foreign language skills and his experience working with tourists. No reaction. He flashed a smile. Nothing.

'Sorry,' said the administrator looking rather bored, 'it's not personal, your language skills are better than most. Normally, that would be of tremendous value. Unfortunately, as I told your uncle, our aeronautic mechanic and pilot programs are full. Maybe next year,' he said as he answered a ringing phone and waved Sam away.

Aware that his interview was over, a disappointed Sam nodded, and left the office. Waiting for the elevator, he got angry. *Why did that man agree to meet with me if there was no chance? This was a big waste of my time.*

Just as Sam stepped onto the elevator, the administrator leaned out of his office and waved at Sam. 'Hey, you, Samir,' he called out. 'Come back here a minute.'

Bewildered, Sam walked back and followed the administrator inside of his office.

'That phone call I just got,' said the administrator, 'ten minutes ago, one of our instructors and a student crashed into the side of a mountain. Bad news for them but good news for you. Now, we've got an opening. You still want it?'

Sam wasn't sure if he should smile, given the circumstances, but he couldn't help himself and shook the administrator's hand. In six months, he would complete his coursework and six months after that he would become a certified commercial pilot. He was on his way. Luck was finally on his side.

The first few months of training were all in the classroom, the actual flying came later. Most of the other students were wise guys, only wanting to get up in the sky. They grumbled about the homework and the studying they were required to do. Sam loved studying and poring over manuals and taking tests. He thrived on it.

'You know what they say,' said Sam to his peers, 'knowledge is power.' The other students only rolled their eyes and dreamed of the day they could leave the four walls of the classroom and go up in the air.

Sam's hard work paid off. The instructors were impressed by his quick processing and retrieval of information. He remembered every command, protocol, sequence and safety regulation and became one of the stars of the flight program. When he finally did get up in a plane, he proved more adept than most of the others at that, too.

One night after school, when Sam arrived home at his uncle's apartment, there was a light blue envelope with a red and blue border addressed to him on the kitchen table. He froze when he saw it. *Was it from America? Was it from her? How did it get to me in Cairo? How did she find me here? I will not forgive her for what she did.*

Confused, he picked up the letter and examined it. He didn't recognize the handwriting and the return address was unfamiliar. He took the unopened envelope to his room, placed it on the small white plastic table next to his bed and stared at it. Trembling, he picked open the fragile blue paper.

August 1994
Hey Sam,

It's been a while since that fun night we had with you in Cairo. We went to London for a few weeks after leaving you before we got home to New York. If you ever get to New York, you must come to see us. We'll show you around.

Sorry it took us so long to look up your friend, Trina Holmgard. Our school year started when we got back and things were so crazy that we totally forgot about it.

We finally took the subway out to Astoria this past weekend. We went to 36-01 37th St., Apartment number 3. Right? We rang the bell, and a man in his sixties answered the door. We explained why we were there. He was pleasant and said he had been living there for a couple of years. He said he didn't know the previous tenant.

We knocked on another neighbor's door thinking maybe someone else in the building might have known her. We spoke to a woman in her eighties. She remembered Trina and said your friend lived there with her grandmother before the older woman died. She said Trina moved out about three or four years ago but she didn't know where. Rest assured, your friend wasn't hurt or dead like you were worried about. Maybe when she moved, she lost your address.

I'm afraid we've failed miserably as detectives. I tried to look her up in the New York phone book but only found the same address and a non-working number in Astoria. Sorry, looks like we're at a dead end, I'm afraid. We liked playing detectives.

Don't forget . . . Come visit us in New York.

Your friends in America,

Jeanette & Walter

Sam crushed the letter in his hand. He had hoped the two Americans were going to give him answers. He was no closer to knowing the truth about his wife than before. It had been six years since Trina vanished. He knew he would find her one day because he would never stop looking. She was, after all, *his* wife — he had every right.

CHAPTER TWENTY-FOUR

New York, 1996

Walking out of her doctor's office in the Tribeca section of Manhattan in a fitted black Armani suit, Kat Sullivan raised her arm to hail a cab. She smiled, thinking she might be the luckiest woman in the world. The OB-GYN had confirmed that she was indeed pregnant and everything looked fine. She decided to keep the news a secret from work for a while. After a few minutes of waiting, a yellow taxi pulled up in front of her.

The journey uptown was slow and when they got to midtown, the traffic was practically at a standstill. Car horns honked continuously while her taxi barely moved an inch. She glanced at her Chanel watch with the little diamonds around its face and frowned. She was going to be late for her two o'clock meeting with the new consultant her boss wanted her to meet with. At the pace her car was going, she might miss the appointment entirely. After ten more minutes of little to no movement, Kat looked down at her feet, resplendent in a pair of gray, suede, three-and-a-half-inch Walter Steiger heels and made a decision. She leaned over the partition to the cab driver and handed him some bills.

'Stop the car. I'm going to walk,' she said.

'You sure?' said the driver. 'We still got a way to go.'

'I'm sure,' said Kat as she flung open the back door, jumped out and dodged her way through the oncoming traffic. Once safely on the sidewalk, she got her bearings, slung her black leather tote over her shoulder and began to walk briskly up Madison Avenue. It was at least seventeen blocks further to her office building, and after crossing only two streets, the balls of her feet started to ache. High heels were not meant for hiking, she thought, as she soldiered on. Despite the New York City chaos around her, she was a million miles away ticking off the many deadlines she had to meet that week.

The monthly overview of all outstanding editorial pieces needs to go to Adam and the managing editor. Production has to get my sign-off on the next month's table of contents and I've got to review all the résumés of the new assistants by end of day. Circulation wants copy for the newsstand promo. Ugh.

Wrapped up in her own thoughts and not paying attention to her surroundings, Kat collided into a shabbily dressed woman, nearly knocking both of them over. Packages and bags went flying.

'I'm so sorry,' said Kat regaining her balance. 'Are you all right? I wasn't paying attention. That was totally my fault.'

'I'm OK,' said the woman bending over to pick up the shopping bag that had fallen during the collision. When the woman stood up, she looked at Kat with a hint of recognition on her face.

'You look so familiar,' said the other woman, dressed in an old gray coat, jeans and ripped-up sneakers.

Clearly, she does not read *Vogue*, thought Kat looking the other woman over.

'I'm Kat Sullivan,' she said straightening out her bags. 'Sorry, but you don't look familiar to me.'

'I know you,' said the persistent woman. 'Give me a minute and it will come to me.'

'I'm afraid I don't have a minute. I'm seriously late for a meeting,' said Kat turning to walk away.

'Wait,' shouted the woman. 'I do know you. You're Trina Holmgard from Astoria, right? We went to the same high school. You were a year ahead of me. I'm Lizzie. Lizzie Mainelli. My brother Jake was in your class. Did you know him? Jake Mainelli?'

Kat stopped dead in her tracks and she felt the familiar flush start to cover her body. She remembered how she had been so certain that Jake Mainelli had loved her, only to watch him take another girl to the prom. She slowly turned her head and stared at Lizzie. Kat hadn't seen or heard from anyone from her previous life in years. With the exception of Jenn, she had almost forgotten there had been a Trina Holmgard, having so completely become Kat Sullivan, the polished New York *GQ* editor. Long before Drew came into the picture, she had abandoned the name Trina, in favor of the more sophisticated sounding Kat. She didn't identify with Queens anymore. She was a Manhattan girl now.

'Did you know my brother Jake?' the woman asked again.

'No,' said Kat as she turned to walk away. 'I didn't know him.'

It felt like only yesterday that she had been on her honeymoon in Australia with Drew, the love of her life. Her wedding to the handsome Australian ex-pat had been held in a trendy downtown loft in Soho, right near the condo they now owned.

The flowers had been done by the florist to the stars, Manuela Cortez. The twenty-eight-piece band rocked the room, and the party went into the early hours of the morning. Dinner was comprised of a series of international food stations with a menu crafted by famous chef Wolfgang Puck, who was a close friend of Kat's boss, Adam Cantor, editor-in-chief of *GQ* magazine. The five-tiered wedding cake was made by the same person who made cakes for Oprah. The whole affair was spectacular — picture-perfect in every way.

Her wedding gown was personally designed by Vera Wang. Her hair, was styled by Noreen Clarke from the

Pierre Michel salon, a mainstay for society ladies. Noreen had loosely piled Kat's hair up on top of her head and placed a single gardenia behind Kat's right ear. Everything had been flawless, just as she had envisioned. Kat often replayed her wedding memories in her mind. It had been a spectacular day.

Being an executive editor at *GQ* had its perks. Those *GQ* credentials and her boss' influence on both coasts gave Kat access to restaurants, caterers, musicians, designers — whatever she desired. All she had to do was give someone her card or have her assistant make a few phone calls, and she was in. People went out of their way to curry favor with her hoping they'd receive coverage in her magazine. If they played ball with her, they might see their names in print. Maybe.

Only a handful of Drew's friends and family had made it to the New York ceremony. After their Manhattan wedding was over, she and Drew flew to Sydney and did it all over again — Australian style, hosted by Drew's parents for the Australian contingency. This time, instead of Wolfgang Puck and champagne, it was a fancy barbecue with Australian beer and wine, grilled lamb chops and meat pies. Drew's father, a quintessential Aussie from Queensland, and a professional bookie, played the part of an Aussie raconteur and the party went on for two full days, followed by a 'recovery party'.

Drew's family kept the newlyweds busy for the week, taking them on a whirlwind tour of sunny Sydney. They ferried to Manly Beach, saw koalas at the Taronga Zoo, and wandered around Luna Park. They strolled through the city's botanical gardens and walked over the bridge to Kirribilli taking pictures of the harbor and the famous Sydney Opera House.

Busy days, long nights and a significant number of beers later, Kat and Drew said goodbye to his family and flew north to Cairns to get their diving certification on the Great Barrier Reef. Scuba diving was something Kat had always wanted to try, and the Great Barrier Reef was the number one diving destination in the world.

'If I'm going to learn to dive, why not learn to do it in the best place?' she had said on more than one occasion. Kat had grown fond of having the best of everything; it made her feel good, it made her feel important. She had learned to appreciate beautiful things since joining *GQ*. Growing up, she had to settle for second best, but not anymore. Kat Sullivan had arrived — she had a great job and an amazing husband. Her future was so bright, it nearly burned her eyes.

In the two years since their wedding trip to Australia, Kat had focused all her energies on her career, and it had paid off.

Promoted several times, she was given more responsibility and moved to a higher position on the magazine's masthead. Now, she oversaw some of the junior editors and regularly received praise for her quarterly *GQ* travel column, *Road Scholar*, an 'off the beaten path' travel guide for young men, ironically written by a woman. The column had been the idea of her editor, Adam Cantor.

'You've got the chops to write this column, Kat,' Adam said. 'Don't let me down.'

Road Scholar had been well received by the *GQ* audience from the start and had since become a reader favorite. Her first column covered Vietnam and Cambodia, still a mystery for Americans after the war in the sixties and seventies. American tourists had finally started trickling into the poor country. Magazines like *Travel + Leisure* or their own *Condé Nast Traveler* had not written much about Vietnam. Adam especially liked when *GQ*, considered a men's fashion and lifestyle magazine, 'out scooped' the travel books. He relished the idea of beating the travel magazines with a 'never done before' travel story. Covering a destination on the cusp of exploding before the mainstream travel books did it, was precisely how Adam Cantor liked to roll.

'We might even get an ASME award for that piece,' Adam boasted to some of his cronies.

Working at *GQ* was fast-paced. Adam had been at the helm of the magazine for over ten years and during that time advertising revenue had quadrupled, circulation soared, and the magazine had won numerous literary awards. Condé Nast's owner, the legendary S.I. Newhouse Jr., insisted on the absolute best content for his large stable of magazines that included household names like *Vogue*, *GQ*, *Glamour*, *Architectural Digest*, *Gourmet* and *Vanity Fair*. The company hired the best writers and photographers in the country and Newhouse was willing to pay whatever was needed to get them. Powerhouse editors like Tina Brown, Anna Wintour and Graydon Carter were given free rein. Kat thought herself extremely lucky to have landed such a plum job working for an editor like Adam Cantor. He elevated her professionally and she knew she owed her soaring career to him and she was grateful.

When she first met her future boss, Kat's polished good looks helped her sail through the first thirty seconds of her interview. In the end, it was her brains and writing skills that got her the job offer. Adam was known to appreciate attractive women, but if you couldn't back it up with smarts and grit, he soon lost interest. The most important thing in the world to him was his magazine. With no children of his own, *GQ* was his baby, and he fiercely protected his child.

Before *GQ*, Kat had been a junior editor at *Rolling Stone*, covering their lifestyle and celebrity beat. The first time she had walked into the Condé Nast building she felt intimidated as she pushed through the oversized revolving doors. Even now, she sometimes felt like a fraud, like she still didn't belong. Condé Nast employees were glamorous. Every highlighted hair was in place, women dressed from head to toe in black. The sound of a thousand heels clicking on the lobby's white and gray marble floor echoed off the walls when she entered the building.

Now, only a few years later, she was a senior editor. She was the one looking glamorous with every highlighted hair in place, wearing black and clicking her ridiculously expensive Manolo Blahnik heels. Things had changed so dramatically for her in just a few short years.

Drew and Kat bought a three-bedroom condo in Soho near Drew's old apartment on Spring Street. His career at Spencer Financial was going well, and while the apartment was expensive, even by New York standards, they decided to stretch their budget and go for it and buy a place large enough to raise a family. Life was good, and Kat was happier than she thought she had a right to be.

When Kat told Drew she was pregnant, he was over the moon with excitement. Today had been her first check-up with her obstetrician.

'Everything looks the way it's supposed to, Kat,' said her doctor. 'The baby has a nice strong heartbeat.'

While in the cab on her way back from the doctor's office, Kat contemplated her life, and she felt gratitude flood over her. The day she met Drew everything had fallen into place. He was the love of her life. They had a beautiful home, a nice car, money in the bank and now, best of all, she was pregnant with their first child. Next year, they would have their baby, and she would finally have a real family. One day, they'd get a dog, too.

It was practically a miracle that she and Drew met at all — a chance meeting that almost didn't happen.

It was 1993. An exhausted Kat was on her way home from a business trip to LA. The flight to New York was full, and the airline had asked if anyone was willing to give up their seat in exchange for a free voucher. Exhausted, Kat had no intention of giving up hers even though she was stuck in a middle seat. She wanted only one thing, to go home, take a hot shower and climb into bed.

Boarding the plane, she reluctantly settled in between two men and hoped neither talked to her. A young guy wearing a headset was to her left by the window, and an older man was on the other side talking to someone across the aisle. *Perfect, neither guy looks chatty.* She buckled her seatbelt, put her head back, shut her eyes and waited for takeoff. She was almost asleep when the older man sitting next to her tapped her on the shoulder.

'Excuse me,' he said.

Kat opened her eyes.

'My wife,' he said, pointing to a woman sitting in the middle seat across the aisle, 'is sitting way over there and I was wondering if you wouldn't mind swapping seats with her so she and I could sit together?'

'Sure, a middle seat is a middle seat,' said Kat as she gathered up her things. Everyone changed places. 'Thanks, thanks a lot,' said the man and his wife. Kat settled into her new middle seat across the aisle. A young woman was on her left on the aisle reading *Glamour. Good choice, that's a Condé Nast magazine.* On the other side, a quietly handsome man with light brown hair was looking out the window. She could tell even from his seated position that he was very fit by the way his suit hung on him. Possibly sensing she was looking at him, the man turned and looked at her. She felt herself blush.

'That was nice of you to switch seats with those people,' said the handsome man with a surprise Australian accent. Kat liked his voice immediately.

'I was stuck in a middle seat anyway. Might as well make someone on this overcrowded misery of a flight happy, right?'

'And so you did. I'm Drew, by the way,' said the handsome man with a twinkle in his blue eyes as he put out his hand.

'Kat. Nice to meet you,' she said smiling and shaking his hand. When their hands touched, they both felt the electricity between them.

The new seatmates talked nonstop for the next five hours as the plane crossed the country. Neither could believe it when the captain announced they were beginning their descent to New York. They had talked about everything and nothing. She told him about her role as an editor at *GQ* and of her previous job at *Rolling Stone*.

'Sounds like you lead quite a glamorous life, meeting celebrities and going to big parties,' said Drew. 'I, on the other hand, work at an international finance desk where I push numbers around all day. Compared to what you do, my job is rather boring.'

She told him about growing up in New York City and he talked about his home city of Brisbane, Australia in an area called Queensland. Kat started to laugh.

'What's so funny?'

'I grew up in Queens, and you come from Queensland,' said Kat. 'Why do I have a sneaking suspicion that those two places are totally different?'

'I've been to Queens, New York,' said Drew with a laugh. 'I assure you, it's nothing like Queensland. Not even close. There are definitely no kangaroos in Queens, New York.'

Kat giggled and shook her head.

'My family doesn't live in Queensland anymore,' said Drew. 'They live further south in Sydney, now.'

Though Kat and Drew came from opposite sides of the world, it somehow didn't matter. They were connected in a strangely deep and profound way and Kat felt herself completely drawn to him.

While the plane landed at JFK and taxied to the gate, Kat had a knot in her stomach. The last five hours had possibly been the best five hours of her life. *Do I just walk away and never see him again or should I say something? He's not wearing a wedding ring, but he might have a girlfriend. A girlfriend isn't a wife.*

They got off the plane and walked into the terminal together. As they neared the exit, Drew asked her if she wanted to share a cab into the city.

Yes, please. Kat smiled and nodded.

'I'm sure you're exhausted after that long trip,' Drew said hesitantly as their taxi cruised down the FDR Drive, 'and I would totally understand if you didn't want to, but are you up for having dinner with me tonight?'

'I would love to,' said Kat without missing a beat. She loved that he asked and didn't let the moment pass. She fell in love with him that very night.

'I'm going to take you to my favorite restaurant,' said Drew. 'We'll have the cab drop off your bags at your apartment on Fifth Avenue. Then, we'll go to my place on Spring

Street and drop off my stuff. We can walk to the restaurant from there.'

'My favorite restaurant is on Spring Street,' said Kat. 'Are you talking about Balthazar?'

Drew smiled and nodded.

Balthazar was crowded on that Tuesday night. Drew, a regular, was warmly greeted by the stunning blonde hostess with the British accent who regularly flirted with him, and quickly found them a quiet table in the corner. The place was lively and everyone appeared to be having the time of their lives. Kat and Drew were no exception and their conversation flowed effortlessly. In sync on every topic, they laughed at the same jokes, and their hearts mutually ached over the same stories. That night, they found out they both loved crème brulée, and in particular, the sound when the spoon broke through the hardened sugar shell.

After several hours, the once noisy restaurant was quiet. The couple hadn't noticed. They were the only customers left in the place.

'I think the staff is cleaning up,' Drew sheepishly looked around the restaurant.

'Where did everyone go?' said Kat glancing around the room.

Kat looked into Drew's eyes. *I've found him. He's the person I've been looking for my entire life. The one perfect one.*

Walking outside into the cold night air, Drew took Kat's hand and intertwined his fingers with hers. The intimate gesture made her melt inside. A moment later, Drew turned towards her, leaned over and gave her a kiss. She could barely feel her legs underneath her.

Still holding hands, they walked all the way back to his apartment. From that day, they were never apart again. Soulmates, forever.

Now, three years later, she was pregnant. Life could not have been rosier.

CHAPTER TWENTY-FIVE

Cairo, 1996

Sam graduated from the pilot training program and soon was co-piloting cargo flights within Egypt. Once he was above the clouds, he felt like there was nothing between him and God, if there was a God, and he still wasn't sure about that. For him, flying was the most fantastic feeling in the world. Nothing else mattered when he was up in that plane. He was one with the universe and felt that excitement every time he was high in the sky. Now that he was a pilot, people treated him with respect and deference.

Every few weeks he sent money home to his family, who desperately needed it. Earning a living in Kashmir had become extremely difficult. His parents would depend on him for most of their income until things improved politically. Sam didn't make much, but it had to be enough for all of them.

Life in Cairo turned out to be fun. Sam made many new Egyptian friends and often went to clubs and parties and relished the dancing, drinking, and flirtations with foreign girls. The European girls were much more fun to talk to than the Egyptian girls. The Western women wore sexy clothes, and made provocative comments. He liked spending time with women from Europe or America; they were more open and freewheeling. The Muslim women were demure and more guarded, while the European girls were bold and sassy and put it all out there. He liked that. It was hot.

There was a new sensation in downtown Cairo called an 'internet café' that had become very popular with the locals. You could pay to use their computers and use this new thing called the internet. He tried this internet a few times and soon realized it might be the way to find his wife. Internet computer time was expensive, but worth it and several times a week he went to the café to search for any information he could find that might lead him to Trina.

It had been more than six years since he had any contact with his wife, but he still wanted to find out what happened to her. Nothing had changed for him over the years, rather his feelings had intensified. He needed to know if she was alive and if she was, where was she? Why didn't she come back for him and was she with another man? He had to know the truth.

One day, he paid his money for an hour of internet time and pulled up a Lycos search. He typed in 'Trina Holmgard', something he had done countless times before. Most of the results he got were in Swedish or Danish, and he couldn't make out what they said. He tried 'Katrina Holmgard'. He got more of the same, but this time there was an obituary of a Katrina Holmgard in Minnesota in America. His heart beat faster when he saw the listing, only to realize, somewhat relieved, the obituary was for a Katrina Holmgard who was eighty-four years old and died of heart failure.

Over and over Sam tried different combinations, using any bit of information about his wife that he could remember: 'Trina New York', 'Katrina New York', 'Holmgard New York', 'Katrina Holmgard Astoria', 'Katrina Holmgard Astoria New York', 'Trina Holmgard NYU', 'Katrina Holmgard Queens', 'Katrina Trina', 'Holmgard Trina Astoria New York', 'Mae Holmgard'. Time and time again, he either got no results or the listings that came up were the wrong people, not his wife.

Week after week, month after month, pound after pound, Sam tried new search terms and new combinations of words hoping one of them would work or that there would be something new posted that hadn't been there before. He often got results for a fashion designer named Trina Turk and thought maybe she was his wife. Trina Turk was about the right age and looked a bit like his Trina except the fashion designer had dark hair. He scrutinized the online photos of the designer carefully and decided she was not *his* Trina.

Because he spoke English and German, Sam applied for a new position within his company. He got a new route to fly mainly within Egypt, but occasionally he would fly cargo internationally between Egypt and Germany.

He was now an international pilot. Granted, he only carried cargo and not people, but still, he got to wear a pilot's uniform with a cap and that made him important. He flew short trips within Egypt and once a month flew a long haul to either Frankfurt or Hamburg. Sometimes, he would have a layover in Germany for a day or two before his return flight. On those days, he experienced the European lifestyle, and he loved it. He was never happier than on his layovers in Germany.

The Germans were open-minded, just the way they had always been when they stayed on his family's houseboat. They didn't have all the social rules like they had in India or Cairo. They did what they felt like doing. He liked German food, beer, and clubs and when he wore his pilot's uniform, the young German girls would come over and buy him a drink. Sometimes, they would end up on his lap. Egyptian or Kashmiri girls would never do that.

Whenever he had downtime in Germany or Cairo, he would always make sure to stop at an internet café. During one session in Cairo, he tried a search term he hadn't used before. Trina once told him her dream was to work for the biggest and best magazine company in New York. When Sam searched on 'New York magazine company' he got hundreds of results. *What did she tell me about one company in particular? Was it the biggest or the best? What was the word she used?*

Sam typed in all sorts of search combinations. 'Affluent magazine', 'high-end publisher', 'expensive magazine' and on and on. After exhaustive searching, he narrowed it down to two magazine companies. Hearst and Condé Nast. Both published the top lifestyle magazines in America. From what he read, either could be the type of company Trina had referred to and described to him so long ago.

He typed in 'Trina Holmgard Hearst'. Nothing. Then he tried 'Katrina Holmgard Hearst'. Still nothing. Frustrated, he typed in 'Katrina Holmgard Condé Nast'.

When he saw the results he leaned back in his chair. He had found her.

CHAPTER TWENTY-SIX

It was a wedding announcement in The *New York Times* from two years earlier.

'Ms Kat Holmgard married Mr Andrew Sullivan on Saturday, June 9, at the Pershing Loft on Mercer Street. Mrs Sullivan, who will take her husband's name, is a senior editor for *GQ* magazine, a Condé Nast publication. She received her graduate degree in journalism from NYU and is currently working on a book called *Men's Contemporary Style in the 20th century*. Mr Sullivan is a vice president, senior finance analyst in the international group at Spencer Financial. He received his undergraduate degree from the University of Sydney and his MBA from Harvard Business School. The couple will reside in New York City.'

Sam couldn't breathe. *She's not dead. She's married to another man! She's an editor with some fancy men's magazine. She's so important that The* New York Times *had an announcement about her marriage. Where was the announcement about our wedding? I'm your first husband, the only one that counts.*

'THAT BITCH!' he screamed out loud while pounding his fist on the table.

'Hey, keep it down, man,' said the café attendant.

You left me without a single word. I looked for you for all these years wondering if you were sick or dead. All the while you were having a wonderful life. Hatred overtook him and he wanted revenge.

Shaking, he got up and left the internet café touching the walls to steady himself so he wouldn't fall. Stumbling along the busy Hamburg streets, Sam's fury grew. His and Trina's story played over and over in his mind. *She threw me away. She pretended to love me and then she discarded me.*

With each step his anger grew stronger. He wanted to punch someone; to hurt somebody. He wanted to hurt her. He wanted her to feel real, unexpected, staggering pain and he wanted to be the one to administer it.

* * *

Two weeks later, Kat Sullivan arrived at her office early that morning to prepare for a big editorial meeting that was to take place that afternoon. She was giving the main presentation. Procrastinating, she picked through a metal tray on her desk that held her mail and examined various invitations to art gallery openings and the upcoming New York fashion shows. *Yes, on that one. Definitely no on this one.* She sorted through the pile until she reached the bottom and saw a blue *par avion* envelope with red and blue chevron trim. Staring at it for a minute, she held her breath and then laughed at herself for having a crazy moment. *Don't be ridiculous.* She opened the letter. One sentence in block letters was written at the center of the page.

I'M GETTING CLOSER

Kat's eyes widened and her heart started to pound. There was no return address and it was postmarked from Cairo. She felt an adrenaline rush go through her entire body and clutched her stomach. She hadn't yet told anyone at work that she was pregnant, deciding to wait as long as possible because so often she had seen smart, successful women's careers marginalized once management knew they were having a baby.

She grabbed her phone and punched in Jenn's number. It rang once, twice, three times. 'Come on, come on, pick up, Jenn.' The phone rang a fourth and a fifth time and then went into voicemail. Kat left a semi-coherent frantic message for her friend as she stared down at the blue document laying on her desk. *It can't be him. This letter came from Egypt. Sam is in India?*

Her phone rang.

'Oh my God, Jenn,' said Kat in a loud whisper into the phone.

'What's going on? I could barely understand your voicemail,' said Jenn.

Kat relayed what had happened and Jenn took a moment to consider the information. 'Calm down. You've gotten this kind of crap before. Remember that guy who used to write to you all the time and tell you that he was in love with you because of that article you wrote on relationships,' said Jenn.

'I guess.'

'This is just another one of those. I wouldn't worry about it.'

'But it's on the blue paper.'

'Big deal. I've used those blue envelopes myself,' said Jenn. 'Does that make me a stalker? Besides, you said it was from Cairo. That's nowhere near India.'

After her call with Jenn, she felt a little better but was still queasy. *Jenn's right, it's just another kooky reader. Every editor gets whacky mail. It comes with the territory. Get over it.*

She ripped the blue letter up into little pieces and then took the remnants out to the big garbage can in the main hallway not wanting the tiny fragments in her office. That afternoon, she gave her presentation to a roomful of editorial people including Adam Cantor and some of the higher ups from Condé Nast management. It was all over by three o'clock.

'Nice job, kiddo,' said Adam as everyone filed out of the conference room. 'Based on your presentation, I think we've got a shot at some awards this year. Maybe I'll win Editor of the Year?'

'You never know,' said Kat half-listening because of the pain in her groin.

'Are you all right?' asked her boss. 'You look pale. I noticed that when you were presenting. Why don't you take off the rest of the afternoon.'

Kat nodded gratefully and went back to her office to get her coat. It was in the taxi on the way home that she started to bleed. She called Drew from the car and he met her at the emergency room but there was nothing anyone could do. They lost the baby.

CHAPTER TWENTY-SEVEN

Egypt and Germany, 1997

Over time, Sam had learned a lot about Katrina's life. He now knew where she worked and what her 'illegitimate' husband's name was. All that time, he had been searching for the wrong name. Nothing about Kat Sullivan was the same as the girl he knew or the woman he married. Even her first name 'Trina' had been abandoned and replaced with Kat, just the way he had been replaced by Andrew Sullivan. The Trina he knew didn't exist anymore. She was now Kat — sneaky and conniving, just like a real cat. A perfect name for a perfect bitch.

Throughout the next year, Sam flew to Germany often and used much of his free time there to search for more information about his wife, all the while formulating a plan. Internet connections in Germany were far better and faster than anything he could find in Cairo. With each internet session Sam learned even more details about Kat's life. Whenever he found something new, he paid the extra money to print it out and compiled organized files to keep track of every piece of data.

The one thing he hadn't been able to find was her picture. He had not uncovered a single photo of her and he desperately wanted to see what she looked like. *Maybe she got fat and ugly? Maybe her skin sagged and her blonde hair fell out. I wonder if Andrew Sullivan likes having a fat ugly wife?*

He knew Kat was an editor for *GQ* magazine and worked on Madison Avenue in New York. Her office was on the twelfth floor. *GQ* was owned by Condé Nast Publications and he even knew her work phone number. Her boss was a man named Adam Cantor, the editor-in-chief of *GQ*. Sam found pictures of him, an older guy with a closely cropped salt-and-pepper beard. *I wonder if Kat is sleeping with this Adam Cantor? She always said she would do anything to work for a big magazine. So, she's a slut, too.*

Sam read several *GQ* articles written by Kat Sullivan. Her columns were on dieting, body type, dating and grooming breakthroughs. *This is what she went to school for? She said she wanted to become a great journalist. I guess she lied about that too or maybe she wasn't good enough. Maybe this is all she can do, stories about shaving and ten minutes to perfect abs.*

He read Kat's *Road Scholar* columns. The one on mountain biking chronicled a trip with her new husband. *That bitch had a wonderful life while my family and I struggled. It should have been me biking in Utah with her, not him.*

With each trip to Germany, Sam compiled more random facts about Kat and her new life. The wife stealer, Andrew Sullivan, went by the name, Drew. *What a stupid name. Drew.* Kat and Drew had been married in 1994 and lived at 256 Spring Street, apartment 202 in Manhattan. They owned a condo that had three bathrooms. *Who needs three bathrooms? She's greedy as well as deceitful.* Their apartment had a balcony and was on the second floor. They bought it in 1994 for $400,000, right after their wedding. *Drew has money. Was that it, Trina? You abandoned me to marry a rich guy. What a conniving Kat you are.*

Sam also learned Kat and Drew went to Australia for their honeymoon and in addition to a law degree, Drew had also gone to Harvard Business School. *He thinks he's important because he went to Harvard. We had guests on our houseboat who went to that school. Most of them thought they mattered more than other people. I wonder if Drew knows about me? Did she ever tell him that she already had a husband in India? Maybe he didn't care and the two of them had a good laugh about it. Poor, uneducated Samir, alone and pathetic in Kashmir. I hate Drew, too. I hate them both.*

With more research, Sam figured out that Drew worked downtown in New York City near Wall Street for Spencer Financial. He had Drew's direct phone number as well. *Maybe I'll call him one day and we can compare notes on our mutual wife and what it's like to sleep with her.* He found out that Drew was a guard on the Spencer Financial after-hours basketball league. He had been born in Brisbane, Australia. *Interesting Trina . . . you married someone else who needed visa documents. Funny you were able to do it for him but not for me. Was that because Drew had money? Is that what appealed to you?* He read that Drew provided free legal counsel work for various causes like homelessness and Make-a-Wish Foundation, whatever that was. Sam wanted to make a wish too: he wished to destroy them both.

Carefully cataloging every minute piece of information, Sam knew Drew donated fifty dollars to the election campaign of someone named Rudolph Giuliani who ran for Mayor of New York in 1993. He gave even more money to the election of the American president, Bill Clinton, the one who slept with all those women right under his wife Hillary Clinton's nose. Sam knew all about Bill Clinton and now he knew all about Drew Sullivan. If Drew gave money to Bill Clinton, then he must approve of Clinton's behavior.

Keeping track of it all, he printed copies of all the articles Kat wrote or edited. He followed the business functions and press parties she attended. He even stumbled upon the occasional financial article that quoted Drew Sullivan. Sam kept it all. Anything that was published or posted on the internet about either Kat or Drew was saved and meticulously filed. He didn't know yet what he was going to do or how he was going to do it, but it would be something big. Something everyone would remember.

Midway through the following year, Sam got a higher paying job within Egyptian Air Cargo. With his new responsibilities, he flew from Cairo to Germany three times each week. His new schedule allowed him to have a lot more ground time in Germany. He met a bunch of other airline employees at a bar near the Hamburg airport and made some friends. Exposure to the clean, organized, efficient German society only underscored the chaos and filth of the Cairo streets and the poverty of the family he left behind in Kashmir. He still sent money to his parents but the exchange of letters grew fewer over time. He was sick of the social rules in Egypt and disenchanted seeing women covered from head to toe, some of them showing only their eyes. He wanted to live in a Western country full time, eat their food and sleep with their women. A few months later, Sam put in a request with EAC to be moved permanently to their German hub. The following spring, he officially moved to Hamburg, only making trips back to Cairo a couple of times a month.

Now, he was even closer to her.

CHAPTER TWENTY-EIGHT

New York, 1998

In the years since Drew and Kat had gotten married, she had carefully crafted every aspect of her new life and family, weighing each decision, big or small, with equal consideration.

The first years of their marriage were filled with romantic dinners, weekends in the Hamptons and brunches with coffee, croissants and long lazy Sundays reading The *New York Times*. Saturday mornings often included walks over the Brooklyn Bridge to their favorite coffee place in Brooklyn Heights. Every time they crossed the iconic bridge, Drew always stopped in the middle to point at the Manhattan skyline.

'There's my office, Kat.'

'You point out your office every time we cross this bridge,' Kat said smiling and punching him gently in the arm.

'Yup. Want to make sure you're paying attention and that your world always revolves around me,' he said winking and gently punching her back.

Life was good for the Sullivans. Their nights consisted of off-Broadway plays, museums, gallery openings, basketball games and concerts. They ordered Thai food twice a week, because it was Drew's favorite even though Kat didn't like it that much. Every day was filled with fun and laughter and Kat could not have been happier. She was living her dream. *If only Nanna Mae could see me now. She'd be so proud. She could never have imagined me in such a glamorous life.*

The couple's mutual passion was traveling. Sometimes Drew accompanied his wife on business trips for her *GQ* travel column. *Roads Scholar* came out quarterly and each year she wrote two domestic and two international columns that took months of prep and research. When Drew could take time away from work, he'd join his wife on some of her trips, often to exotic locations.

They went to Moab, Utah and went mountain biking on the red rocks. Her column was a big hit with the *GQ* readers. A few months later, she and Drew flew off to Ecuador to sail around the Galapagos Islands. Kat and Drew lived on a boat for a week, hiked around the islands, swam with sea turtles and sea lions and even saw an albatross.

'You know something,' Kat said as they wandered around the magical islands, 'we are very lucky people.'

'I'm the lucky one,' Drew replied, squeezing her hand, 'because I got to marry you.'

When she got back to New York and turned in her article and pictures of Galapagos, her editor was pleased. 'I think you've got a winner here, kiddo,' Adam said. 'I'm proud of you. This is your best work to date.' Adam never aimlessly flattered his staff, if he complimented you, he meant it. Kat felt herself blush a deep red. Her editor had been right. A few months later, Kat, Adam and *GQ* were nominated for an ASME award for her Galapagos story. She didn't win, but the nomination validated her writing and moved her up a few notches within the editorial pecking order at Condé Nast. That in itself was a win.

A few weeks after the awards in March, Kat got an email from Adam about her next *Road Scholar* column.

Kat
Have idea for next R *Scholar. Had dinner with friends in travel biz last night. Something big happening in India. Lots*

of travel co's investing and visa numbers from US to India are up for past five years. Looks like a trend. Houseboats on lake in place called Kashmir, sound interesting? Travel just opening after years of political upheaval. Too dangerous until this year. We could be first to cover, maybe do political angle. Dalai Lama lives in north India with Tibetan refugees, too. Would be great story. Maybe another ASME? Plan to go in about 8–10 weeks.
Adam.

Kat couldn't get air into her lungs. She read Adam's email a second, a third and a fourth time. Frantic, she called Jenn.

'I'm freaking out. I'm going to lose it,' whispered Kat into the phone.

'Take a deep breath,' said Jenn. 'Talk to me, what's going on?'

Kat read the email from Adam.

'Oh God,' shrieked Jenn. 'You can't go back there. You've got to get out of this trip.'

'I don't know how. Adam rules *GQ* by suggestion, almost like a mob boss. He poses statements as if he'd be open to an alternative but he's not. He's already decided I'm going to India. That wasn't a suggestion, it was an order.'

'Tell him you can't go.'

'You don't say no to the editor-in-chief of *GQ* magazine. It would be professional suicide. But, there's no way I can go to India and I definitely can't go to Kashmir. What if I ran into Sam? I feel sick. No one knows anything about what happened there except you. Drew knows nothing.'

'It's been almost ten years since you've seen or heard from Sam. He might not live in Kashmir anymore.'

'Are you kidding?' said Kat with a laugh. 'He'll spend his entire life on that houseboat. I know that, like I know the sky is blue. I have to figure a way out of this.'

The rest of Kat's day was a blur. By the afternoon, her skin looked ashen and clammy and she was so distracted that several of her co-workers asked her if she was coming down with the flu that was going around the office.

By the end of the day, she had a plan.

A week later, after the editorial assistants had put together preliminary travel plans for Kat's India trip, Kat marched into Adam's office.

'Got a minute, Adam?' said Kat with a big smile.

'For you, always.'

'I have some news.'

'I hope it's something good, because I've had a shitty day,' said the editor growling. 'My top photographer, just up and quit. Got an offer to go to Hearst. I gave that guy his big break when he was just taking black and whites for the *New York Post*. The piece of crap *New York Post*!'

'I'm pregnant.'

Adam's jaw dropped but soon he slowly smiled. 'That's wonderful, Kat. Congratulations,' he said walking around his desk to give her a hug. 'I couldn't be more delighted.'

'Thank you,' said Kat. 'There is something else. Due to some medical issues that I'd rather not get into, my doctor doesn't want me traveling at all during the pregnancy. I have to stay close to home.'

Adam, knowing nothing about Kat's previous miscarriage but being of the old school, didn't question women about anything to do with their lady parts. 'Say no more,' he said quickly. 'The main priority is that you have a healthy baby. I'll pass the India assignment to another editor. Trust me, one of your envious colleagues will be more than happy to jump into your shoes. They're probably sharpening their knives already.'

Kat solved one problem but in doing so had created another. There was no baby and no doctor. She lied about being pregnant, and now she had to produce a baby in nine months. She and Drew had agreed to wait a while after the miscarriage but that night, she declared she was ready to be a mother and suggested they start trying again. Drew gladly complied and soon thereafter, he learned he was to be a father.

By early 1999, nearly nine months later, the Sullivans welcomed their son, Conner, into their lives. Kat finally had the family she had always longed for.

Eleven months after Conner was born, their second child, a girl they named Sophie, arrived and Kat's perfect family was nearly complete.

They hired a live-in nanny from Guyana named Imelda, who quickly became a valued member of the family. The Sullivans adored her and she them. Kat's life had fallen into a comfortable and cozy place but there was still one last piece needed to complete her perfect picture.

A year after Sophie was born, on a rainy Saturday afternoon, Kat, Drew, the kids and Imelda marched into an animal shelter in their neighborhood. Drew carried little Sophie on his shoulders while Conner scrambled over to the cages containing dogs who needed a home. The little boy instantly pointed to a little black and white terrier-mix.

'Is that the one you want?' asked Drew.

The little boy nodded. 'That one.' Conner eagerly tried to pet the dog through the cage's openings. Drew handed Sophie to Kat and followed his son over to the cages.

'He is really cute. What do you think, Soph?' Kat asked the little girl with the golden curls in her arms as she moved closer to the puppy. Sophie was still very young and her vocabulary was limited. All she could muster up was 'dog', which was good enough for her parents. Imelda also agreed, the little black and white puppy was the one. They brought the small pup home, named him Beasley and at last, Kat's thousand-piece life puzzle was complete. She was married to the 'most wonderful man in the world', had two beautiful and loving kids, a thriving writing career and now, her dog. Of course, Beasley occasionally chewed up a few of her expensive shoes but one look at his sorry little face and floppy ears, and she melted, even when she caught him with one of her Jimmy Choos in his mouth. Kat wished for nothing more and prayed everything would stay exactly the way it was.

But nothing stays the same, especially when someone's hunting you.

CHAPTER TWENTY-NINE

In Hamburg, Sam shared an apartment with a few Egyptian guys from his company and was enjoying his new German life. He and his roommates still marveled at how open the lifestyle was in Europe and more importantly, how free-spirited the German women were.

'At the beach, I look directly at their breasts when they take off their tops to sunbathe and the German girls don't even care,' Sam boasted to his friends. They bought the local girls drinks, danced with them, made them laugh and were often rewarded by an invitation to spend the night.

There was even the occasional day when he didn't think about Kat/Trina or Drew at all. He met a cute girl who was half German and half Lebanese and went out with her a few times. She helped pass the time until he was ready to set his plan in motion, a plan he hadn't yet completely figured out. Until he had clarity, he would continue flying, partying and searching the internet for more information about his wife.

On a Sunday morning when Sam had the day off, he got up early and walked through the streets of Hamburg. He picked up a coffee at a shop and then headed to his favorite internet café. He paid the clerk in the front of the café for his computer time and sat down in the back to begin his session.

'Hey,' said the clerk looking over at him, '*kein Kaffee in hier erlaubt.*' Then he said quickly in English, 'Sorry, no coffee allowed in here. The computers.'

'You don't have to translate, I speak German,' said Sam proudly.

'Big shit,' said the unimpressed clerk as he turned to help another customer.

Sam dropped his half-finished coffee in the trash bin and turned back to the computer. He began his session the way he always did by putting dozens of combinations of search words into Yahoo. 'Kat Sullivan', 'Drew Sullivan', 'Kat Sullivan *GQ*', 'Kat Sullivan fashion show', 'Kat Sullivan author', 'Drew Sullivan finance', 'Drew Sullivan Spencer Financial'. He clicked on time and date parameters and searched for images. The technology behind internet searching had gotten more sophisticated and his exercises were reaping more and better results. This time a photo came up. Several recent group shots of some *GQ* party in honor of Ralph Lauren had been posted in a fashion newsletter. The first photo had a bunch of people Sam didn't know, but one person in the middle he recognized: Adam Cantor, *GQ*'s editor. *I've seen his picture before: that's the old man who Trina screwed to get her job.* He looked at all the names underneath the photo and none of them were familiar. The next picture was another group shot with the designer, Ralph Lauren, standing in the middle next to Adam Cantor. *That's what Ralph Lauren looks like? I have a few of his shirts. I thought he'd be taller.*

He looked carefully at each face in the photo and then he saw something familiar. He zoomed in on the picture. *It's her! It's Trina. I know that face.* He examined the photo carefully. It had been ten years. Trina was a woman now, not a girl. Her hair was much lighter and the style was different but he knew it was her. *She's still pretty, not at all fat. Too bad.* Tiny flutters of emotion crept into his heart but he quickly squashed them.

He looked underneath the picture at the caption to be certain and read the names. There it was: *Kat Sullivan,* GQ *Editorial. Finally.* Next to Kat's name it said *Drew Sullivan.* He looked back at the picture. The tall handsome man next to

Kat was Drew, the man who had replaced him. *The man who stole my wife. The man who stole my life.*

A germ of an idea formed in his mind. Soon it was crystal clear what he would do. What he was destined to do. He knew exactly how he was going to reconnect with Kat and how he would get her attention. His only obstacle was financing the endeavor. It would take a lot of planning and require a lot of money but in the end, it would all be worth it.

* * *

Kat's plane landed at three p.m. at Kennedy Airport after a hectic four-day business trip to San Francisco where she had interviewed up-and-coming young entrepreneurs in Silicon Valley. The valley was crawling with guys barely in their twenties who had become overnight millionaires many times over. Her editor had sent her out there to talk to some of the most notorious bad boys. This was a topic that would be of high interest to the *GQ* reader. She was pleased with most of the interviews she'd done and was looking forward to putting the piece together.

A car was waiting for her when she walked out into baggage claim and she arrived at her apartment building by four fifteen. When she entered, she was surprised to find the apartment was empty. *Oh right, Imelda takes the kids to gymnastics from four to five thirty on Thursdays.*

She wheeled her bag into her bedroom and changed out of her work clothes into a T-shirt and jeans.

In the kitchen there was a shopping list written by Imelda listing various food and cleaning items they were out of. Next to the shopping list was a large catch-all wooden bowl. Everything went into the bowl: keys, loose change, invitations, bills, mail. She poked around in the bowl to see if there was anything new or important.

> *Conner and Sophie are invited to Annabel Crawford's birthday party next Saturday at the Jumpy Gym. Remind Imelda to pick up a couple of gifts this week.*

She sifted through several more bills and spotted the corner of an envelope in the center of the pile. The color was familiar — a specific shade of blue. She moved the other envelopes out of the way to get a better look. It was a blue *par avion* envelope with red and blue chevron trim. She felt the fight-or-flight rush race through her veins and her hands began to tremble. She picked it up and stared at it. It was addressed to her. The postmark was from Hamburg, Germany. *I don't know anyone in Germany.* With trepidation, she opened the blue envelope. A single line in block lettering was in the center of the page.

I'M EVEN CLOSER NOW

Kat grabbed for the back of a kitchen chair. She sat down and took a few slow breaths and tried to calm herself. She needed to see Jenn. It was nearly five and Jenn would be getting out of work.

Kat called her and asked if she would meet her in fifteen minutes at a pub near Jenn's office. Kat scrawled a quick note to Imelda letting her know she had a few errands to run and would be back later. She grabbed her Louis Vuitton bag and stuffed the blue envelope inside, ran out to the street and hailed a cab. Twelve minutes later she was standing out in front of McQuade's, a popular Irish restaurant and pub. After another five minutes, Jenn appeared, gave Kat a hug and the two went inside and sat at a quiet table in the corner and ordered their customary glass of Chardonnay.

'What was so urgent?' said Jenn. 'I canceled my manicure for you so this better be good.'

Kat opened her purse and pulled out the blue envelope and put it on the table between them. Jenn's eyes bugged slightly when she saw the letter. Kat pushed it towards her friend. Jenn opened it and read what was inside. '"I'm even closer now"? What the hell is that supposed to mean,' she said wrinkling her forehead. 'Who is even closer now?' She looked at the postmark. 'Do you know anyone in Hamburg?'

'No,' said Kat. 'Don't you remember? I got that blue letter at work last year from Egypt. It was exactly like this one. It said almost the same thing and it was written in the exact same way.'

'I remember. We thought it was from some mental case *GQ* reader,' said Jenn.

'This letter was mailed to my home,' said Kat. 'How would a *GQ* reader know my home address? Why wouldn't they just send it to my office?'

'You can find almost anything on the internet these days,' said Jenn. 'I wouldn't let it freak you out. It goes with the territory. You told me lots of editors get crazy mail and packages.'

'What if it wasn't a *GQ* reader?' said Kat. 'What if it's him.'

'It's been almost ten years,' said Jenn. 'Besides, you said he'd never get out of India. Now you've got him going to Egypt and Germany. That's a lot of traveling for a dirt-poor guy from the north of India.'

'You think I'm being ridiculous?'

'Getting that letter twice is definitely creepy, but I think it's just some random loser. Not Sam.'

'Don't say his name.'

Kat let out a big breath wanting to believe that Jenn was right and that her imagination had got the best of her. Several friends in the business, both male and female, had received alarming fan mail and none of it ever amounted to anything — just lonely guys with unrequited fantasies. She tore the blue envelope up and dumped the remains into a public trash receptacle on Fifth Avenue.

She would say nothing to Drew. He didn't know anything about Sam and that's the way she wanted to keep it.

CHAPTER THIRTY

While Sam carefully planned the plot points of his revenge, his life in Hamburg remained fast and furious with long nights and parties going on all hours.

Some of the guys were into the Muslim thing, going to the mosque all the time — he wasn't into that. He didn't tell anyone the way he felt because he knew they wouldn't understand. When he was young, his father and his father's friends would say their daily prayers and make him join in, but it never made sense to him. He had gone along with it, but he never believed. The truth was, he didn't think there was a God. Since his wife abandoned him, he didn't believe in anything. He wasn't sure if he even had a soul. At one time he had believed in love, but not anymore.

When you die, you're dead. No afterlife, no heaven, no hell, only darkness. It's like turning a light out in an otherwise dark room. Everything stops. People spend too much of their lives worrying about God and all his rules. God needs to lighten up and go to a disco and have a beer. Religions have so many rules. Why do I have to pray five times a day facing Mecca? Why not six or four? Rules. If you're Jewish, you can't eat pork. If you're Hindu, you can't eat beef. Too bad for them because a bacon cheeseburger tastes damn good. If you're Catholic, you can't get divorced. What if your wife is a bitch? Sam remembered he and Trina had talked about this on one of their trips and were in sync on all these things. It was one of the ways they had connected. None of that mattered now.

Throughout 1998, Sam pursued several different possibilities for securing the money he needed for his master plan. Most roads proved to be dead ends.

Then, he heard about a powerful and dangerous man with endless resources, who operated in the shadowy world of black-market arms and other assorted criminal activities. He heard this man, while extremely elusive and difficult to reach, was looking for new innovative projects to invest in. Someone Sam met, knew people who said they might be able to get him in touch with this power broker. From what Sam had learned, the arms dealer might be open to an extraordinary idea. Sam's plan was indeed that, but would require a lot of money and would be difficult to pull off. However, if it were executed properly, all the time and money would be worth it. There would be quite the payday.

On the other hand, if the man didn't like Sam or his idea, he might have Sam killed for wasting his time. Sam didn't care about the danger. He only cared about one thing: revenge. With no other viable options, this was the chance he was willing to take. Through his social circles, Sam let it be known that he had a proposition for the arms dealer. He floated out the bare minimum of information through an underground grapevine and waited.

A few weeks later, while sitting at his regular lunch place near the airport, deep into a book, a small, fat, bald man sat down next to him. The bald man said he represented the arms dealer and had been sent to get additional information.

'Before my boss meets with anyone, he needs to know the stakes and the details,' said the bald man. 'So far, it sounds only a little bit interesting. He needs to know more to determine if it's worth a meeting.'

'I don't even know who you are. Maybe this is a trick. How do I know this isn't a setup?'

'You don't,' said the bald man. 'If you want to do business with my boss, you have to go through me.'

'Maybe you're police.'

'Maybe.'

Sam hesitated a minute as he considered the risk and reward. He decided to take a chance — the bald man was too fat to be police. The bald man ordered a coffee and waited patiently for Sam to provide the additional details his boss required. Calmly, Sam laid out the tent poles of his big idea. Nothing more, nothing less. He shared only enough to get the meeting, but not too much that they could steal his idea and do it without him. He wanted to be a part of it, to be the one who lit the match.

Several weeks passed and Sam received a message. The meeting with the arms dealer had been arranged. It would take place the next time Sam was back in Cairo. He was given a date, time and address but nothing more.

He was told to go to one of the oldest hotels in Cairo, the Windsor Hotel on Alfi Bey Street in the old section of town. Sam knew where it was. The Windsor was an inexpensive hotel where he had stayed once when he and another pilot had a layover on their way back to Hamburg. It was a small but beautiful old building with intricately tiled floors and arched windows. The rooms were basic but clean. It was simple and unassuming and Sam understood why they would want to meet there, rather than at a place with a higher profile. Nobody watched you at the Windsor because it wasn't on anyone's radar.

After much anticipation, Sam was nervous on the morning of the meeting. He showered and put on his best pair of pants and his favorite linen shirt. He knew he had a great idea but he also knew first impressions were critical.

He walked through the old neighborhoods of Cairo towards the Windsor and passed a tea shop. Several old men were sitting out front smoking and drinking their morning tea. *Look how content they are. Their minds are calm. It must be nice to feel relaxed like that.*

Sam checked his watch. It was ten fifteen and his meeting with the big man was at ten forty-five. He liked to be in control but knew if he wanted to work with these people, he would have to give up all control. The boss was a leader who could never be questioned. Sam was willing to do whatever it took to make his vision a reality. In the end, it would all be worth it.

When he turned the corner, the Windsor Hotel loomed in front of him. He had been told to go to the front desk and ask for the meeting room for Primus Pharmaceuticals. It was still early so Sam walked around the block again to kill some time. He didn't want to look too eager. He needed to play this exactly right or they wouldn't want to work with him. He had to be cool.

As he circled the block again, thoughts entered his mind. *What am I getting myself into? I could turn around right now and run away. I could stop this before anything got started.* Another voice in his head told him to turn and run. *Go back to the airport. Fly back to Hamburg.* Still the first voice reminded him of why he was there. *She left you to rot. She married another man while she was married to you. She has a wonderful life and left you with nothing.*

Sam shut down the noise in his head, crossed the street and walked directly towards the Windsor Hotel.

CHAPTER THIRTY-ONE

The hotel's doorway was decorated with green iron grates and the words Windsor Hotel were written in gold on a pane of glass high above the door. Sam walked through the front entrance. *No turning back now.*

The dark, mottled wooden floors in the lobby were covered by old Persian rugs. To his left, Sam passed an open dining room with arched windows. An older man and woman were seated on a shabby sofa in the lobby reading a newspaper. A dusty old upright piano, that looked like it hadn't been played in years, sat in a corner. A bored bellman stood by the front desk picking at a stain on his lapel. In the adjacent dining room, a group of middle-aged men were eating breakfast, drinking coffee, smoking and laughing. Every few seconds their laughter got louder as plumes of their smoke drifted through the air.

Sam looked at his watch. It was ten thirty-five. Go time. He walked up to the front desk and waited for the attendant to finish a phone call. 'Excuse me, I'm looking for the meeting room for Primus Pharmaceuticals,' said Sam.

'Did you say Primus Pharmaceuticals?' said the desk clerk standing up straighter and treating Sam and their conversation with more respect.

‘That’s what I said,’ replied Sam.

‘Take the elevator to the second floor and go to room 202.’

When the elevator doors opened, Sam saw a sign pointing to room 202. He followed the sign and turned the corner in the hallway where he came upon three tough-looking muscular men. They puffed up their chests and looked suspiciously at Sam as he approached.

‘What do you want?’ said one of the thugs.

‘I have a meeting with someone from Primus Pharmaceuticals,’ Sam said to the menacing gatekeepers.

‘Identification.’

Sam handed over his pilot’s license and his Egyptian Air Cargo ID that had his picture on it. The three passed Sam’s documents between them and examined them for what Sam considered an unnecessarily long time. Satisfied, they opened the door to the meeting room and let Sam in.

‘Sit down. Don’t touch anything,’ said the first thug.

‘When will he be here?’ asked Sam.

‘When he gets here.’ The thug closed the door.

Alone, Sam looked at his surroundings. It was a small meeting room with a wooden conference table and eight chairs. There was a closed door at the other end of the room. A pitcher of iced water and six semi-clean glasses were arranged on a tray on the table. His mouth was dry so he poured himself some water. It tasted good. He was about to pour another when a young man wearing a skullcap came through the door of the adjoining room and closed it behind him.

‘Are you ready?’ the young man asked.

‘I have been waiting for this day for a long time,’ said Sam.

The young man nodded and knocked three times on the door to the adjoining room and opened it. He gestured for Sam to follow him.

Sam walked into the second room. A small older man with a beard and glasses, head tilted down, was seated at a wooden desk writing on a piece of paper. Next to the small man was a computer. Stacks of papers and folders in boxes were spread across the floor. Two new thugs with rifles hanging over their shoulders stood on either side of the wooden desk. *So that's him? He looks rather ordinary.*

Sam waited patiently for the man to acknowledge him. A full minute passed and finally the bearded man looked up and gave Sam a warm smile. He gestured for Sam to take a seat across from him. Then he reached out and shook Sam's hand with both of his and thanked him for making the long trip.

'We finally meet. My colleagues have told me you've been trying to reach us for a long time.'

'You're not an easy group to find,' said Sam.

'That's the way we want it,' said the man. 'Why don't you tell me the details of your proposition.'

Sam slowly outlined his masterpiece. As he talked, Sam saw the man's eyes light up and he knew he had him.

The man listened carefully to Sam's words and nodded with admiration. He appeared to be truly impressed. Sam and his idea were exactly what his organization and, more importantly, their leader, Osama bin Laden, had been looking for.

CHAPTER THIRTY-TWO

Sam's plan was simple. They would hijack two commercial planes from Boston going to California and strike both towers of the World Trade Center in New York. Sam would pilot one and hit the North Tower while the other plane would strike the south. Everything would happen at the same time — one giant boom.

'Transcontinental flights would have full tanks of gas and will make a bigger explosion causing greater damage,' said Sam. 'I've studied the flight patterns for those flights on the internet. The Boston flights would bring us the closest to New York City and to the World Trade Center without attracting attention. It would be easy for us to divert slightly from the expected route long before air traffic control knew anything was wrong.'

'I see you've given this a lot of thought,' said the small bearded man. 'I applaud your creativity.'

'Al-Qaeda tried to blow up the World Trade Center in 1993, but something went wrong,' said an emboldened Sam. 'Now, you could be the one to make that dream a reality and the whole world would know and fear al-Qaeda.'

The whole world will pay attention, especially my wife, when my plane flies directly into her husband's office building.

The bearded al-Qaeda deputy listened carefully to Sam's entire plan and smiled when the young man finished. He thanked Sam for bringing such a clever and grand idea to them. 'It isn't often we are brought conceptions of this magnitude,' said the bearded man. 'Most proposals involve blowing up cars, buses or weddings. Those have all been done and are so uninspired. A bus isn't going to put al-Qaeda on the front pages of international newspapers.'

'That's why I brought this to you,' said Sam smiling.

The bearded man nodded and smiled back thinking that Sam's idea was nothing short of genius. Still, he wanted to give the plan more thought and find out more about the young Indian before he let him into al-Qaeda's inner circle.

He took both of Sam's hands in his and shook them for several seconds. 'I have one final question for you, Samir,' he said. 'Why are you willing to do this?'

Sam paused for a moment. 'I have personal reasons, my own private reasons,' said Sam offering no more than that.

The bearded man merely smiled. His boss could easily find out what Sam's true motivation was. He told the pilot he would be in touch once they made their decision.

After Sam left, the bearded al-Qaeda official sat for a while and pondered all they had discussed. He was intrigued by the Indian man who spoke five languages and flew planes. It was rare to find Kashmiris circulating in the world. Most of them lived and died in the north of India and never ventured further. But this one was different, unique. He also knew that his boss, Osama bin Laden, didn't get to his powerful position by taking unnecessary risks or by being reckless. Before they took another step with Sam, they had to find out what motivated the young man. One thing the bearded man knew for sure — he loved this idea. It was exactly the global event al-Qaeda had been waiting for.

The official adjusted his skullcap. For years, Osama had tried to move his organization to the center of the world stage. Time after time their efforts had been thwarted or their 'events' didn't deliver the cataclysmic wallop they had envisioned. The nations of the world barely paid attention to the ten-year-old al-Qaeda organization. Occasionally, they got coverage from the international news community if they blew up a random truck in Somalia or car in Yemen. The official made some notes in his worn leather notebook and pushed his glasses up on his nose. If they really wanted to get their movement off the ground, they needed something massive. They had to create an event with images that people couldn't wipe from their minds. It had to be tremendous, something that would make every government and every person in the world stop and pay attention. The bearded man smiled and made a few notes. Their goal: America and all their allies had to feel violated and permanently unsafe. The Western world had to collectively spin out of control.

Sam's plan could achieve that end.

The bearded man packed up his bag and waved to the guards at the door who snapped to attention when he walked out of the room. America attacked al-Qaeda's people in Somalia. Americans supported atrocities against Muslims in Chechnya and aggression against Muslims by the Jews in Lebanon. Even in Kashmir, Americans supported the Indian oppression of Muslims. As far as the tall al-Qaeda leader was concerned, Americans were the criminals and murderers, not them.

The bearded official got into the back seat of a waiting car. The American people voted for and chose their leaders. Americans pay taxes that fund the planes bombing Afghanistan. The US Dollar is used to buy tanks and bombs that destroy Muslim homes. Americans give their tax dollars to Israel to attack and penetrate Muslim lands that knock buildings over on top of Palestinians. The American people fund these attacks against Muslims through their elected candidates and are one hundred percent responsible. The official took off his glasses and rubbed his eyes as the car moved through the streets. Every American civilian must be held accountable. They deserve whatever happens to them.

He looked out of the car window, his mind elsewhere. Al-Qaeda had had a few successes and some failures. They tried to blow up the World Trade Center in 1993: that was a failure. There was the assassination attempt on Mubarak in 1995: that wasn't a win but they still got some good press. Over the years, there were dozens of other one-off attacks all around the world. Most got little attention because none of them were of significant proportions. They all lacked largesse and drama. Sam's idea had the scale they needed and would finally put al-Qaeda on every front page in the world.

CHAPTER THIRTY-THREE

Before he presented Sam's ingenious plan to Osama bin Laden, the bearded official needed to learn more about the Kashmiri man. *If he doesn't check out, I'll have him killed and take his idea and make it mine.*

It didn't take the al-Qaeda organization long to get information on Sam. Their vast network of sympathetic parties around the world could find out anything in a surprisingly short period of time. They weren't all working in back alleys; some people were in highly visible strategic positions. All it took was money. You could accomplish almost anything if you had enough money, and they did.

Money was never their problem. Aside from Osama's own personal family fortune of billions, their coffers were constantly replenished by 'interested parties' supportive of their organization's objectives. Those supporters gave him free rein to do whatever they wanted, providing it was the same as what the donors wanted. So far, their mutual missions had been in alignment. His boss, Osama bin Laden, wasn't stupid and knew well how to play the game. He needed them as much as they needed him.

Al-Qaeda reached out to sources in Kashmir, Delhi, Dharamshala, Cairo and Hamburg. In two short weeks, they had an extensive dossier on Samir Ayad. The bearded official reviewed the reports and sent out follow-up questions for clarity. Using all the data, he formulated a full picture of Sam and better understood the young man's motives. When he read the dossier, he knew instantly that Sam was exactly the right person to be part of their inner circle.

Seventy-two hours later, Sam was summoned to Cairo. Four thugs in a sedan picked him up, blindfolded him, put him in the backseat and drove for over an hour. When the car stopped, they opened the door and led Sam up a short set of steps. It was only after he got inside the doorway that they took off the cloth covering his eyes.

They walked Sam down a hall and up a flight of stairs and then led him to a room at the top. Inside, the small bearded man he had met with before conferred with an older man with a long white beard, his head covered by a white turban. The younger bearded man looked up, saw Sam, smiled and beckoned him to enter.

'Come in, Samir. Please, sit down.'

That appeared to be the cue for the old man to move away and stand by the door, out of earshot. Sam's heart pounded in his chest as the bearded official got right to the point.

'We have given your ideas and proposal a great deal of thought,' said the al-Qaeda official. 'I had a background check done on you and learned a lot about what motivates you. After reading through everything, we've determined you are exactly the right person for our team.'

Sam smiled and let out the breath he had been holding.

'You see,' continued the official, 'I know all about Trina Holmgard and Kat Sullivan. I know about your marriage and how she left you in India. She betrayed you. Then, she married someone else while she was still married to you. That must have made you very angry.'

Sam's stomach flipped over several times. *How could they know all this?* He tried to ask but the man silenced him with a wave of his hand.

'It's unimportant how I know,' he said. 'I learned what I needed to know. You are angry and you want your righteous and proper revenge. I read about your wife's second husband and I've put all the pieces together. I don't blame you for feeling the way you do,' he continued. 'Revenge is a very powerful thing. Most of the world believes our organization is filled with religious zealots. Not so. All the top aides, the people who run al-Qaeda, are not the least bit religious. Nor am I. Nor is our leader.'

Sam's eyes grew wide.

'Does that surprise you?' said the al-Qaeda official. 'We are all people who have lost something precious. A wife, a child, a mother, a father, a sister, a brother. We want the same thing you want — revenge.'

Sam was amazed, intrigued and terrified all at the same time. This is not at all what he thought al-Qaeda was all about.

'I'll let you in on a little secret,' said the bearded official. 'A man of faith can lose his way in the blink of an eye. For centuries people have lost hope and lost faith. Faith makes men weak. But not revenge. Revenge will rot in a man's stomach until he completes what he set out to do. When you seek retribution, you don't stop until you finish the job. Our army isn't full of people blindly following Allah. Our army is full of men who have lost something and are filled with hate. They are people who have had their homes and families destroyed and their children murdered. They are men who have been betrayed or lied to just like you. You are one of us, Samir. You want revenge and that makes you a valuable asset. That was the one piece of information we needed to know about you. A man who pledges his allegiance based on faith could have a change of heart, run scared, join the enemy, betray us. But vengeance is single-minded.'

Sam searched for words but none came.

'We've been thinking,' said the bearded official slowly smiling, 'about how we can make the plan even better and bigger.' He paused for what seemed like an eternity and then a look of clarity came across his face. 'We'll add more planes and hit the Pentagon, the Capitol, and the George Washington Bridge,' he said with a bigger smile. 'It will all be quite spectacular.'

Ultimately, they settled on commandeering four US commercial planes and destroying American symbols of democracy that included the Pentagon, the Capitol and the World Trade Center. All symbols of American greed. Through this act, al-Qaeda would finally make their mark on the world, and shine a spotlight on all the crimes Americans had committed. Sam was put in charge of the entire American operation. Forever after, America would live in terror and Muslim deaths would be avenged.

The bearded official smiled, everything was coming together nicely.

CHAPTER THIRTY-FOUR

Florida, spring 2000

It was a hot and sticky Friday night on Atlantic Avenue in Delray Beach. A water mist sprayed the people crowding around the perimeter of Johnnie Brown's hamburger joint on the corner. A Rolling Stones cover band played on a small stage while the inebriated barflies sang along to every word of every song.

Hot young waitresses wearing short-shorts and skimpy halter tops slammed down bottles of beer as fast as customers could drink them. 'Keep 'em coming' was the order of the night.

Sitting around a big table in the crowded pub, twelve Middle Eastern men easily blended in. Dotted with bars, cafés and boutiques, the busy thoroughfare cut a swath through town down to a deep white sandy public beach.

Not a bad place to spend the last year of my life, Sam thought on the day he arrived in sunny Florida.

No piece of the plan was random. Sam had finally met Osama bin Laden and the al-Qaeda leader had personally selected each man for the team. Every man had extensive knowledge of Western culture and solid English language skills. A few had even attended college in the United States, making their assimilation that much easier. English proficiency was not the only criteria. Osama had hand-picked them because each one had lost someone important and retribution fueled their soul.

Most of the men were from Saudi Arabia and the free-wheeling life in Florida was like being on the other side of the rainbow. Days were spent at the beach listening to rock and roll, smoking cigarettes and weed, drinking, working out and chatting with pretty girls in bikinis. They even flirted with the ugly girls because there were no bikinis in Saudi Arabia. American women in thongs walked along the beach as if it was perfectly normal. The Saudi men despised and wanted the women at the same time.

Their accommodation was varied. They shared apartments and hotel rooms scattered around towns in southeast Florida. Some had rented rooms at a seedy efficiency motel that was also a mecca for drug addicts and prostitutes — the perfect place to hide in plain sight, a strategy al-Qaeda often employed.

Since Sam was the mission leader, he leased a two-bedroom condo at the Delray Racquet Club and shared it with two of the older men in their group. The Racquet Club looked like a resort: pristine grounds with winding grassy paths; two pools; a lake; and a few dozen tennis courts. There was a gym and even a hot tub. Paradise.

Sam's rented condo was nicer than anywhere he had ever lived. It came fully furnished and had cream-colored marble floors, and a wide-open balcony with a big round table and six chairs where his guys would smoke, play cards and down shots of vodka. This was the lifestyle Sam had imagined he would have had with Trina, before she left him like an unwanted dog to die in India.

Clubs, drinking and weed helped them all forget why they were there. Sam's job was to keep each man focused on his mission. Sure, they could let off a little steam now and then, but every person had a specific and important role. As long as they were accomplishing what they were there for, Sam saw no reason they couldn't also have a good time.

For the overall plan to work, Osama bin Laden knew his disciples couldn't attract attention, and had to adopt the American way of life. Their arrival into Florida had been staggered over a period of months. With dark complexions and foreign accents, they were already at a disadvantage and any unusual behavior could draw dangerous scrutiny. Sam's job was to make sure they acted like typical American guys, even supervising their clothing purchases to make sure they looked 'American'.

'Go out, go dancing, have a good time,' he told his crew. 'But, don't lose your heads. We're here for one reason. Our al-Qaeda family is counting on us. Remember your oath. When we complete our assignment, each one of your families will be richly rewarded,' said Sam to his men. 'At the same time, it will not be good for them if we fail. Remember, don't draw attention to yourselves,' he told them. 'Do normal American activities. Act like stupid, macho American guys. Hang out at bars. Listen to rock and roll. Flirt with girls. Sleep with them if you want to, they're all whores, anyway. Be American, but always remember why you're here.'

The men took road trips to Orlando spending days at Disney World and Universal riding the rollercoasters, screaming when the cars careened down a steep track. They ate giant turkey legs and drank beer at the food halls and arcades. They went to waterparks and played like kids. On Miami's South Beach, they hung out with Latina glamour girls. They rented motor scooters and rode around Fort Lauderdale and Palm Beach. They joined gyms, did odd jobs and bought hot used cars. They slept with women, tried drugs, gambled, drank alcohol, and watched pornography. They rationalized all their behavior was a way to keep their cover. The truth was — they were having the time of their lives.

Sam had many logistics to work out. Middle Eastern passports would send up red flags at the airports. Each man had to get proper identification for travel. Once they established residency, every man on his team applied and received a Florida driver's license as well as their own social security number. It was all too easy, thought Sam after they received their US government IDs. They signed up for flying lessons at Huffman Aviation and Florida Flight Training to keep their skills sharp and familiarize themselves with US aviation protocols.

Though half of them were already licensed pilots, they needed to get United States certification to be familiar with American instruments and commands. Each team member had to know how to fly the planes in case one of the trained pilots, like Sam, was injured or prevented from taking over the controls. The men had to be interchangeable in every aspect in the event of something unexpected. Any one of them should be able to take their mission to its ultimate conclusion. Osama bin Laden had left nothing to chance.

* * *

Kat was at an ASME award luncheon in New York City. None of her pieces were nominated this year but *GQ* was up for a general excellence award and Adam Cantor wanted all his senior editors with him like an entourage.

When the announcements were made, *GQ* didn't secure the big prize but did win one for photography and a special feature. Not the big brass ring they had hoped for, but it was still a win. After having a glass and a half of wine at the event, Kat was feeling a little loopy when they all returned to the office. The lunch had run long and it was nearly three thirty when the black limos finally pulled up in front of their office building. Sailing down the hallway towards her office in a mellow mood, Kat waved to her young assistant to let her know she was back and plunked herself down at her desk to check her messages.

She was listening to a voicemail when her assistant appeared at her office door holding a bunch of folders and files. Kat held up one finger to her assistant so she could finish listening to the last of her messages before being interrupted.

When she was through, the assistant came in and sat down across from her.

'I guess you heard. We didn't win the big one,' said Kat looking at her email.

'How did Adam take it?' asked the young woman.

'He wasn't happy. Fortunately he'd had a couple of Ketel One's when they announced it so he was relatively mellow.'

'Kat, I've been going through your correspondence and I've put various invites in one folder, requests for coverage by some of the fashion people in another and general letters in yet another. There was one piece of mail that came in that was a little weird. I didn't mean to open it. I usually don't open mail if it looks personal. I guess I wasn't paying attention. I'm not really sure what it is or what to do with it.'

Kat looked up from her screen because somewhere it registered that her assistant's voice sounded strange. The young woman pulled a pale blue *par avion* envelope with red and blue chevron trim out of a folder. Kat froze when she saw the color and the block letter print on the outside. The assistant held the letter out to her.

'Where is it from?' Kat asked feeling faint.

'I don't know. There's no return address on it.'

'Where is it postmarked from?' said Kat beginning to tremble.

The younger woman looked carefully at the outside of the letter.

'Orlando, it was sent from Orlando, Florida,' said the assistant. 'I didn't understand what it meant. It's addressed to you and inside all it said was . . . Is this some kind of a joke?'

Kat looked over at the open letter her assistant held in her hand.

I'M SO CLOSE I CAN ALMOST SMELL YOU

The assistant watched all the blood drain from Kat's face. 'Are you all right, Kat?' said the young woman. 'You look like you're going to be sick.'

Kat took a deep breath. 'Did anyone else see this?'

'Only me. Should I send this to our security people. It sounds so creepy.'

Kat tried to compose herself. She definitely didn't want the Condé Nast security involved. She forced a smile and faked a laugh. 'No, it's a joke,' she said still smiling. 'One of my college friends went to Disney World and she always sends creepy stalker postcards and letters. It's just a joke. Funny, right?'

'Thank God,' said the young woman now also smiling. 'That's a weird kind of joke, though.'

Moments later after her assistant left her office, Kat called Jenn.

'I thought that ASME lunch would never end,' said Jenn. 'At least you guys won a few awards. I was thinking . . .

'Jenn! I need to tell you something,' said a highly agitated Kat. 'I got another blue letter.'

Jenn gasped. 'Where was it mailed from?'

'Florida.'

CHAPTER THIRTY-FIVE

Florida, 2001

By June 29, the last member of Sam's team had arrived in Florida. There were still some outstanding issues to be resolved, like exactly how they were going to hijack the planes once they were in the air. Also, how would they get through airport security without being flagged?

They purchased knives and various chemicals from Lowe's Home Improvement store and experimented with different explosive compounds. At one point, Sam developed a severe rash on his hands from some of the chemicals. Not wanting to go to a doctor or a hospital for fear it would attract unwanted attention, he went to Huber's Drugstore in downtown Delray and got medical help from a pharmacist. They couldn't afford to take any chances.

Still, on July 5, Sam, who had a weakness for fast cars, was stopped for speeding in Delray. He had proper documentation and was given a warning by the police officer who let him go. Sam was angry with himself for putting his mission in jeopardy over something so stupid.

A month later the bits and pieces leading to their final mission were put into place. On August 6, Sam rented a white Ford Escort. He had been instructed to travel to a final meeting with a two-man team set up in a safe house in New Jersey. In his rented car he drove from Florida to Hoboken, NJ. It was over 1,200 miles and took him nearly twenty hours to get there. It was on that trip, from the shores of Hoboken, that Sam for the very first time, finally saw New York City — the place that at one time was going to be his home with her.

Across the blue-green murky water of the Hudson River he could see all of Manhattan and the two towers that made up the World Trade Center. Though it wasn't part of his original plan, after his meeting with the men in New Jersey, Sam found himself driving through the Holland tunnel under the river into Manhattan.

When his car came out of the long, dark, underground roadway, the sunlight made him squint. He was finally in New York City. He drove around the streets, marveling at the vibrancy around him. *I would have liked living here. I should be living in one of these tall glass buildings with my wife instead of doing what I'm doing. It's all her fault.*

He pulled over, reached into the glove compartment and pulled out a map of Manhattan that he had purchased at a gas station. He drove towards the east side of the city watching the numbers on the buildings. There was one specific number on Spring Street he was looking for — 256. Trina's address. Kat's address. *256 Spring Street is where my wife lives with the man who stole her from me and then had his children. Those children should have been mine. Now, I'll never have any. That was stolen from me, too.* His heart pounded and he could feel the blood rushing through his veins as his car moved slowly down Spring Street.

Number 256 was a plain beige brownstone with six big steps in front and a dark polished wood front door. *Not so special,* he thought. All those months, he had spent so much time thinking about this place and now it was right in front of him and it didn't look so grand after all. His idling car blocked the entire street and several cars behind him honked to get him to move. He pulled away but circled the block. On his second pass, another car was just pulling out and he moved into a parking space about forty feet from the front of his wife's building and turned off the engine. For two hours he sat there, staring at her house and thinking about his life, his journey, his mission and all that had been taken away from him.

The summer sun overhead drifted down towards the horizon turning the blue sky orange. It was six p.m. and the evening rush hour foot traffic had picked up on Spring Street. Then he saw her. After twelve years, he knew it was her right away, even from a distance. On some level, he knew he would see her that day. Maybe that's why he went there. Her hair was different, blonder, longer, smoother. It had been a long time but he recognized her walk. The way her legs moved to a certain rhythm only she had in her head. He knew that walk even before he could make out her face. It was Trina, his wife, and she was still beautiful.

From the other end of the block, two small children barreled down the street with an older woman running behind them. 'Mommy, Mommy!' they screamed as they ran to Kat and clung to her legs. Sam slouched lower in the car so he would not be seen but continued to watch. Kat bent over and picked up the little girl, and gave her a kiss. She passed the girl to the older woman and lifted up the little boy and kissed him as well. Sam couldn't hear what they were saying but the body language told the whole story. The older woman was talking about the children and using big hand gestures. The children giggled and danced around their mother, vying for her attention. Kat split her conversation between the older woman and the kids responding alternately to both. Everyone was smiling and laughing.

She's still stunning. She hasn't changed much over the years. She looks more polished, more groomed, but still the same. His heart filled with the old familiar emotions he had felt so many years before. *There's my wife. She's so close to me, laughing, smiling. I remember that. It's the smile of my soulmate.*

Many times, over the past year, Sam had thought about abandoning the entire plan. *I could walk away from al-Qaeda, from all of them. I could find a job in America, live in a nice place, have a great life.* And then he'd soon remember, you can't walk away from al-Qaeda. They don't allow that.

As he continued to watch the happy group on the street, the two women stopped talking and turned around. The children squealed and Sam saw them run down the sidewalk. 'Daddy!' they shouted as they catapulted themselves into a tall man in a dark gray suit.

Sam had seen pictures of Drew. He was taller than Sam had imagined. But he knew it was him, Andrew Sullivan. The man who stole his wife and his life.

Drew dropped his briefcase, picked up both kids and gave them each a hug. Kat and the older woman caught up with them and the group moved noisily along the street laughing and smiling and up the steps of 256 Spring Street. One big happy family. The older woman took the children and went in through the front door first. Just before Drew and Kat walked through the doorway, Drew leaned over and kissed his wife. That's when Sam's softening heart turned to stone again.

The moment Sam saw Drew kiss *his* wife, all of his doubts about the mission dissolved. Thirty minutes later, after a short stop, Sam was on his way back to Florida to set the final steps of his master plan in motion. He had a twenty-hour drive south to let his hatred fester.

* * *

On August 13, Sam returned his rental car with almost 2500 miles on it and moved out of his apartment in Delray Beach. Three days later on August 16, Sam rented a single-engine Piper Archer from the Palm Beach County Airport in Lantana. For three days straight, he took up a different team member and instructed them on the finer points of the controls. Everyone had to be ready to take over at a moment's notice.

An Arabic-speaking instructor on the ground overheard Sam speak in that language on the radio. He heard Sam say '*Allahu Akbar*' which means 'God is Great'. He thought nothing of it because many people say a prayer when they fly. Sam and some of his other pilots went to the SimCenter at the Opa-Locka Airport and spent six hours in the training cockpit of a Boeing 727 simulator, a machine similar to the 767s they would eventually be piloting over New York and Washington D.C.

* * *

Those last two weeks of August, Kat's kids' nursery school was closed so Kat and Drew took two weeks off from work to give Imelda a much-needed vacation and to spend some family time going to Jones Beach and the Bronx Zoo. It was a hot August and the kids were never happier than playing by the edge of the water with their proud parents looking on.

Even though Kat was on holiday, Adam Cantor emailed her on her fourth day of vacation saying he needed her to weigh in on an important piece. One of the other senior editors had a death in the family and Adam needed all hands to help out. Not wanting to disappoint the kids, Drew offered to take them to a petting farm in Westchester to give Kat the peace and quiet to get her work done. Grateful for his support, she kissed her husband and kids goodbye as they left for the farm and sat down to edit the article. After a couple of hours, she was hungry and decided to walk to the corner store to pick up a smoothie and a sandwich. When she returned she picked up her mail and went inside to eat her lunch. She completed the editing assignment, sent it back to *GQ* and called her husband to let him know she was free and clear and he could come back with the kids at any time.

She picked through the mail tossing circulars for discounts on tires and chimney cleaning in the garbage. She separated out a stack of bills and the tuition that was due on the kid's fall semester of nursery school. Midway through the pile, she saw it — a blue *par avion* envelope.

She felt her lunch climb up into her esophagus, and threw up in the kitchen sink. Trying to breathe deeply she stared at the envelope for almost fifteen minutes. The postmark was from New York. Shaking, she opened it. Inside, there was a single sentence in block lettering.

I SAW HIM KISS YOU ON SPRING STREET.

Kat threw up a second time and called Jenn.

* * *

On August 17, a few of Sam's men drove to Miami to buy a cockpit instrument diagram of a Boeing 757 so they could study it.

On August 23, Sam's driver's license was suspended for failure to appear in traffic court. That same day, two of his team went to the Delray Beach Public Library to download information on crop dusters and check commercial flight times. By August 28, several on his team had purchased their final one-way airline ticket through Travelocity. They used a public internet terminal in a branch of Kinko's.

Two days later, on August 30, they bought cheap box cutters at Lowe's Home Improvement and Sam and a few others moved into a motel.

Sam sent a FedEx package to the United Arab Emirates on September 4. The package would ultimately be routed to Osama. It was Sam's final written report of the entire operation and his last communication to al-Qaeda.

Two of the men went to Passage Tours in Fort Lauderdale on September 5 and bought one-way tickets to Newark. So they didn't attract attention or trigger any suspicion, three of the other men bought their tickets to Newark from a different travel agent in Fort Lauderdale.

Chemicals and bombs had been ruled out as too risky. They might be stopped before they could board the planes. It was a very simple plan. Each man would carry a box cutter:

the blades were under the four-inch maximum allowed by the airlines. No one would stop them, it was all perfectly legal.

Sam reflected on the past year of his life. He had a good run in Florida. Life had been fun and a part of him liked the American lifestyle. Back in Kashmir, he remembered he used to enjoy Americans when they stayed on his houseboat. They liked to have a good time and didn't care if he was from Egypt or India. America was comprised of people from all over the world and the only class anyone cared about was money. If you were successful, you belonged. It didn't matter where you came from or what language or religion you were born into. What mattered in America was what you made of yourself. Sam appreciated that. *If I had lived in America I would have been very successful. I probably could have gotten a job as a pilot here if I wanted to or have been an architect designing tall buildings. Life in America would have been just fine.* There were many times over that last year when Sam almost changed his mind, but there was no turning back after the day on Spring Street.

* * *

September 7 was Sam's last day in Florida. He and two of his men went to Shuckum's Oyster Bar. They spent four hours playing video Trivial Pursuit and drank a lot of vodka and orange juice.

At the end of the night, there were issues with their high bar bill and the waitress asked them whether they had the money to pay their check. Drunk and angry, Sam yelled out, 'You think I can't pay? I'm a fucking pilot for American Airlines. I can pay my fucking bill.' Tensions were red hot.

On September 8, some of the men, including Sam, flew to New York. That night, Sam and a few others had drinks at Harry's Bar at the Helmsley Hotel on Madison Avenue. Later that night Sam and another guy drove to Portland, Maine. The remaining men in Florida flew to Boston.

By September 9, all the chess pieces had moved into place. Checkmate.

On the night before their mission, September 10, all nineteen men in various northeast locations went out and got extremely drunk at local bars. One group was overheard laughing and talking about 'how stupid and dumb the Americans are' and how 'they would find out how dumb they really are the next day'. Other bar patrons thought they were just a bunch of loud drunken men and paid no attention to them. That turned out to be a fatal mistake.

CHAPTER THIRTY-SIX

September 11, 2001

Sam and his co-pilot Waleed, arrived at the Portland, Maine, International Jetport for an early morning flight to Boston. They had already purchased one-way tickets on American Airlines flight 11 traveling from Boston's Logan International Airport destined for Los Angeles.

At the same time, three other teams boarded planes in a similar way. One group would take over United Airlines flight 175, going from Boston to Los Angeles; another team would be on American Airlines flight 77 from Dulles International Airport in Washington D.C. headed to Los Angeles. The last team would takeover United Airlines flight 93 leaving from Newark heading to San Francisco. All the flights would have full tanks of gas.

Sam and Waleed waited on the ticket line to check in for their flight to LA. They had bought first-class one-way tickets. That was Sam's idea: he figured that nobody looks twice at people with first-class tickets and, after all, he deserved to be in first class for this final flight. The other three guys were in coach because they needed people stationed in the back of the plane, too.

Sam approached the first-class ticket counter. The female ground agent asked him where he was going and for some identification. Sam handed her his Egyptian passport.

She looked at the passport and the picture, then back at Sam. She noticed his thick black eyelashes and wished her own were thick like his. 'Samir Ayad,' she said, slowly reading his passport. 'Did I pronounce your name correctly?' she asked Sam.

'You said it exactly right,' said Sam smiling. 'Most people in America don't pronounce it right, but you said it perfectly.'

The American ticket agent blushed as she completed the transaction. 'Have a wonderful flight,' she said, noticing the man looked nervous when she handed him his ticket. 'I looked at the weather forecast this morning, Mr Ayad, and the skies are completely clear. Don't worry, you should have a smooth trip.'

'Thank you. I hope so,' said Sam forcing a smile as he turned to walk towards the gates. His plan was simple. Fifteen minutes into the flight, with the box cutters hidden in their carry-on bags, he and Waleed would casually walk up to the cockpit, swing the door open and enter. His team would breach the compartment and take over the plane. They would overpower the captain and first officer; then Sam would take over the controls. Chances were all the fat cats in first class would be so absorbed in their movies, champagne and warm nuts they wouldn't even notice two passengers entering the cockpit.

They would wait until the first-class flight attendant walked away for a moment and then make their move. Everything had to seem normal so air traffic control didn't notice anything was wrong. That's why Sam's language skills were so important. It would all work perfectly if they stuck to his plan.

After they had control of the plane, Sam would gently guide the aircraft to its final destination — the ninety-eighth floor of the North Tower of the World Trade Center. Around the same time, Marwan, piloting another plane, would hit the south tower. As far as Sam was concerned, Marwan could hit any damn floor he wanted, it was irrelevant to him. All he cared about was hitting the ninety-eighth floor, where Drew Sullivan would be sitting at his desk having his morning coffee.

One of his guys sitting in coach also had a box the size of a loaf of bread in his carry-on bag. There was nothing inside the box besides bits of paper, gum, cardboard and rocks but it was wrapped up with duct tape and wires, making it appear like a homemade bomb. They would tell the passengers it was an explosive but that everyone would be okay if they all stayed in their seats. They would explain that the plane would land sooner and no one would get hurt if everyone cooperated. That was the plan.

Box cutters, fake bomb, impact, boom.

CHAPTER THIRTY-SEVEN

Everyone had agreed it was a spectacularly beautiful Tuesday morning and American Airlines 11 took off right on time. When the plane reached a cruising altitude, Sam and Waleed waited for just the right moment. A red-haired first-class flight attendant served drinks to her small group of elite passengers. When she stepped out of first class and walked back to coach for a moment, Sam and Waleed exchanged glances. That was their opening. It was time.

Both hijackers got up and casually walked towards the cockpit, opened the door and stepped in. They closed the door behind them before either of the American Airline pilots turned around. When the two pilots looked back and saw Sam and Waleed standing there, they were confused more than anything else. Several thoughts rushed through their minds before they understood what was happening. *Who are these guys? They're not supposed to be in the cockpit during the flight. Where's that flight attendant?*

Before the co-pilot could say anything, Waleed reached around from behind him and cut his throat with his box cutter. The pilot didn't have time to react before he met the same fate by Sam's hand. It had been much easier than Sam had anticipated. He thought he would have felt something more as he dragged the blade of his boxcutter along the pilot's neck and watched the blood at first trickle and then spurt out. The captain hadn't even put up a fight, seemingly stunned by what was happening to him.

Sam considered for a brief moment that he had just killed a man. A man he didn't know. Someone who might have been a father or a husband and was probably looking forward to going home that night and watching a ball game with his kid. Sam was also aware that he didn't care. Killing the pilot was a means to his end. He did what he had to do and he would do it a thousand times if that's what was required. Waleed locked the cockpit door, and the two men moved the dead bodies to the side as they took control of the plane. While Waleed familiarized himself with the controls, Sam changed the direction of the plane to steer it gradually towards the final destination — New York City.

A few minutes later, Sam heard a commotion outside the cockpit door. The three others on his team had made their move in the main cabin. Sam heard shouting and screaming and was glad he was inside the quiet of the small compartment. He didn't like chaos. He liked order. *Let the rest of them deal with all those frantic passengers.* He had only one job and that was to fly this plane, something he could do with his eyes closed and ultimately would.

In another twenty minutes they would be flying over New York City. The sounds of panic outside the cockpit grew and Sam wondered if the passengers could possibly overwhelm his people. They had all been well trained on what to do, but still, there were only three of them and over a hundred passengers. If all the passengers attacked his men at the same time, they would overpower them. The passengers might also knock the cockpit door in. If that happened, Sam knew exactly what to do — take the plane straight down.

An urgent call from air traffic control came over the radio. Someone on the ground had noticed American flight 11 was off-course as well as a United flight.

'American Flight 11, this is air traffic control at Logan Airport. You have veered off the appropriate flight path. Please advise and reset your co-ordinates.'

Silence.

'American Flight 11, we can't hear you. You are off your flight co-ordinates. You are not in the right flight path. Do you copy?'

Silence.

'American Flight 11, is there a problem? Let us know what's going on.' Pause. 'American Flight 11, urgent request for communication. Is there a problem? I repeat, is there a problem?'

Sam turned the volume down. He could hear the passengers' hysteria through the door and opened up the intercom.

'Hello,' he said over the microphone with a soft, gentle, calming voice. 'Hello. Everyone, please calm down. This is your captain speaking. I have complete control of the plane. Rest assured, I am a fully licensed, trained and accredited commercial pilot, so you need not worry about that. I know what I am doing. Right now, I need all of you to take your seats, buckle your seatbelts for your own safety and remain quiet. No one will be hurt by my men if you all do what we ask. We do have a bomb but we won't detonate it, if we get what we need. All we want is for the American government to release some of our people that they have detained.'

At first there was a panic when passengers heard the word bomb but Sam's reassuring voice had its desired effect and the noise and chatter in the plane diminished.

'We only want the American government to release some of our brothers who have been wrongly imprisoned in American jails. I am going to turn the plane now and take you all to New York.'

Through the door, Sam could hear the people in the back talking loudly and shouting again.

'If you don't cooperate,' he continued over the loudspeaker, 'we will detonate the bomb. So please, for your safety, take your seats and I promise, this will end soon when we arrive in New York.'

It's true, you will all end up in New York.

The plane moved closer to its final destination. In just a couple of minutes, Sam would be able to see the World Trade Center. He instructed Waleed to go back into the main cabin and help the others. He could handle everything in the cockpit by himself. When Waleed left, Sam locked the door and reached into the breast pocket of his shirt. He took out Trina's old battered New York State driver's license with her picture on it. He placed it on the control panel in front of him so he could look into her eyes as he flew the plane. Her face would be the last thing he ever saw.

Though Sam was unaware of it, when he spoke on the microphone to the passengers, he had simultaneously broadcast to air traffic control. That inadvertent communication put the people on the ground on high alert. They now knew for sure that something bad was happening on flight number 11. A few minutes earlier, two flight attendants on Sam's flight contacted American Airlines using a phone in the back of the plane. They gave the authorities on the ground information about the hijackers, told them what was going on, who was injured, how many people were involved.

Sam didn't know about any of this. It didn't matter. They couldn't stop him, it was too late. He was almost there.

In front of him, directly ahead in the clear blue sky, he saw two giant columns — the Twin Towers of the World Trade Center. He guided the plane towards them. The North Tower was directly in front of him. That was his target. Drew Sullivan's office was on the ninety-eighth floor of the North Tower. The building had 110 stories. As the plane glided closer, Sam counted down from the top floor . . . 109, 107, 105, 103, 101, 99, 98 . . .

As the plane made contact with the building, Sam looked at Trina's picture and shouted, 'I never stopped loving you, Trina,' and closed his eyes.

* * *

On September 11, 2001, nineteen men took down four 767 commercial jets, both towers of the World Trade Center, the Pentagon and changed the world forever. They did it all with only four-inch box cutters purchased from a Lowe's Home Improvement store in Boynton Beach, Florida.

CHAPTER THIRTY-EIGHT

New York, September 11, 2001

That Tuesday morning in New York City, the sun was shining, and the sky was a bright blue. A warm gentle breeze blew at just the right temperature as it caressed the skin. The air was dry and the city even smelled good for a change.

Drew and Kat got up extra early to spend time with their kids before they left for work. Imelda made breakfast while Sophie and Conner watched their favorite *Little Mermaid* video. Kat and Drew took their vitamins, kissed the kids goodbye and told Imelda they'd be home early to celebrate Imelda's birthday. Together they walked out of their building and down Spring Street towards the number six subway. Kat would take the train uptown and Drew downtown.

Walking past the Balthazar Bakery they both caught a whiff of the freshly baked bread and pastries at the same time. They stopped there so Drew could get a coffee and a croissant, something he did almost every morning.

'That reminds me, since you'll get home before me tonight, will you stop and pick up a birthday cake for Imelda?' asked Kat.

'Sure,' said Drew. 'Chocolate?'

'Duh, of course,' said Kat laughing. 'I don't even know why people eat cake that isn't chocolate.' She kissed him on the cheek and saluted. 'See you tonight, honey pie,' she shouted as she darted across the street through the traffic towards the uptown subway entrance. Drew smiled and waved back, took a sip of his coffee and walked down the stairs to the downtown train.

Minutes later, Kat got off the subway in midtown and walked across town to her office in the Condé Nast building at Times Square. She flashed her ID, which allowed her to go through the turnstiles and got on the elevator to the twenty-fourth floor — *GQ* Editorial and Sales.

Once a month on Tuesdays, she and a few other editors accompanied their boss, Adam Cantor, to the *GQ* advertising sales early-morning meeting. At those meetings, Adam gave the sales team a review and heads-up on the features and stories from upcoming issues. Occasionally, an editorial story dovetailed nicely with an advertiser's campaign and a salesperson could leverage it for more advertising dollars. Issues closed two months prior to publication, and this week they were reviewing the November 2001 issue. Kat was to present the highlights of the cover story on Ben Affleck.

The edit staff filed into the conference room. Coffee, bagels and bottles of water were on the sideboard. All the salespeople were already seated at the large conference table waiting for Adam's entrance. He always started promptly at eight thirty. You didn't come late to these meetings.

Kat grabbed a bottle of water and sat next to Adam's empty chair at the head of the table. Behind her was a huge flat screen television often used for big presentations, but they wouldn't need it today. At eight twenty-nine, Adam strode into the room and took his seat.

'Good morning, everyone,' Adam said with his confident booming voice and a smile. 'I have to tell you, I'm really pleased with our November issue.'

He eloquently described the various writers, photographers and features of the upcoming issue. The salespeople ooh-ed and ahh-ed over some of the clever articles while trying to figure out how they could use the advance information to sell more advertising. Adam talked for about fifteen minutes and was about to wrap up when the conference room door was opened. Heads turned as Adam's assistant stuck her head in the room.

'Adam, excuse me for interrupting but I thought you would want to know about this right away,' the assistant said. 'Apparently, a plane just hit one of the World Trade Towers.'

Everyone in the room started talking at the same time. 'What kind of plane? A little two-man plane? How could a pilot hit such a big building? Was anyone hurt? Why would a plane be flying so close to the World Trade towers? Wasn't the plane flying too low?'

'That's all I know,' said the assistant helplessly. 'I heard it on my desk radio. I ran down here to tell you right away.'

Kat's stomach flipped over. She leaned over to Adam and told him she wanted to go to her desk and call her husband.

'It's a big building, Kat, it was a small plane,' Adam said reassuringly. 'I'm sure Drew is fine. Of course, go call him.'

Kat excused herself and walked briskly back towards her office telling herself that she was needlessly worrying. As she walked she noticed small groups of people had gathered around radios on desks. She didn't stop until she got to her office, picked up her desk phone and called Drew. It was busy. She dialed again. Still busy. She tried ten times and it was busy each time. Feeling queasy, she tried his cellphone, it went directly to voicemail. She tried his assistant, also voicemail. She called his cellphone again and left a message.

'Drew, it's me. I just heard a small plane hit the World Trade Center. Don't know if it was even your building but you need to call me. I tried your office and got a busy signal. OK, so call me, OK? Love you.' She tried Imelda and got the busy signal, too.

'Hey, everybody,' a female voice shouted from down the hall, 'they've got the TV news crews at the Trade Center. We've got it on the big screen in the conference room if you want to come down.' Kat jumped up, grabbed her cellphone from her desk and ran to the packed conference room. As she entered the room, before she looked up at the screen she saw expressions of disbelief and confusion on every face.

When she turned her head to see the TV screen, she knew why they all looked that way. A huge fire was burning on the side of one of the Twin Towers and the newscasters were saying it wasn't a small plane at all. They said they thought it was a commercial plane, a jetliner. As everyone in the room stared at the horrific images, suddenly, from the left side of the screen, another plane shot across the sky and slammed into the other tower. A collective scream emanated from the room. Kat grabbed at the back of a chair to steady herself as the room began to spin. Somehow, even though she thought she might pass out, she managed to punch Drew's number into her cellphone again. As it had so many times before, it went directly to voicemail.

'Drew, it's me. Please call me. I'm watching it on TV. What's going on down there? It looks like a plane might have hit near your office. Listen, honey, get out of the building. Just get out. Just go. OK, call me when you get outside. Please get out as fast as you can. I love you.'

The conference room was a ball of confusion and panic. 'What's happening? Why did two planes hit the buildings? Did air traffic control mess something up? Was it a computer glitch? How could something like this happen?'

Many people in the room had friends who worked in or near the World Trade Center but Kat was the only one at *GQ* whose husband worked in the building.

'I'm sure Drew is OK, Kat,' said one co-worker trying to reassure her but Kat was not sure at all. Drew's company phone lines were down and he wasn't answering his cell. Over and over she called and left message after message until finally his voicemail was full.

She tried calling Imelda to see if she had heard from Drew. The home line remained busy.

On the TV the newscasters said that the cell towers at the World Trade Center had been destroyed and that was affecting all communication. Everyone in the conference room stared at the screen, watching the horror unfold while they cried. No one spoke. There was nothing to say. None of it made any sense.

At nine twenty-one the Port Authority closed all bridges and tunnels leading in and out of New York City. That's when the newscasters began to introduce the idea of terrorism. At nine twenty-four the news reported there might be another hijacking happening on another plane. There was a report that passengers on the third plane had called family members. At nine thirty-one, President George W. Bush announced an 'apparent terrorist attack.'

'I can't reach Drew,' Kat said, tears streaming down her face. 'I have to go downtown and find him,' she told her boss.

'Kat, listen to me,' Adam said, 'I know you're worried and upset. I don't blame you. But, you can't go downtown right now. I don't even think the subways are running. Look out the window.' Adam and Kat peered out the window onto the street. Tens of thousands of people were pouring out of buildings and walking in every direction. It was total chaos.

'We're in midtown. Look at the streets, it's bedlam out there,' said Adam. 'It's going to be a million times worse downtown. Stay here and wait for him to contact you. I'll stay with you until you hear from him.'

Kat tried to call Imelda at home again, still busy. She tried again and again.

At nine thirty-seven, six minutes after the president announced a possible terror attack, American Airlines flight 77 crashed into the Pentagon in Washington, D.C. At nine forty-two, the news announced that the FAA had grounded all flights over the continental United States. At nine forty-five, the US Capitol and the White House were evacuated.

At nine fifty-nine, little more than an hour after the first plane hit, the south tower of the World Trade Center collapsed. A collective scream went through the conference room, the building, the city, the world. Every face wet with tears.

Seven minutes past ten, there were new reports of another hijacked plane, United Airlines flight 93 had crashed in a field in Pennsylvania. The final blow came at ten twenty-eight, when the North Tower, the tower that Drew Sullivan worked in, also fell.

In 102 minutes, the world as everyone knew it had changed forever and a piece of America died.

Kat cried out as Drew's building collapsed and she began to sob uncontrollably. 'I'm going downtown. I have to find my husband and family,' she said running out of the conference room leaving behind a room full of sobbing people. Half an hour later, New York City Mayor Rudolph Giuliani ordered an evacuation of more than one million people from Lower Manhattan.

CHAPTER THIRTY-NINE

Kat tried to get on an elevator to the ground floor. Hundreds of people, were leaving the building all at once and the elevators were completely full. After the seventh fully packed elevator opened on her floor, she stuck her arm in to stop the doors from closing.

'Please, my husband works in the World Trade Center,' she cried. 'I need to go down there.' Three women immediately stepped off the elevator to let Kat on. The doors closed; the faces inside were a mix of terror and tears. No one spoke. Someone tried to make a joke. Nobody laughed. Everyone knew someone who worked downtown.

Outside on 42nd Street and Broadway, it was insanity. Crosstown, uptown and downtown traffic was at a complete standstill. Sirens and horns sounded off in every direction. People walked into the streets, crossing wherever they were with no regard to crosswalks or lights. There was no order whatsoever. Oddly, in all their haste to get home, people were surprisingly polite to each other, as if they somehow knew they were all in whatever it was together, as Americans.

Everyone looked up as the loud roar of US fighter jets flying low between the buildings buzzed right over Kat's head. People were in a panic and not knowing where to go, but determined to go somewhere. By this time, all bridges, subways and railroads were shut down and anyone who lived outside the city was trapped. People abandoned overflowing buses that simply stopped in the middle of the streets, immobilized by the frozen traffic.

All Kat cared about was finding her husband and kids. The only way to get to them was on foot. She would have to walk the many miles downtown to her apartment and the World Trade Center.

Walking south, she noticed the faces of people working in the stores and restaurants along Madison Avenue. Because it was a warm beautiful day, many stores had their front doors open and their employees stood outside by the open doors watching the chaos in the streets. Nobody knew what to do. There was no protocol for this kind of thing. Store managers wondered if they should close for the day and tell their employees to go home. At the same time, the employees wondered if they should tell their bosses they were leaving and go home to be with their families. As she walked, Kat saw the same look of bewilderment on everyone's face. Nobody knew what they were supposed to do. There was no playbook for this.

She had only gone seven blocks, a fraction of the journey and already her feet were in agony from her three-inch heels. Passing an open athletic shoe store, she went in and bought a pair of socks and the first pair of size seven sneakers they brought out. She jammed them on and started to run downtown towards Spring Street.

Still in midtown, she could see the smoke and fire from the World Trade Center. Her apartment was midway between midtown and what had been the Twin Towers. Everyone was walking or running uptown, away from the burning buildings. She was the only person heading downtown, towards the fires.

What if Drew didn't get out? What if he's dead? I have to find him. A steady stream of tears flowed down her cheeks. *Maybe Imelda heard from Drew. Please let my kids be OK. Please, let Drew be OK. What if there are more attacks? I have to find my kids.* She called her nanny and husband over and over as she walked and continued to get busy signals.

At some point on her long walk, her phone's battery died. She felt like an empty shell. Like a stick person with no blood or feelings. Nausea bubbled up in her gut and into her throat. *What if my whole family is dead?*

She kept going, trying to calm her mind as she continued her trek. *The plane hit the north side of the tower. Drew's office looks south. His office is on the opposite side from where the plane hit. He would have had time to get out. He could take those steps three at a time. But what if he stopped to help someone? Drew is always helping people.*

Out of breath, she stopped for a moment to get oxygen into her lungs and then continued on, passing hundreds of bedraggled, exhausted people all walking uptown.

'You're going the wrong way,' they yelled at her. 'Turn around.'

'I have to find my family,' she shouted back without stopping. 'I have to get home.' The further south she walked, the bigger the flames and smoke coming from the towers became. The stench was overwhelming. Police cars, motorcycles and ambulances with blaring sirens raced past every thirty seconds.

Adrenaline still pumping, she moved quickly towards downtown when she saw something strange in front of her. She blinked her eyes and squinted, it looked like there was an army of zombies walking towards her. As they got closer, she realized what it was.

Men and women in suits were covered from the top of their heads to the soles of their feet in a thick, white powder. They looked shell-shocked but determined to get to wherever it was they were going. Kat knew where they all wanted to go. They wanted to go home, just like her.

'Were you in the towers?' Kat shouted at them as they passed.

'No,' the first man shouted without stopping, 'I was on the street near the towers. I need to get home to my family.'

Kat understood, she needed to do the same. A woman covered in powder passed by and Kat called out to her, 'Were you in the tower? Did everyone get out?'

The woman stopped and gripped Kat's forearm. 'I was on the next block. I saw the buildings fall. I don't know who got out. But you're going the wrong way. Turn around.'

Kat pulled her arm away from the woman. 'I'm going home,' Kat shouted over her shoulder and continued to walk south. *Please, Nanna Mae, let my kids and husband be OK.*

Finally, she saw the Spring Street sign in the distance. *Only a few more blocks. I'm almost there.* She quickened her pace and when she turned the corner onto her street she broke into a full run and thought her lungs were going to burst. At the front door of her building, she thrust her key into the lock and pushed the door open. She ran up the stairs and stopped just outside her apartment door, afraid of what she'd find. She took a deep breath and opened it.

The scene inside at first looked so normal. Sophie and Conner were sitting at the kitchen table coloring and eating grilled cheese sandwiches, oblivious to everything that was happening in the world. Imelda stood in the hall between the kitchen and living room with her eyes on the TV. Tears ran down Imelda's face as she watched the video of the falling towers. The nanny was so engrossed in what was on the TV, that she didn't hear Kat when she entered.

'Have you heard from Drew?' shouted Kat gasping and out of breath. 'I haven't been able to reach him.'

'Kat, you're okay!' yelled Imelda running over and throwing her arms around her. 'We tried to call you so many times.'

Kat, tears running down her face, went over and hugged both her kids. 'Have you heard from Drew?' she cried. 'I couldn't reach him. Have you heard from Drew?'

'I'm all right, Kat,' said Drew, stepping out from the bedroom, tears streaming down his cheeks. He walked towards her and wrapped his arms around her and held her tight.

That's when Kat started to shake and convulsively cry.

‘I’m here. I’m okay, don’t cry. Shhh,’ he said over and over. ‘I’m okay. Look at me, see, I’m fine.’

‘I tried to call you so many times and the phone was always busy,’ she sobbed and hyperventilated, ‘and then the plane hit your building and then the towers fell and all I wanted was to come home and I ran all the way here and there were people covered in dust . . .’ She couldn’t go on and collapsed in his arms.

The following awful days were a blur for New Yorkers, America and the world. At first there was hope that there might be survivors. Families wandered from hospital to hospital looking at wounded, burned and broken people, praying their loved one was one of them.

Over the next few days, thousands of pictures of missing friends and relatives were posted all over the city on walls, fences, online, anywhere something could be posted. The first week after the World Trade Center fell, people still thought there could be survivors in hospitals or survivors trapped under debris who needed to be rescued. After a week, hope turned to resolve. There would be no new rescues, only a recovery of bodies. The terrorists had done their job very well.

The city and the country were awash in patriotism. American servicemen in fatigues, armed with rifles and grenades became a new fixed presence at all landmarks and transportation hubs. The streets of New York were lined with thousands of American flags. If it wasn’t all so sad it would have looked festive.

September 11, 2001 changed America forever. Any innocence they had before was now gone.

CHAPTER FORTY

Two weeks later, the Sullivan's apartment was swarming with people. Drew's mother and father had flown in from Australia. Imelda, the kids and assorted cousins and friends were scattered around the apartment. Old sandwich platters and half-eaten cakes were strewn about the kitchen, living room and dining room. Drew's parents and most of the others stared for hours at the CNN coverage of the 9/11 attacks. Two weeks had passed since that awful day. The people of the United States and the world had reluctantly accepted that the victims at the World Trade Center were not coming back.

New explanations about who, what and why emerged each day since the attack. Drips of information were disseminated as the US government tried to piece together what had happened. New words were heard by Americans for the first time: *al-Qaeda. Muslim extremists. Radical terrorism.*

Most Americans were surprised that there were so many people in the world who didn't like them. 'We're Americans,' they'd say, 'everyone loves Americans, don't they? What's al-Qaeda? Why did they hurt us? Why did they kill all those innocent people? They killed all those fathers and mothers who were going to work on a Tuesday. Why do they hate us?' None of it made any sense to most Americans.

Devastated, Drew had worked in the North Tower for years. His department at Spencer Financial shared the ninety-eighth floor with Marsh & McLennan and had been directly hit by the American Airlines flight 11 out of Boston.

Most of Drew's co-workers had died, except for the handful of people like him who were mercifully out of the office that day. Everyone else was dead. His boss; his assistant, MaryAnn; Matt, his trading partner. All of them. Gone. No one on his floor made it out alive. They didn't have a chance to evacuate. Marsh & McLennan had lost 295 people and Drew's department lost forty-three. He had worked there for ten years and those forty-three people were like a second family to him. He knew their birthdays, their families, even their dogs' names.

Drew was inconsolable because all his friends and colleagues were dead and because of the intense guilt that he had been spared. He had spent the better part of the first two weeks after it happened crying, and asking himself why he was alive. He had survived 9/11 for the stupidest of reasons.

'You should eat something, Drew,' said his mother gently. 'You haven't eaten anything in days and you look awful. You're getting so thin. Let me make you a toasted ham and cheese sandwich.' Drew nodded. He was glad to have his mother there. *I shouldn't be alive. I should be dead like everybody else in my office.*

Kat had warned her husband so many times not to bring an open coffee onto the subway but he did it almost every morning. That cup of coffee and a sudden jolt the subway made when it went too fast around a curve is what saved his life.

He had been sitting on the train reading the *Wall Street Journal* with one hand while holding his hot drink with the other. The train sped up around a corner, hit a bump and lurched to the right. Many of the straphangers fell onto the sitting passengers. A large woman in orange spandex bike pants and a middle-aged man in a navy-blue suit both fell into Drew who wound up spilling his coffee all over himself and them.

With his shirt, tie and pants soaked with hot brown liquid, he had no other choice but to go home and change. He got off at the next stop and called his assistant, MaryAnn, and asked her to move his morning meetings to the afternoon. He got back on the uptown train and went home.

After he changed, he played with the kids for a few minutes and was about to leave his apartment when footage of a plane hitting the North Tower cut into the *Today Show* that Imelda was watching on television. Drew's life had been spared because of a cup of French roast coffee and a large woman in orange spandex bike shorts.

Kat looked around at all the people milling around her apartment. CNN had been playing twenty-four hours a day and she couldn't bear to hear it anymore. It was the same thing over and over and it was all bad news. No one knew anything. They didn't know why. They didn't know who. She closed her eyes and tried to remember what life was like before September 11.

Just two weeks earlier on Saturday, September 8, she and Drew and the kids took Beasley for a walk in Central Park. It was a warm September day. The weather was dry and breezy and the park was brimming with people. There were frisbees flying, skaters skating, runners running, bikers biking, and tanners tanning. Families, couples and people walking around by themselves, everyone enjoying New York on a beautiful Saturday afternoon. Now, it was all gone. Life had changed forever. There was no joy in New York and Kat wondered if there ever would be joy again.

'Breaking news,' blared the CNN newscaster, 'the State Department has issued pictures and bios of the nineteen hijackers believed to be behind the attack on the World Trade Center, the Pentagon and the plane that crashed in Shanksville, PA. The investigators now believe the downed flight in Pennsylvania was originally headed to the Capitol before the brave passengers on board intervened.'

Kat opened her eyes to see the faces of the monsters who had murdered nearly three thousand mothers, fathers, sisters and brothers and had devastated countless families. Those men killed people she knew. They killed all of Drew's colleagues, his friends. Kat had known those people for years. She had been to many of their homes and even to their weddings.

She looked at the terrorists' faces on the TV screen.

They don't all look like monsters. Some of them look like teenagers. She saw their ages listed under their pictures. Some of them were kids, a few were twenty or twenty-one. She scanned each face slowly trying to see the evil in their eyes as the newscaster profiled what little information he had on each man. She found herself crying again, something every New Yorker had been doing all day, every day since it happened. *Who were they? Why did they murder so many innocent people? Why do they hate us?*

When the fifteenth photo came onto the screen, she saw something familiar and moved closer to the television. She knew that face, the hair, the lips — those eyelashes.

'What we know so far is, this man, Samir Ayad, was considered the leader of the entire operation. Ayad was thirty-three years old and believed to be the person who piloted American Airlines flight 11 that slammed into the North Tower,' said the CNN correspondent.

Kat froze.

It can't be him.

CHAPTER FORTY-ONE

An hour later, there was a loud knock on Jenn's apartment door. When she opened it, a wild-eyed Kat flew in. Jenn reached out to give her a hug but Kat pushed her away and walked over to the window and stared out.

'You sounded absolutely crazy on the phone,' said Jenn. 'What's wrong?'

'Turn on the news,' said Kat abruptly. 'Turn on CNN.'

'Why, what happened?' asked Jenn as she grabbed the remote control and put on the news.

The CNN newscaster was going over details of 9/11 and the aftermath like they had been doing all day, all week. Since September 11, the only news reported was about the attack and attempts at recovery. It had been like this twenty-four hours a day since the planes hit, as if the rest of the world had ceased to exist.

'I've seen all this coverage before,' said Jenn looking at the TV. 'This is what's been on all week.'

'Keep watching,' said Kat.

Jenn sat in front of the TV and listened to the news for a few minutes until something new came up on the screen.

'Today the State Department released the names and photos of the men they believe to be the perpetrators of the September 11 attacks,' said the CNN newscaster.

The screen on the TV showed photos and faces of men with dark hair and dark eyes. Under each face was a name, an age and a country of origin.

'These are the nineteen men responsible for the attack on the World Trade Center, the Pentagon and the downed plane in Shanksville, PA.' The newscaster systematically did a short bio on each man. All of them were from Saudi Arabia except for one from Egypt, one from Lebanon and two from the UAE. All the men were in their twenties or thirties. The TV screen slowly panned the face of each man citing his age and name. Then, the camera rested on one face. He looked vaguely familiar to Jenn.

'His name was Samir Ayad,' said the newscaster. 'He was believed to be the ringleader and pilot of the plane that hit the North Tower.'

Jenn's head cocked to one side as she looked at the picture. The face on the TV looked familiar, she had seen him before. It took her a minute and then she gasped.

'You see it, too,' said a stone-faced Kat. 'It's Sam. Samir. His full name was Samir Ayad.'

'No, it can't be Sam. That's crazy. It couldn't be him,' said Jenn. 'Samir is a very common name in the Middle East and Ayad probably is, too.'

'It's Sam, I know it. I know him,' said Kat wringing her hands. 'Look at his picture. That's him.'

'It can't be. C'mon, it's been thirteen years since you've seen him. That guy resembles Sam a little. I'm sure it's not the same person. Sam was sweet. He wanted to open a rug shop,' said Jenn. 'This has to be a different guy.'

Kat was motionless. 'I know it's him.'

'Wait, hold on a second,' said Jenn. 'I'll prove it to you.'

Jenn went to her bedroom and after a few minutes came back with a big box that contained dozens of yellow packets full of developed photos and negatives. She dug through the packets until she found one with the word 'Kashmir' written across the top.

'Here it is,' she said as she sifted through the pack of photos pulling out four different pictures. One was of Sam,

Kat and Jenn posing by a temple. There was also a shot of Sam and Kat sitting on one of the shikaras. Another picture was of Sam and Jenn goofing around on the houseboat. The last picture was of Sam alone, holding a book, standing in front of a tree. The pictures were somewhat grainy but they gave a clear shot of Sam's face.

Jenn took the photos over to the computer screen and searched online for the FBI's website. She found information on the hijackers posted on the front page along with their current photos. She scrolled down to Samir Ayad's photo and held up her old picture next to the image on the FBI site. The picture of the man Jenn knew as Sam was much younger and thinner with an innocent look in his eyes.

'There is a little resemblance,' said Jenn half-heartedly, 'but he's not a dead ringer. Of course, my pictures were taken thirteen years ago. It's possible he could look like this guy, now.'

She paused as she read from the site. 'Wait a second, it says here this Samir Ayad was from Egypt. Sam was Indian, so it can't be him,' Jenn said, relieved.

'Sam's father was Egyptian, his mother was Kashmiri,' said Kat. 'Sam told me he could have dual citizenship.'

Jenn continued to scroll through the FBI information on her computer. 'Wait, according to the FBI, this Samir Ayad was the leader of the group. He was a pilot and had lived in Germany and Florida. That doesn't sound like your Sam. How could he have done all those things. He was a penniless guy in India. He wasn't a pilot. Remember, you said, and I quote, "he'll never get out of India".'

'First of all, he's not *my* Sam and I don't know how he did it or when, but it's him. He was always very resourceful. Somehow, I think all of this is connected to me,' said Kat. 'Remember those stalker letters I got?'

Jenn nodded.

'They were postmarked from Egypt and Germany and the last one was from Florida.'

'That could be just a coincidence,' said Jenn as she scrolled further through the FBI site. 'Do you remember Sam's birthday?'

Kat wiped away a tear and closed her eyes to think. 'His birthday was the same as Nanna Mae's, September 1,' Kat said.

Jenn turned slowly around and looked at Kat, her mouth wide open.

'Oh my God. This Samir Ayad's birthday was September 1. We've got to call the FBI,' said Jenn. 'We've got to tell them what we know.'

Kat walked over to the computer, sat next to Jenn and they read the FBI page together.

> *This is a list of the nineteen individuals who have been identified as hijackers aboard the four airliners that crashed on September 11, 2001, into the North and South Towers of the World Trade Center in New York, the Pentagon, and Stony Creek Township, PA.*
>
> *American Airlines flight 77: Boeing 757, departed 8:20 a.m. from Washington Dulles for Los Angeles; 9:37 a.m. crashed into the Pentagon in Washington DC.*
>
> *United Airlines flight 175, departed 7:58 a.m. from Boston for Los Angeles; 9:03 a.m. crashed into South Tower of the World Trade Center*
>
> *United Airlines flight 93, departed 8:01 a.m. from Newark, New Jersey, for San Francisco; 10:10 a.m. crashed in Stony Creek Township, Pennsylvania*
>
> *American Airlines flight 11, departed 7:45 from Boston for Los Angeles; 8:46 a.m. crashed into North Tower of the World Trade Center*

'Look down at the fourth name on the list,' whispered Jenn her eyes glued to the screen. 'It says Ayad lived in Florida and Hamburg.' Kat stared at the line listing Samir Ayad as Jenn continued reading the remainder of the names.

> *1) Satam Al Suqami — DOB: 6/28/76; UAE.*
>
> *2) Waleed M. Alshehri — DOB: 9/13/74/ Possible residence: Hollywood, FL/ Believed to be a pilot.*

3) *Wail Alshehri — DOB: 7/31/73; Possible residence: Hollywood, FL. Believed to be a pilot.*
4) *Samir Ayad — DOB: 9/01/68; Residence: Delray Beach, FL/ Hamburg, Germany; Believed to be a pilot.*
5) *Abdulaziz Alomari — DOB: 12/24/72 Possible residence: Delray Beach, FL; Believed to be a pilot.*

'Kat,' said Jenn touching her friend's shoulder. 'We have to call the police. Kat, are you listening to me? We've got to go to the FBI and tell them everything we know.' Getting up abruptly, Kat walked across the room to the window and looked out.

'We know nothing. I don't know anything. He was someone I knew for a few weeks more than a decade ago,' cried Kat. 'My husband is traumatized. We've lost so many friends. I don't need any more insanity in my life. I'm not going to the FBI.'

Jenn walked over to the trembling Kat and put her arms around her and let her cry. After a few minutes, Kat sat on the couch and blew her nose.

'Listen to me. We *are* going to call the FBI,' said Jenn quietly determined. 'We are Americans first. We need to do this for our country and for all the people who died. There might be more terrorists out there planning something else. Maybe we know something that could help. It's not for us to decide what's important or not. It's our duty to our country to tell whatever we know. If you won't go, I will.'

Kat sighed and nodded her head as Jenn picked up the phone and called the FBI.

CHAPTER FORTY-TWO

For two hours, Jenn and Kat waited in an interrogation room in the FBI field office at 26 Federal Plaza in downtown Manhattan. During their twenty-minute walk there, they detected the noxious smell from the tower disaster that lingered in the air. Smoke could still be seen rising from the remains of what soon would be known as Ground Zero. Outside the FBI building, hordes of reporters stood in front waiting for any bit of new information. Inside the building, it was like a beehive of organized chaos: agents running up and down halls; phones ringing; files of papers being moved. A soft-spoken FBI woman ushered Kat and Jenn to a back room and offered them coffee. They declined.

'It's going to be all right,' Jenn said to Kat reassuringly. 'We're probably all wrong. We'll tell them what we know and they'll thank us and send us home. At least we'll know we did the right thing and our conscience will be clear.'

Twenty minutes later, a young male FBI agent entered the room and closed the door. 'I'm Special Agent Nick Ricci. I'll be taking your statements,' he said.

While Kat thought he looked like he was still in high school, Agent Ricci was all business, no nonsense and direct.

'I'm sorry for the long delay but as you can imagine, under the circumstances, it's been crazy. Right now, we don't have enough manpower to follow up on all the leads,' said Agent Ricci. 'You contacted the bureau this morning because you believe you both have had contact with one of the hijackers, is that correct?' said the agent looking at some papers in his folder and then directly into Kat's eyes.

It feels like he's looking into my brain and reading my thoughts.

'We're not sure, but we think we might know one of the hijackers,' volunteered Jenn. 'We met a guy in India about thirteen years ago who kind of looks like the guy we saw on TV. On the news, they said this hijacker was Egyptian.' She handed the agent the three photos of Sam and began to tell the story of their trip to Kashmir in 1988.

'We met this nice guy named Sam in Srinagar,' said Jenn. 'He spoke five languages and dreamed about opening an Indian rug shop in Europe or America. He was really sweet. Then, I left to go home but Kat stayed for another three or four more weeks.'

Nick Ricci turned his eyes on Kat. 'Tell me what you remember, Mrs Sullivan,' he said gently. 'It's important. We have information that the Samir Ayad who piloted American Airlines flight 11 was born in Egypt while his parents were on a trip to visiting relatives. They apparently went back to the north of India when Ayad was only a few weeks old. Ayad later moved to Egypt, we think about ten years ago, and apparently had dual citizenship. So, it's logistically possible he could be the same person.'

Kat told the agent about the lazy days exploring the Kashmir province, boat trips on Dal Lake, normal tourist activities. She said there was nothing from her trip that foreshadowed the event that happened so many years later. She didn't mention a romantic relationship. She told the agent she and Sam had become friends and were even pen pals for a while.

'Do you still have any of his letters?' asked Ricci.

'I threw them away years ago.'

Agent Ricci interrogated Kat for a full half hour and was finally satisfied. 'That's all for now,' he said. 'Thank you for coming in. Every bit of information helps. We need to learn as much as we can about the background of these people to understand what makes them tick. We'll be in touch if we need help filling in some of the blanks. Anything else you want to add?'

Kat shook her head. Jenn stared at her friend in disbelief. The agent thanked them again and Jenn and Kat left the building without speaking. When they were outside and a block from the FBI office, Jenn spoke. 'You didn't tell them the whole truth.'

'I told them enough,' said Kat. 'I helped identify Samir Ayad. They don't need to know the details of my personal life. It's completely irrelevant.'

'You should have told him the whole story. Let the FBI decide what's important and what's not.'

'My life is a mess,' said Kat. 'Our friends are dead and my husband is depressed. I don't need to add to the pandemonium.'

'But I just think . . .' Jenn started.

'It's my story to tell or not and I want it to remain private,' said Kat grabbing Jenn's arm and squeezing it. 'Drew doesn't know anything about Sam or the marriage and he never will. Is that clear?'

'Painfully,' said Jenn as she pulled her arm away and rubbed it.

CHAPTER FORTY-THREE

Three Saturdays after that awful day, Kat was at home in a fog, staring out a window, something she did often since September 11. The FBI had called several times asking for clarification on parts of her statement but it seemed they found no material connection between her and the hijackers. Kat convinced herself that it was all a bizarre coincidence and put it behind her.

That day, Drew was out, attending another memorial service for a colleague who had died. Kat had been to so many services in the past few weeks that she begged off this one. She hadn't known this person well and going to each one was emotionally draining.

Like every American, many times each day, sadness and tears overcame her. She thought she had cried more over the past few weeks than in her entire lifetime. When Drew had offered to go to this service without her, Kat was relieved to have the time to be alone with her thoughts.

Imelda and the kids had gone to a neighborhood park and Kat was completely by herself for the first time since September 11. She wandered around the apartment picking up the kids' toys and putting them in their proper place. CNN was on the TV with its endless news about planes, people and the horror of the aftermath.

A knock sounded on her front door. It was one of her neighbors from downstairs. 'Hey there, Kat,' he said. 'I signed for a certified package for you this morning. The guy said he rang your bell but no one answered.'

'Everyone is out except me, it was probably when I was in the shower.'

She thanked him and threw the oversized envelope on the kitchen table not particularly interested in who it was from or what was inside. Nothing really interested her much these days.

She found herself staring out the window again. After a few minutes, she looked around the room. *This apartment is a wreck. Nobody has cleaned anything since it happened. I need to create some order here so things can get back to normal.*

She picked up old newspapers and piles of mail, hung up clothes that had been tossed on chairs and put away what looked like a million Legos. Wiping down the kitchen counters, the certified package on the table caught her eye. She picked up the cardboard envelope and opened it.

A thin blue *par avion* letter with a chevron border floated onto the table. The blood rushed to her head as she stared at the familiar blue paper. With her heart pounding, she gasped for air. Leaning against the refrigerator to steady herself, she picked up the envelope and stared at it for a full minute, afraid to open it. Then slowly and carefully, she unfolded the delicate paper.

Dear Mrs Ayad,

That is your name, did you forget, Trina? You are Mrs Katrina Ayad. Should I call you Trina or your new name, Kat? I will call you Trina because that's who you were when you married me, when you became my wife. For years I searched for you, not knowing if you were alive or dead. My heart was broken into a million pieces, my life ruined, my dreams gone. I wanted to die. I had to leave Kashmir because it was full of memories of you. Every street, every tree, every flower reminded me of my beautiful wife. I had to leave my own family, my home and my country to start a new life, all because of you. But I couldn't find you.

But there was a new thing — the internet. That's how I found you and learned all about your new life. You had a new name and a new husband named Andrew. But, you already had a husband — your first husband. Did you forget our wedding in 1989?

I learned you were an important writer for a big American magazine, just like you planned. You always get what you want. Just like you got your locket back.

You have two children who should have been my children. But even after all your lying and deception, over time, my heart softened. I almost moved on until that day in New York when I saw you with him and your children on Spring Street. Yes, I was there, watching you and Drew, with my own eyes. I watched my wife kiss another man and walk away with his children and my heart became forever hard.

Now you know what it feels like to lose the one person in the world you love the most. You will feel the same pain I had when you lied and abandoned me. You gave me your locket and promised your love and a lifetime together. You married me and then left me without a single word.

If you're reading this, then I have been successful and your illegitimate husband is dead. If you had just treated me with the respect and honor I deserved, none of this would have happened. His death is all your fault. His blood is on your hands. You have to live with that. Even today, as I write this last letter, God help me, I still love you.

You are my heart.
Your First Husband,
Sam

Gripping the letter in her hand, Kat ran out of her apartment and into the street not knowing which way to run. She couldn't breathe and was having a panic attack. She needed air. The sky was a bleak gray, full of clouds, it looked like it was about to rain. She started to run up the street. She didn't know where she was going, but somehow, she did. Clutching the blue envelope in her fist, she eventually found herself on the pedestrian walkway of the Brooklyn Bridge. She walked to the center of the bridge and stared out.

A light rain had started to fall but she didn't notice. From where she stood, she could see the still smoldering steam and smoke from the wreckage that was once the World Trade Center. She and Drew had stood in that same spot many times, him always joking that he could see his office from there. Now, it was all gone. She looked at the empty hole in the skyline. The only two men who had ever loved her were both connected to that spot.

For one final time, she read Sam's letter, her temples pulsing. Over and over she read the last line. *God help me, I still love you.*

She took a deep breath and let the air out slowly. *He couldn't have loved me. He just wanted to get to America. He used me and I had to get my locket back. He was the liar, not me. He's the murderer.*

While keeping her eyes on the smoking sky, she ripped the blue letter into tiny pieces. *No one will ever know about this letter, not Drew, not Jenn, not the FBI. Not anyone.*

She opened her hand allowing the wind to lift the tiny pieces of blue paper from her palm. She watched the confetti-like fragments swirl into the air and then slowly drift down one by one into the gray river below. Unhooking the clasp of her locket she held the silver charm in her hand as she considered all the things she had done. *Are all those people dead because of what I did?*

The locket felt like it was burning a hole through her hand and she stared down at it. She raised it over her head to hurl it into the East River and wondered if her grandmother would forgive her.

After a long time on the bridge looking at the empty sky, Kat looked around. She wasn't the only one there. Many other people were looking at the place where the two soaring towers had once stood. Hundreds of New Yorkers had made the same pilgrimage — everyone staring, praying, crying.

The rain was coming down harder and Kat walked home to be with her family. When she opened her front door, Sophie and Conner ran to her.

'Mommy, Mommy,' they shouted.

Flinging her arms around them both she hugged them as hard as she could. The love from her kids immediately lifted her and renewed her spirit. She clung to them not wanting to let them go until they got antsy and wriggled away.

'Imelda, I'm going to take a long, hot shower,' she said as she walked into her bedroom. She turned on the shower in her bathroom. The sun had just come out and was making stripes on the wall as it streamed through the blinds. The bathroom mirror steamed up and she wiped it with her hand so she could see her face. She looked bone tired. She had felt that way every day since it happened. *I don't want to think about this anymore and I don't want to think about him ever again.*

Wet and cold, she kicked her shoes off under the bed and threw her jeans into the hamper. She put her earrings in the jewelry box on the dresser. Automatically, she reached up to her neck to remove the locket when she remembered — it was gone.

Walking back to the clothes hamper, she pulled out her dirty jeans, reached into the front pocket and retrieved the silver locket and chain with a fancy clasp. She stared at the familiar charm for a moment and opened it. Inside it said: *You Are My Heart.* She closed it, opened her top drawer and dropped it into her jewelry box.

She had promised her grandmother she would always keep it.

CHAPTER FORTY-FOUR

October 20, 2001

A little before seven in the morning, Dave DeWitt walked out of the rain into the lobby of his midtown office building carrying his briefcase along with a cup of coffee and a bacon, egg and cheese sandwich on an English muffin. Fewer people were traveling into the city since September 11, making his morning drive from his home in New Rochelle much faster than it used to be. He was glad his commute took less time but saddened by the reason why. Since that day, people were scared to come into New York City. It was awful. He loved his city and ever since, everyone had been inconsolable and frightened. It was on people's faces when he passed them on the street. Entering his building, Dave stopped at the newly installed makeshift security desk in the lobby.

'Morning, Mr DeWitt,' said the security guard.

'Good morning,' said Dave putting his coffee and sandwich bag on the high desk so he could fish out his wallet and ID. Six weeks ago, this same security guard, who he had seen every day for the past twelve years, would have simply waved at him as he entered the building. Since September 11, everyone had to show proper ID. He showed the guard his company card, gathered up his food and briefcase and walked slowly to the elevator.

His floor was dark and quiet when he stepped off the elevator. He turned the lights on as he moved through the halls. Except for that one eager-beaver junior reporter who occasionally beat him in, Dave DeWitt was usually the first person in the office every morning. The eager-beaver wasn't there today. Must have had a late night, he thought.

Walking to his desk, Dave DeWitt reviewed what he had to do that day. He had been running Metro for the *New York Post* for a long time. Given that it was a New York paper, and his division covered the news in the city, his department had become the most important editorial group in the company since 9/11. Washington D.C., Pennsylvania and New York had all been hit but it was the Twin Towers that became the poster child for that awful day. Dave DeWitt's Metro team had been working twenty-four seven ever since it happened and he was exhausted.

Turning down another hallway towards his corner office he noticed his assistant's empty desk piled with stacks of mail and memos. She had taken a leave of absence since 9/11. Her brother was a NYC fireman who had died in the south tower. Dave told her to take as much time as she needed. He knew a lot of people who had died in the towers since he had been covering the NY beat for over twenty years and had done countless interviews with police and fireman during that time. And of course, he knew Father Michael Coyle; everyone in the press knew him.

Dave's eyes welled up with tears, as they had so many times over the past six weeks. He had interviewed and met with Father Coyle many times. The priest had been a constant figure on the New York City scene, always there to lend a hand, much beloved. Dave always thought he was one of the purest souls he had ever encountered. True to form, right after the planes hit, the priest, along with hundreds of firefighters, went straight into the towers. Father Coyle had been the first identified casualty of the 9/11 attacks. A total of 343 firefighters also perished. It was a tremendous loss to the city, he thought. Dave wiped a tear from the corner of his right eye and looked over at the mess on his assistant's desk.

Digging through the piles of unopened papers, he grabbed a few armfuls and brought them into his office. He had to go through the mail himself or something would be missed and he couldn't afford that. A newsroom was all about timeliness. If you missed a tip, you missed the story. Missing a story couldn't happen, not now. He prayed his assistant would be back the next week so he could focus on more important things than opening mail.

Sitting at his desk, he opened his egg sandwich and took a big, satisfying bite. It tasted good, greasy and salty, exactly what he needed. He took a swig of his coffee and sifted through the mounds of papers. Internal memos on new protocols for company security; a board of director's agenda for next week; invitations to meetings at City Hall with Giuliani; invitations to more memorial services. He put those in a separate stack. He couldn't go to all of them and would send some of his reporters to those.

There was a ton of junk mail and a couple dozen FedEx envelopes containing press releases about various events around the city, all of which had to do with 9/11.

It's all so awful. Every day is gray. Everything is so different now. He opened another FedEx package and pulled out a thin light blue *par avion* envelope with a red and blue chevron border.

Sam had been thorough. He left one last parting gift for his wife. Just as he had arranged for a letter to be mailed to Kat after his death, he also made sure twenty other letters would go to all the major newspapers and news organizations in the United States. *Reuters*, The *New York Times*, The *Washington Post*, *CNN*, The *Wall Street Journal* and many others all received the same blue letter with a red and blue chevron border.

My name is Samir Ayad. I presume you now know who I am. I was one of the pilots of the planes that hit the World Trade Center.

I was the pilot who flew into the ninety-eighth floor of the North Tower. My colleagues would have done the same on the south building as well as the Pentagon and Capitol in Washington D.C.

I wanted to tell you about my beautiful American wife, Kat Sullivan. She lives in New York City and is an editor for GQ magazine. She married me in Dharamshala, India in 1989. We never divorced but she still married another man and had his children. That man, Drew Sullivan, worked on the ninety-eighth floor of the World Trade Center's North Tower. In order to avenge my honor and my marriage, I flew a plane into the ninety-eighth floor so my wife would know how it feels to lose someone, to lose her heart, to watch her world disintegrate.

For a long time, Kat Sullivan's help and commitment to our cause was instrumental in our planning of this al-Qaeda mission. While she ultimately betrayed me personally, she deserves recognition for our success on September 11. She deserves all the credit. We couldn't have done it without her.

Samir Ayad, Pilot, American Airlines flight 11

CHAPTER FORTY-FIVE

Dave DeWitt never finished his bacon, egg and cheese that morning. After he recovered from reading and then re-reading the letter in the blue envelope, he called the editor-in-chief of the *NY Post* at home and woke him up. Then, he stopped all the presses.

The following day, the front page of the *New York Post*, and every American newspaper and TV news station, carried a picture of Kat Sullivan with headlines like *Sami's Girl!*; *9/11 Black Widow Lives in Big Apple*; *Ayad's Wife: Editor at GQ*; and *Bride of Terror*. You could not turn on the TV or pass a newsstand without seeing Kat Sullivan's face.

Around the same time the headlines hit the news, Agent Ricci, along with several other FBI agents, was on his way to the Sullivans' apartment. Only minutes before, Kat and Drew's phones started to ring as friends and colleagues heard the shocking news and called them in confusion and disbelief. Drew turned off his incessant phone and turned on the TV and watched the story of his wife's life being played on every channel.

'According to our sources,' said the newscaster, 'Trina Holmgard, who now goes by the name Kat Sullivan, met Samir Ayad in 1988 and married him in 1989. It is not confirmed if or how involved Ms Sullivan was in the attacks on the World Trade Center on September 11, though Samir Ayad has implicated her.'

'Kat, what are they talking about? Why are they saying this about you?' said Drew changing the channel and seeing his wife's picture on every network.

'I don't know,' said a panicked Kat.

'What's happening?' shouted Drew his face contorting. 'You knew this guy? You knew Samir Ayad, the guy who killed all my friends?'

Kat stared at him.

'Answer me!'

'Yes. I knew him,' shouted Kat. 'But barely. I met him thirteen years ago on a trip to India. I haven't seen him or spoken to him since. I don't know what this is all about or why they are linking me to it.'

'Why are they saying he was your husband? Why are they saying that?'

'I don't know.'

There was a knock at the front door. 'It's the FBI, please open the door.'

Drew let five agents enter. They were there to bring Kat downtown.

'Are you charging my wife with something?' asked Drew.

'We just want to ask her some questions,' said Agent Ricci.

'We just heard about this on the news ourselves. Why are they saying my wife was married to that terrorist?' asked Drew.

'Mrs Sullivan?' Agent Ricci looked directly at Kat.

'I met him in India thirteen years ago and we hung out for a few weeks,' said a wild-eyed Kat to her husband. 'But, I don't know why they are saying those other things. I haven't been in touch with him since then.'

'This doesn't make any sense,' said Drew to the FBI agents. 'So what if my wife met this guy thirteen years ago. I'm sure a lot of people crossed his path over the years. Why are you connecting my wife to him? Why are they saying she's *his* wife?'

'That information came from a letter that Mr Ayad sent to a number of news companies earlier today,' said Ricci. 'It said your wife helped his organization and that he was and still is married to her.'

'How do you know it came from Ayad?' said Drew. 'It's probably a hoax. Some nut.'

'Our experts believe the letters were created by Samir Ayad,' said Ricci. 'One of the FedEx offices has footage of Ayad mailing a stack of large envelopes. They have a record of where they were mailed to. It was him. They made a positive identification.'

'If you haven't been in touch with this guy for thirteen years,' said Drew turning to his wife, 'why would he do that?' Kat shook her head but no words came out. 'Why, Kat? He was practically a stranger. Why you?'

'When I met him in Kashmir, we had a little vacation fling,' said Kat. 'It was nothing, but he must have been obsessed with me.'

Minutes later the agents escorted Kat through the crowds of photographers already camped in front of her building and put her into a dark-windowed government limousine. They drove to the FBI offices and placed her in a large interrogation room with a female agent. The rest of the large team watched on monitors down the hall fed from remote cameras. Kat, completely numb, sat motionless, stunned by the media frenzy of the past two hours.

She remembered the look on her husband's face when the FBI agents filled him in on more of the details. Drew's emotions had run the gamut from desperately fearful to accusatory and angry. She had sworn to him that it was all a lie, that everything being reported on the news was false or inaccurate. Drew said a few comforting and protective things, but it was obvious he had some doubts and even more questions.

She put her head in her hands and laid her head down on the table in the interrogation room, still trying to make sense out of all that had happened.

The female agent minding her leaned over and touched Kat's shoulder. 'I'm Special Agent Linda Mason. Are you okay?'

Kat didn't lift her head or move at all. She couldn't. She was floating somewhere, a prisoner in an abyss.

'We have a number of questions vital to national security that we need to ask you,' said Agent Mason.

Kat didn't respond.

'People's lives may be at stake.' Agent Mason's voice was becoming more urgent. 'Do you hear me?'

The one-sided conversation continued with the agent gently trying to coax Kat into speaking. After another ten minutes with no reaction, Linda Mason glanced back at the hidden camera behind her and made an exasperated face before she turned back to the immobile Kat.

'We need to find out what you know about the hijackers,' said Mason.

Kat remained still.

'Mrs Ayad? Are you, all right?'

Kat's head jolted up and she stared icily at the agent, her nostrils flaring. 'Don't you call me that! That's not my name. Do you hear me? My name is Mrs Kat Sullivan,' she bellowed.

'I'm sorry, a slip of the tongue. Of course, I meant to say Mrs Sullivan.'

Down the hall, the FBI counterterrorism team watched the two women's exchange on a screen.

'Here we go,' said the older FBI supervisor right after Kat blew up. 'Linda just brought the ice princess to life. Now, that lady is spitting mad. I guess she doesn't like being called by her real name. Good to know. Ricci, get in there and handle her. You're the only one in the bureau who has any previous experience with Mrs *Ayad*.'

'Yes, sir,' said Special Agent Ricci walking to the door.

'How did she respond to you the last time you met?' asked the supervisor.

'She was reticent and not terribly forthcoming at first,' said Ricci as he opened the door.

'She didn't marry you, too, did she?' said the supervisor with a bitter smirk.

Agent Ricci walked down the beige halls and entered the room where Kat and Agent Mason were still poised in a Mexican standoff. He nodded at Mason, which was her cue to leave, and pulled up a chair sitting directly across from a still fuming Kat.

'She called me Mrs Ayad,' said Kat through clenched teeth. 'That's not my name.'

'I'm sorry about that. Agent Mason shouldn't have said that. It was way out of line.'

'I want to go home,' said Kat starting to cry. 'I'm tired. I want to see my kids. They need their mother.'

'I'm afraid we have to sort through some things before you can leave,' said Agent Ricci gently. 'This whole thing must have been extremely difficult. I want to try and untangle as much of it as I can for you. Does that sound fair?'

Kat peered at him and reluctantly nodded. *Whatever. Just make it all go away.*

'Ms Sullivan, when you came down here the first time, you appropriately let us know that you had previous contact with Samir Ayad,' said Agent Ricci. 'More recent information now contradicts your statement to the FBI. Our intelligence indicates that your relationship with Mr Ayad was far different from the one you reported on the day you came here with Jennifer Fairchild. Would you like to add anything at this time?'

Motionless, Kat stared over Ricci's head but said nothing. Exasperated and worried that every precious minute wasted might result in another act of terrorism, the senior director of Agent Ricci's unit, who had been watching the scene remotely, strode down the hall and entered the interrogation room with several other agents in tow.

'Ms Sullivan, I'm Director Lewis Fauch. What we are discussing with you is very serious and a matter of national security. Do you understand?' the older man continued in measured tones. 'We need to know everything you know. This is not a request. We will keep you here until you tell us the truth. You have young children. You wouldn't want them to visit their mother in jail, would you?'

'Leave my kids out of this!' Kat shrieked and then buried her head in her hands again.

'Ms Sullivan?' said Agent Ricci gently, trying to calm her down.

Kat lifted her head and stared up at the older director. 'Is whatever I tell you completely confidential?'

'Of course,' said Director Fauch. 'Always.'

For the next five hours Kat recounted as many details as she could remember of the two years she had known and been in contact with Samir Ayad. She told the agents about the stolen glances, their first kiss, romantic nights and the first time she left India, when she gave him her grandmother's silver locket.

'I told him he could keep it until our wedding day.'

'Did you mean that?' asked Ricci.

'At the time.'

She told the agents about the series of blue letters she received and how eventually she suspected that Sam's professions of love was only an act; a ruse to get his American citizenship.

'If you thought that, why did you go back to Kashmir?' asked Ricci.

'I wasn't a hundred percent sure. I went back to see for myself. I needed to know if he wanted me or if he was only after a new life in America. Also, I had to get my locket.'

'Go on,' said Ricci. 'Then, what happened?'

Kat paused, looked down at the floor and breathed in deeply several times. 'Once I got to Kashmir, he said he'd only give the locket back to me after we got married, like I had promised him. He suggested we get married the next day. I wanted to see how far he'd go. So, I called his bluff.'

Kat paused again.

'His bluff?' asked Ricci.

'I didn't think he'd go through with it. But, he did. I went through some idiotic ceremony that lasted two minutes and he gave me my locket back. Once I had it, I told him I'd go home and apply for his visas to bring him to America,' said Kat. 'I left India a few days after that and never communicated with him again. That's the truth.'

Agent Ricci displayed no emotion. 'I see,' he said, making some notes and glancing over at Director Fauch.

'Surely, he reached out to you,' said the director.

Kat squirmed in her chair. 'For eighteen months after I left India, I received dozens of letters but never opened any of them,' Kat said robotically without emotion. 'Why would I? He used me. He made a fool of me. One day, I burned all of them and threw the ashes away. A few years later, I met Drew, got married, moved and changed my name. I never heard from Sam again.'

'Let me make sure we fully understand what you've told us. You married Ayad just to get your necklace back,' Agent Ricci said, trying to tamp down his astonishment. 'You never had any intention of being his wife or bringing him to America. Is that correct?'

'Yes. That's correct.'

'You agreed to the wedding as a ploy to retrieve your property?' asked Director Fauch.

'It was my grandmother's locket. What other choice did I have?'

'And, you maintain that you never had any further contact with Samir Ayad or anyone else he was associated with,' said Director Fauch. 'You have never had any contact with anyone in al-Qaeda.'

'Of course not,' said Kat quickly. 'Sam didn't know where I was or who I was. The last letter I received from him was eleven years ago. He only knew me by my maiden name, Trina Holmgard, and my old address in Astoria. I got married a long time ago. I've been Kat Sullivan for the past eight years and live in Manhattan with my husband and kids.'

'It is quite a coincidence that your husband, Drew, worked on the same floor that Ayad flew his plane into, wouldn't you say?' said Director Fauch.

'I don't know why he wrote those letters about me helping him and al-Qaeda,' Kat said, her voice getting louder and more agitated. 'I never heard of al-Qaeda until September 11. I never communicated with him or even thought about him, not once. And, I definitely didn't talk to his friends. You've got to believe me, I don't know anything about al-Qaeda.'

'But you were technically still his wife, right?' asked Agent Ricci.

'Look,' said Kat starting to lose it. 'He took me to some broken-down shack in the mountains in northern India. A little man in a dirty gown said words in a language I didn't understand. Sam put a cheap ring on my finger and said we were married. How did I know if it was real?'

'It sounds like a wedding to me,' said Ricci.

'To me it was a joke. He was also supposed to send me all the marriage documents. I never received anything.'

'Maybe he didn't send them because you never wrote back? Maybe he kept them as proof.'

'I never took him or any of it seriously.'

'Looks like he did,' said Agent Ricci as he glanced over at Director Fauch.

CHAPTER FORTY-SIX

'Tell me again what happened, but slowly,' Drew said to Imelda while trying to comfort his shaken mother and daughter.

'We got to the park and the kids were on the monkey bars in the playground when a group of photographers began snapping pictures and it . . . it was terrible,' said Imelda while stealing a glance at Kat who had been reading on the sofa. Kat had been on a leave of absence from work because the FBI was still questioning her daily.

'Tell us. We need to know,' Kat said as she stood up.

Drew's mother, her face red, took a breath and said quickly, 'Some crazy woman screamed at Sophie over and over, "Your mother is a goddamned murderer!" When that happened, we came straight home.'

This had not been the first time his family had been attacked. Previously, when they tried to venture out of the house, it had proved to be a disaster. Twenty-four hours a day, crowds of media mixed with protesters were fixtures in front of their building. If they stepped out the front door, they were surrounded by reporters and New Yorkers who followed them wherever they went. The Sullivans were harassed so much that they abandoned any kind of normal activities, even grocery shopping. Anything they needed, Drew's parents would fetch or it was ordered by phone and delivered. Once a reporter pretended to be a delivery guy and actually got inside the Sullivans' apartment. Drew went nuts. It didn't end well for the reporter.

The incident in the park with his children was the final straw. Because of the FBI investigation, Drew and Kat couldn't leave the country but his parents could certainly take their kids far away from all the chaos and hate.

An hour later, after much soul-searching, Drew went into the bedroom to tell Kat what he proposed.

'You want to send our kids to Australia? For how long?' Kat asked.

'Until things calm down. We can't put them through this. Sophie is traumatized.'

'You want to send my kids away?'

'It's the best thing for them,' said Drew. 'My parents are on board. They're trying to get a flight for all of them right now. I talked to Imelda. She said she'd go with them to help. It's just until things blow over.'

On some level, Kat knew her husband was right. It had been extremely hard on her kids and they couldn't put them through any more. She wished more than anything that she could go with them but she couldn't leave the country because her passport had been confiscated by the FBI — indefinitely.

When they told their children, Kat and Drew had to fight back tears and tried to make it sound like a cool holiday with Gran and Grandpa. The kids had been to Australia a few times before and loved spending time there. It was a scramble but the flights got booked, the bags were packed and two days later a car picked up the kids, Drew's parents and Imelda and they were gone.

Unable to go anywhere, the apartment on Spring Street felt very small and tension between Kat and Drew mounted over the following weeks.

'Your story doesn't add up,' said Drew bitterly one afternoon.

'He was crazy. Obviously, he had some sick obsession with me,' said Kat. 'He tied me into his plan just to screw me.'

'But why, Kat? Why did he want to screw you so badly?' said Drew. 'The way you tell it, you hardly knew the guy.'

'I don't know why. Stop asking me the same questions over and over. I get enough questions from the FBI.'

'Why would someone you barely remember go to such lengths to get you?' Drew asked.

'I told you already. I had a little fling with him in India thirteen years ago. It was nothing,' said Kat emphatically.

'Did you sleep with him?'

'That's all you really want to know, isn't it?' said Kat glaring at her husband. 'No, I never slept with him. Happy now?'

'You swear you never married him?' Drew asked for what was probably the tenth time.

'He must have been stalking me for years. I'm the victim here. Look what's happened to my life.'

'Actually, the people who went to work at the World Trade Center and the Pentagon on September 11 are the victims,' Drew sneered as he walked out of the room.

After their fight that day, Kat made a decision. She needed to make things more normal again and decided it was time to go back to work. The following morning, she put on her navy Armani suit, her favorite pair of gold hoop earrings and a pair of red suede Manolo Blahnik four-inch heels. It wasn't safe for her to take public transportation because everyone in New York knew her face and the paparazzi were everywhere. When she was ready to leave, she called a car service to pick her up and Drew helped her fight her way through the reporters and onlookers waiting outside and put her safely into the town car.

'Wish me luck,' said Kat with a forced smile as Drew closed the car door.

'Yeah,' he mumbled as he slammed the door shut.

Sitting in the back seat of the limo, Kat let out a sigh of relief. It felt good to finally be outside of her apartment after being cooped up for so many weeks. She told the driver to pull up to the rear door of the Condé Nast building.

When they got there, there were a few reporters waiting at the back entrance. When the car stopped, she took a deep breath and dashed into the building before the reporters had a chance to surround her. Once inside she pulled out her Condé Nast ID and slid it through the opening at the top of the turnstiles. The machine made a buzzing sound. Puzzled, she looked at the ID and slid it through a second, third and fourth time. Each time it buzzed but would not let her pass. A lobby security guard walked over to see what the problem was.

'For some reason my ID isn't working,' said Kat to the guard.

'Are you an employee here?' said the guard suspiciously. Everyone in New York was on high alert in the aftermath of 9/11.

'I've worked here for years. My office is on the twenty-fourth floor at *GQ*,' said Kat. 'Don't you recognize me? I walk past you several times a day.'

'Thousands of people come in and out of here every day,' said the guard. 'Maybe the strip on your card is corrupted. I can call someone to come get you and then you can have your card replaced.'

Kat stood off to the side while hundreds of employees filed through the lobby, many carrying cups of coffee and bags of breakfast food. Several people stared at Kat, whispering and pointing as they passed through the turnstiles. When a few of Kat's *GQ* colleagues entered the lobby, Kat smiled and waved to them. Their eyes widened but they didn't acknowledge her in any way. Mortified, Kat turned away and faced the wall in the corner while she waited for someone to come get her. She looked at her Tag Heuer watch. It had been nearly ten minutes since the guard had called upstairs.

'Excuse me,' Kat said impatiently to the security guard, 'do you know what's holding things up? I'd like to get in to my office.'

'Someone's coming right down.'

A moment later, the senior vice president of human resources for all of Condé Nast appeared in the lobby and signaled for Kat to follow her. The security guard immediately buzzed Kat through the gate.

'Come with me,' said the SVP as she pushed the elevator call button.

'What's going on?' asked Kat. 'My ID card isn't working.'

'Let's talk in my office,' said the SVP ending the elevator conversation.

Ninety seconds later, Kat was seated in the HR offices on the third floor. 'Why did you come down to get me?' she asked suspiciously. 'Can you fix my ID card here?'

'Ms Sullivan, given what's transpired, we've had to make some staffing changes.'

'What do you mean? What staffing changes?'

'Surely you didn't think you could just come back to work as if nothing had happened,' the SVP began. 'Besides the 9/11 hijackers and Osama bin Laden, you're the most infamous person in America, maybe even in the world. Our organization can't have an association with you. We're a luxury brand company. You being here is very bad for business. It's already cost us clients when they learned you were employed by us. People have pulled their advertising dollars out of six of our titles already. You working here is not an option.'

'But I didn't do anything.'

'I'm not a judge or a jury. At some point, the truth always comes out. I'm sorry but this is the end of the line for you and Condé Nast.'

'Are you kidding me?' said a flabbergasted Kat. 'Does Adam Cantor know about this? I demand to talk to Adam.'

'It was his decision along with senior management. If you know anything about Adam, you know his magazine always comes first. Any personal items left in your office will be sent to your home,' said the SVP looking above Kat's head as two young security guards stepped into the room. 'These gentlemen will show you out.'

'I know how to get out,' said Kat bitterly.

'These gentlemen will show you out,' the SVP repeated.

Speechless, Kat stood up. Each man took one of her elbows and walked her to the elevator.

'You don't have to hold my arms,' she said through clenched teeth. 'I'm not going to run away.' Disregarding her request, the guards held on to her as they had been instructed and escorted Kat Sullivan out of the building and onto the sidewalk.

'Traitor,' hissed one of the guards into her ear as he roughly let go of her arm.

'Murderous bitch,' said the other.

Tears filled Kat's eyes as she looked around for an escape route. Mercifully, someone was getting out of a yellow cab right in front of her. She got in and closed the car door just as a few stray photographers surrounded the vehicle, clicking their cameras until the taxi pulled away.

CHAPTER FORTY-SEVEN

'I can't help you, Kat,' said a managing editor friend. 'I shouldn't even be talking to you. Look, I hear what you're saying. That Ayad guy was a terrorist and maybe you had nothing to do with all those people dying, but right now, you're poison.'

'What do you mean maybe I had nothing to do with it?' said Kat. 'Of course, I didn't have anything to do with it.'

'I'm sorry. No one will hire you. It would look unpatriotic.'

Most of Kat's friends were incredulous, a few were mildly sympathetic, most were not and nobody trusted her. The majority of her phone calls were not returned. Those who did call her back just wanted to ask her questions about 9/11 and get the inside scoop. She even heard one of her friends was writing a tell-all about her.

Most of her job search calls played out the same way. An assistant politely said they were taking her information though Kat could tell they weren't writing anything down. She would wait for a call back but they never came. Six months earlier, she could have had any editorial job in New York. Executive recruiters regularly called about this company or that. Now, those same recruiters wouldn't talk to her. She called Adam Cantor several times to plead her case but his assistant always said he was unavailable. Even her dismissal from *GQ* became front page news and Adam, who had once been her mentor, never called her back.

Drew stayed busy going to church services for his friends and co-workers and visiting their families. Kat was often by herself, alone in their apartment. Her only contact with people apart from Drew was her daily inquiry from one or more branches of law enforcement. No matter how much she protested, most Americans emphatically believed that Kat Sullivan had somehow been involved with the terrorists. Conspiracy theories abounded.

Life in New York had become untenable for both Sullivans. People catcalled and jeered at them whenever they went out and reporters trailed them and relentlessly stuck microphones in their faces.

A visit to the dentist caused such a stampede that her dentist, who she had been going to for six years, said he could no longer treat her. 'Sorry, Kat,' he said, 'you're bad for my practice. Some of my patients have threatened to go to a new dentist.'

Crowds of news vans permanently camped out in front of their condo — the thirst for news about Kat Sullivan was insatiable.

They put their condo on the market and their lawyer arranged for them to rent a secluded cottage in the woods on two acres in southwest Connecticut. The CT cottage had fencing and a gate around its perimeter to keep prying eyes and cameras out.

With all of her friends abandoning her, Kat reached out to the one person she knew would always be there for her — Jenn. They hadn't talked in weeks though Kat had left several messages. Jenn hadn't called her back, which was odd. She tried Jenn again and left a voicemail saying she was going to be in the city and wanted to stop by and see her.

Desperate to talk to her friend, she drove into Manhattan from Connecticut and waited outside of Jenn's apartment building for her. Jenn took a yoga class every Tuesday at five p.m. and Kat knew she would be arriving home around six thirty. She waited in a parking spot a few doors down from Jenn's building.

At six forty-five, Jenn walked quickly down the street carrying a grocery bag and Kat got out of her car. Surprised to see her friend, Jenn stopped and stared at Kat like she had seen a ghost.

'What are you doing here?' asked Jenn looking around for paparazzi.

'I left you a message that I was going to be in the city tonight and that I'd drop by.'

'I didn't get it. Tonight's not going to work for me,' said Jenn as she started to walk past Kat towards her apartment building.

'Jenn,' said Kat in a loud whisper also surveying the street to make sure there weren't any photographers lurking. 'What do you mean? I don't have to stay long, I just thought we could catch up a little, so much has happened that I want to tell you about.'

Jenn spun around and shot her old friend an incredulous look. 'Don't you get it?' Jenn raised her voice, clearly angry. 'You think your life is ruined? Well, guess what? So is mine and I *really* didn't do anything. For me, it's been guilt by association. Don't tell me you haven't seen the headlines about me "Bomber Girl's Bestie — Jenn Fairchild". That picture of you and me and Sam in India has been in every magazine and newspaper in the country. The guy I thought I was going to marry broke up with me because he couldn't handle it and yesterday, I got fired from a job I loved. I'm followed by photographers and reporters, day and night, and people want nothing to do with me. I'm a pariah and it's all because of you.'

'You know I had nothing to do with what happened,' said Kat moving towards her friend.

'Don't come near me,' Jenn hissed, putting her hands in the air in a defensive stance. 'You just *had* to get that goddamn necklace, didn't you? No matter what the cost.'

'I didn't know any of this would happen,' said Kat.

Jenn shook her head with disgust and turned to go into her building. When she pulled open the front door she gave Kat one last look.

'Don't come here again,' said Jenn. 'Don't contact me, ever. We're done.' With that she stepped inside her building leaving an hysterical Kat crying on the street. Jenn's brief friendship with Samir Ayad in Kashmir so many years before had also made her the subject of public fascination and speculation. Conspiracy theorists suggested that Jenn too, might have been involved in the attacks. The one friend Kat thought she could always rely on had turned her back on her.

Drew had taken a leave of absence from his company and spent most of his time watching sports on TV or playing with Beasley out in their large wooded compound. Other than regular visits from law enforcement, the couple saw no one. The highlight of each day was the phone call they had with their kids, who seemed to be thriving in Sydney but still constantly asked when they were going to see their parents.

In early December, three months after 9/11, the FBI picked Kat up and brought her to their offices again. Agent Ricci was there and asked her what seemed to be the same questions Kat had been asked a million times. When he was finished, he dropped a bombshell.

'Ms Sullivan, when we first questioned you about your *friendship* with Samir Ayad you had asked that your personal details regarding your relationship remain confidential,' began Ricci. 'However, the public is demanding to know what happened and the Department of Justice wants there to be full transparency.'

'What are you saying?'

'We are going to release a full report and in it will be information regarding your true relationship with Ayad, your marriage and the incident with the locket. I'm sorry, it's all going to be public,' said Ricci. 'There's nothing I can do about it.'

'You promised me,' said Kat. 'I told you everything you wanted to know. My husband doesn't know. I told him I never married Ayad.'

'That's unfortunate,' said Ricci. 'We believe you most likely had nothing actively to do with 9/11. But it seems pretty clear that all those people are dead because Ayad was trying to settle a score with you. It's going public. There's nothing I can do. My hands are tied.'

Later that day, before Drew heard about the soon-to-be released FBI report on the news, a terrified Kat pre-empted it by telling her husband what it would say.

'You've been lying to me the whole time?' said an astonished and heartbroken Drew with a look of disillusionment and anger. 'Every time I asked you, you denied it right to my face. You didn't even flinch.'

'That marriage was never real to me,' pleaded Kat. 'You have to believe me.'

'Believe you?'

'I never considered him a legitimate husband,' said Kat reaching for Drew's arm that he quickly pulled away. 'The only reason I went back to India and married him was to get my necklace. I had no feelings for him. That's the truth.'

That night, they had a terrific fight that lasted for hours and after that, conversation between them was minimal. Kat took to staying in bed and remaining in her pajamas while Drew kept busy reading in the living room and puttering in the yard with the dog.

'You haven't spoken to me since yesterday,' said Kat one afternoon while Drew was doing a crossword puzzle.

'I have nothing to say.'

'I didn't know anything, Drew, you've got to believe me,' implored Kat. 'He was a liar, look what he did. He was obsessed with me. I never had any romantic feelings for him. It was completely one-sided.'

Drew stared at his wife and walked out of the room. They had become strangers; polite but disinterested and they didn't trust each other.

When the story hit, the media concocted a litany of conspiracy theories involving Kat, Samir Ayad and Osama bin Laden. Kat Sullivan was the centerpiece of talk radio, which was collectively convinced she had been in on the plot. She tried to explain to the media and tell her side of the story but they twisted everything around to sell more newspapers. Fringe press speculated that she was an operative with al-Qaeda and had even had contact with Osama bin Laden himself.

Even those who believed Kat wasn't knowingly involved with terrorists, thought her evil and treacherous for marrying a man for a necklace and leaving him behind to rot. To those people she was still to blame because in their eyes, her appalling, insensitive and selfish behavior might have been what triggered Samir Ayad's plan and his actions.

Everyone had a different opinion about Kat Sullivan and her motives. One thing they all agreed on — Kat Sullivan was a cold-hearted bitch. She became the most vilified person in the world after Osama bin Laden and her first husband.

They had been in the new house in Connecticut for a few months and had only unpacked some of their clothes. Walking by the second bedroom filled with more than forty unopened boxes, Drew picked open a box labeled 'pictures'. Inside were dozens of framed photos of him and Kat and their kids. He pulled out their wedding portrait and thought how truly beautiful Kat had looked on that day. He remembered how much he had loved her when she walked down the aisle. Looking at all the old photos stirred something in him. It wouldn't be easy after all that had happened, but he thought his wife and family were worth it and they could find their way back. *Maybe it's like she said, she had no feelings for him, she just wanted that stupid necklace.* Drew knew if they were ever going to put their broken family back together, they had to make this house feel like a home.

On a mission, he unpacked the kitchen supplies: mugs, pots, pans and spices and put them in the cabinets above the stove. He found a box with knickknacks and candles and scattered them around the living room.

Kat said nothing, watching silently as he placed their treasures on tables and shelves. She didn't feel like helping him. She didn't feel like doing anything anymore.

Drew pulled the tape off a box that contained framed pictures and smiled as he looked at a few pictures of his kids. There was one family photo of the four of them looking so happy. That was taken when Kat had hired one of the top photographers in New York through her *GQ* connections. He remembered that the whole family had gotten dressed up and the kids had giggled and squirmed while they posed for the camera. Afterwards, they all went out for ice cream. It had been such a happy day. Drew placed some of the family pictures on shelves and end tables and it made him feel better.

'I don't know why you're bothering,' said Kat standing in the doorway watching him. 'None of it matters.'

'It does to me,' said Drew, refusing to get sucked into his wife's negativity. 'It makes me happy to have our things around. It makes me feel a little more normal.'

With half of the boxes unpacked, he went back into the second bedroom and opened another that was filled with books. Lining his books up by size in the bookcase in the bedroom he began to add some of Kat's books to the lower shelf. When he picked up a copy of *Wuthering Heights*, a blue envelope with red and blue chevron trim fell out from between its pages and floated onto the floor. He bent down and picked it up. It was old and was addressed to Trina Holmgard in Astoria. The return address was from India and was postmarked from 1989. His hands began to shake as he opened the letter.

Dearest Trina,

It's been three weeks since we got married. My heart aches when I think of you and how beautiful you looked on our wedding day and how even more beautiful you were in my arms on our wedding night. I have never felt such passion and joy at the same time.

I remember our trip to Dharamshala and the first time we made love but it didn't compare to our wedding night because then you were my wife. That made it different, special and amazing. You made my body feel something I've never felt before. I watched you sleeping that whole night. You looked like an angel from heaven. I pinch myself every day because I still cannot believe I am your husband and will soon join you in New York. We are going to have an incredible life, my love. One day soon we'll have the family we talked about. I miss you so much, Trina. Always know I will love you forever because . . .

Drew didn't finish reading the letter because his head felt like it was on fire. *She said Ayad meant nothing to her, that she barely knew him, that she only wanted to get her necklace. She told the FBI she burned all of his letters. What other lies did she tell?*

He walked deliberately into the living room with the blue envelope clenched tightly in his fist. He stared silently at Kat until she looked up at him, his face bright red and snarled into a mask of hatred. Startled by his demeanor, Kat was confused until she saw the blue envelope in his hand.

'Because of you, all my friends are dead,' shouted Drew. 'You're a liar. You married me when you were already married to someone else.'

'I told you. It wasn't a real wedding,' screamed Kat. 'I barely knew him.'

'I read his letter, Kat,' Drew screamed back. 'It was real and you're a liar. You told me you never slept with him, that it was a one-sided relationship. That's bullshit! Almost three thousand people are dead because of you. We are over. I'm leaving for Australia as soon as I can get on a flight. You are on your own.'

Sam had turned the final screw. That night Drew moved his things out and two days later, he was on a flight to Australia to be with his kids. Kat's perfect marriage and perfect life were gone. All that was left was Beasley and she hugged the little dog close to her.

* * *

Despite his anger, Drew was financially generous to Kat. She got their condo in New York and any proceeds that she received from selling it were all hers. The following year, she sold the apartment for a good amount and used that money to live on.

To conserve her funds, because she was still unable to find employment, she moved to a small one-bedroom apartment in her old neighborhood in Astoria. She colored her hair a dark brown, cut it short, added bangs and wore thick eyeglass frames to alter her appearance. The only work she could secure were minimum wage jobs. For years she worked as a cashier at a diner and swept the floors at a hair salon.

When her kids were young, Kat called them once a week. As they grew older, they grew impatient with their mother who had very little to say. More than anything, they didn't understand why she wouldn't see them.

'But why, Mum,' pleaded eleven-year-old Sophie who now had an Australian accent. 'Why won't you come visit us? You could come for Christmas. Couldn't she, Dad?' Her father who always sat in the room when the kids were on the speakerphone with their mother, attempted to change the subject. 'Your mum is very busy right now. Maybe another time.'

'You never will see us, will you, Mum?' said Conner. 'You send us cards and letters and little gifts but you're not like a real mum. Real mums spend time with their kids.'

The truth was that Kat was never given back her passport and was unable to leave the country as the investigation into 9/11 continued. She and Drew agreed on one thing. They were both adamant that their kids not set foot in the United States. They believed it would only result in a horrible media fiasco.

By the time Sophie and Conner were in their teens, they only spoke to their mother twice a year. She called each of them on their birthdays and every Christmas Eve. Over the years, the calls became shorter with neither side feeling very good when they were over. Time and distance had made them all virtual strangers.

As the years passed, public interest in Kat Sullivan waned as the country healed and put 9/11 behind them. She sold her jewelry including the diamond engagement ring that Drew had bought for her. Combined with the money she made on the condo and what little she earned at the diner, she scraped together enough to live on.

Not long after her last painful conversation with her old friend Jenn, her former best friend left New York and moved to a small town in rural Oregon and changed her name. The two women never spoke or saw each other again.

Every Tuesday, rain or shine, Kat took the subway into Manhattan. She'd walk across the Brooklyn Bridge remembering the times she and Drew did it together — when they'd gaze out at the magnificent Twin Towers and joke about seeing his office from the bridge. Right after 9/11, there was a huge gaping hole in the skyline where the towers had once stood. For a while, the city projected two lights the size and width of the towers in its place as a tribute to the lives lost.

In 2006, the new Freedom Tower construction began and finally the new World Trade Center opened in 2014, defiantly filling the empty space in the sky as if to say, 'You will not beat us — we will only come back stronger'. As an odd coincidence, Kat's old company, Condé Nast, was one of the first new tenants in the Freedom Tower.

Four years later at dusk, on the evening of September 11, 2018, Kat Sullivan, wearing her silver locket, walked onto the Brooklyn Bridge and looked out at the gleaming glorious Freedom Tower in the distance. She walked halfway across the bridge to a maintenance walkway. Waiting until it was fully dark, she grabbed the railing with both hands. With two wide steps she climbed onto the safety ramp, took one last look at the shiny new tower and then dove head first over the railing into the dark murky water below.

Katrina Holmgard Ayad Sullivan, along with her wretched locket, sank to the bottom of the river. No one even saw her jump. No one knew she was gone until three days later when her blue swollen body was found floating near the shore in Brooklyn. The locket was gone.

On September 11th 2001, America was attacked. 2,977 people died and the world was forever changed.

THE END

ACKNOWLEDGMENTS

Sometimes, "It takes a village". *The First Husband* is the product of many hands and minds. Four years in the making, many friends, relatives and colleagues were sounding boards, editors and proofreaders.

In the early stages, I bounced ideas off and received encouragement from Faye Kim, Rebecca Farwell, Anne Fitzpatrick and Cindy Sullivan (miss you) who all helped me flesh out the original story. Once my first draft was finished, my sister Diane McGarvey and my husband Peter Black, did the first reads and provided early constructive feedback. Verdict: it needed work.

After a second draft, I cast to a wider net of early readers who also gave me tremendous support and feedback — Lolly Arkin, Jill Chaifetz, Julie Garcia, Lisa Goodman, Fran Hernon, Jamie Holt, Charles "Chuck" Kanganis, Brooke Laffan, Cindy Pabst, Marlene Pedersen, and Regina and Bob Turkington.

My third draft and probably the help that really changed the narrative came from my good friend, award winning author, and writing critique partner, Susan Cox. For five months, Susan and I met regularly and helped each other with our respective works in progress. Her insight and keen story telling sense moved my novel into new places.

After a fourth, and fifth draft, author Virginia Aronson gave it a read as did Marlene Pedersen for a second time (that's right, good friend — read it twice!) and gave me their input. Verdict: getting there but still needed work.

I'd also like to thank Erika Toen who helped me with the German phrases in the book. A lifesaver!

The making of *The First Husband*, did indeed "take a village". My deep thanks to each and every one of you for helping me write the story that's been rattling around in my head for thirty years.

THE JOFFE BOOKS STORY

We began in 2014 when Jasper agreed to publish his mum's much-rejected romance novel and it became a bestseller.

Since then we've grown into the largest independent publisher in the UK. We're extremely proud to publish some of the very best writers in the world, including Joy Ellis, Faith Martin, Caro Ramsay, Helen Forrester, Simon Brett and Robert Goddard. Everyone at Joffe Books loves reading and we never forget that it all begins with the magic of an author telling a story.

We are proud to publish talented first-time authors, as well as established writers whose books we love introducing to a new generation of readers.

We have been shortlisted for Independent Publisher of the Year at the British Book Awards three times, in 2020, 2021 and 2022, and for the Diversity and Inclusivity Award at the Independent Publishing Awards in 2022.

We built this company with your help, and we love to hear from you, so please email us about absolutely anything bookish at feedback@joffebooks.com

If you want to receive free books every Friday and hear about all our new releases, join our mailing list: www.joffebooks.com/contact

And when you tell your friends about us, just remember: it's pronounced Joffe as in coffee or toffee!

ALSO BY MCGARVEY BLACK

TRUST ONLY ME

Printed in Great Britain
by Amazon

26378247R00142